THE
ASCENT
OF DAVE

Andy R

This is a work of fiction. Names, characters, businesses, places, events, locales, and incidents are either the products of the author's imagination or used in a fictitious manner. Any resemblance to actual persons, living or dead, or actual events is purely coincidental.

Vik, would you like a cup of tea?

THE ASCENT OF DAVE

Dave ran his hand across the back of his neck and shook his head: they were eight runs short with just one over left. He imagined the silence of the crowd as the bowler began his run, a solitary figure in white, lengthening his stride, accelerating forward and transferring his momentum into his windmilling arms. There was a cough to Dave's right. Dave kept his gaze fixed on the laptop screen, his hand hovering over the keyboard. The score increased by two runs. Dave nodded, took a deep breath and began gnawing on his fist. They were so close. So close. The cough came again. Dave held up his hand in the universal gesture of 'give me one moment'. He imagined the restrained applause of the crowd as they watched the bowler turning over the hard, red leather sphere in his hands and walking away from the crease. He could picture the bowler once again beginning his run... The cough transformed into a throat clearance. Dave held up his hand again, his head bowed over the laptop screen, his breathing faster. He pressed F5 a few times for good measure, but the live Ashes series information-ticker would not be rushed. A four! He leaned back and let out a long sigh. Yes, surely they would do it now.

"Sir," a voice said to his right.

Dave looked up. "Are you okay?" he asked. The twenty-eight faces of his physics class gazed at him in patient silence.

"I think everyone's finished, sir," the student said. Dave nodded and glanced up at the clock. The exam had finished about three minutes ago. He got to his feet and in his best booming exams voice said, "Right! Pens down everybody: stop writing." Such an instruction would usually be accompanied by a frantic burst of last-second scribbling but this time the students looked at him with the bemused expression of cows watching a passing car. A few looked around to see if Dave was addressing anyone in particular. "Has everyone put their names on the front of the papers?" The bored expressions suggested that they had. "Right, well I'll put the mark scheme up on the board then. Swap your papers with the person next to you." There was a flurry of rustling paper and Dave seized the momentary activity to check the cricket score once more. One run short and with just one ball left. He hit F5 a few more times.

"Are we marking them ourselves, sir?"

Dave nodded and turned on the projector. It was going to be close...

"What's the test out of, sir?"

"Oh, whatever all the numbers add up to," Dave said tapping F5. He clenched his fist and allowed himself a little "Yesss!" under his breath. Four runs on the last ball: they had done it. He breathed out the tension of the last half hour and smiled. The students looked at him expectantly. "Oh right, yes," Dave said and flicked the mark scheme onto the projector and read the answers to the first two questions. "Question one: It gets bigger. Uh, two is twenty-five kilonewtons."

"What if they just put twenty-five?" A student asked.

Dave sighed. "If they've missed out the kilo then it's a thousand times wrong."

"It's basically right though," another student complained.

"No. No, it's not. It's a thousand times wrong. Would you say being paid twenty-five pounds is basically the same as twenty-five thousand?" There was a brief murmur of consideration as the students began to contemplate this idea and then the bell rang. "Right, well that's the end, pass 'em all to the front. We'll finish them off next time," Dave said and the students placed the barely marked tests on the front desk as they filed out of the room. At the back of the laboratory, a man in a grey suit got to his feet. He returned his stool to one of the desks, picked up the pad of paper upon which he had been writing and approached Dave at the front.

"How was that?" Dave asked turning off the projector.

The man rubbed the back of his head with his left hand. "Well, Dave I'd have to say that the sixty seconds of peer assessment at the end was fine."

"That's great," Dave said and made a cheery thumbs-up gesture.

"Yes it is, but I would also have to say that on the whole there wasn't really all that much teaching for me to observe."

Observations were a standard part of teaching and at least once a year, every teacher could expect to be observed by some authority figure. Dave was usually spared the full ordeal of these whimsical observations by his line manager, John, who would conduct his annual observation by dropping in to a lesson for twenty minutes to check that Dave hadn't devolved into violent sociopathy over the summer and then let him get on with teaching for the rest of the year.

"You did say to just teach a normal lesson," Dave said in the cautious tone of one who suspects that they might have been tricked.

John nodded his head slowly. "I did say that, yes. But, I think it's probably worth pointing out that senior management have said they're planning a series of learning walks." Dave sighed heavily but let John continue: "So when they tell everyone to 'just teach a normal lesson' that doesn't mean that you should in any way teach a normal lesson."

"Of course," Dave said, his brow furrowed.

"It means the opposite," John said, noticing Dave's frown. "When they say 'teach a normal lesson' what they mean is: teach a completely unrealistic lesson that hits every buzzword and every bit of edu-guff from this year's guidelines and at the end, pretend it was a normal lesson." John collected his papers and headed for the door. "I know how good you are Dave: I've seen you teach some brilliant lessons, but..." he paused and shook his head. "You know how management are." The door closed behind him.

Dave dropped the unmarked tests into a box as he considered this information. He needed a plan of action. His usual philosophy was to avoid senior management wherever possible but occasionally events forced them together. Rumours had been circulating that government inspectors would soon visit the school and this prospect of external accountability had triggered an outburst of frantic management by the school's leadership team, management that predictably involved a series of "learning walks". It had never been clear to Dave where the learning in a "learning walk" was meant to be taking place. Was it those on the walk who were learning? Or were they simply taking a walk through the learning as though through some academic orchard, marvelling at the bountiful yield of learning. As with many aspects of teaching, the philosophy behind a "learning walk" was largely irrelevant, along with management's insistence that the walks were there to "support good practice". All that really mattered was that in practical terms a "learning walk" meant that Dave would be observed and judged. And whilst Dave had consistently high exam results and was a valuable member of the department, he knew that this meant very little to the senior leadership team who, off the back of a single bad observation, could immediately write off fifteen years of excellent results as an extended anomaly and demand an immediate programme of improvement.

Dave loaded up the Times Education Supplement website and went onto the academic resources. This was where all the keen teachers who paid attention to the latest fashions would upload example lessons and resources. Five years ago, Dave had uploaded some cutting-edge resources on learning styles, but learning styles had now become unfashionable, even heretical and so his once five-star resources had plummeted to less than one star and had even accumulated some enthusiastic hate-comments. "You ignorant fascist," one commenter had written, "how can you live with yourself? Labelling beautiful, complex individuals as being either visual or kinaesthetic learners: it's reductive, outdated and crushes the creativity of the children. I hope you die."

It was unclear how Dave's death was expected to help matters, but he concluded it was probably less of a suggestion and more of an indication that he should withdraw the resources from public circulation. He deleted them from the website but kept a copy on his hard drive: in five years, they would more than likely become fashionable again. It took Dave twenty minutes to get a feel for the current zeitgeist in teaching and then he downloaded some resources for tomorrow's lessons.

LESSON DELIVERY

Dave flicked through the plans he had used for the previous three lessons and at the top of each scribbled "ineffective" in red ink. The students had gone along with the activities, filling in the worksheets that he had downloaded, but it was clear to Dave that none of them had learnt anything useful about physics. He rested the plans on the intricate forest of penmanship and crisscrossing grooves etched into the laboratory desk. He had inherited the desks in something close to their current state and since no student could ever produce enough graffiti signal to cut through a decade's worth of noise, few seemed to bother anymore. He glanced over the plan for his next lesson and then, weaving between the desks, laid out five laptops. The sound of his year tens jostling and shuffling outside the laboratory door grew louder.

"Sit with whoever you want," Dave said, as he opened the door and allowed the group to file into the room.

On the whiteboard, he had written the objective: How is electricity dangerous? And underneath, an extension: How do we protect ourselves from electricity?

"Ah, laptops! Brilliant!" one of the girls shouted and sat in front of the nearest keyboard.

"So what we doing?" one of the boys asked as he grabbed a stool and sat next to the girl.

"I want you to organise yourselves into whatever groups you want and answer this question," Dave said, pointing at the board.

"What's the website?" a short, blonde-haired girl asked.

"I dunno," Dave said. "That's one of the things that you and your group are going to have to solve. Now you can copy each other and share ideas because we're all trying to find out the same thing. And at the end, your groups are going to present what they found to the rest of the class." He handed out marker pens and large sheets of white paper.

"But sir, I don't know why electricity is dangerous?"

"No, I'm aware of that. That's why I'm asking you to find that out," Dave said, pointing to the laptops.

"But I don't know how to do that," another student said.

"Well, talk to the other members of your group. I'm sure you'll figure it out."

The theory was that students were perfectly capable of teaching themselves. All the teacher had to do was provide them with the resources and then step back. The students' natural curiosity and innate capacity for problem solving would overcome the majority of obstacles and the teacher would be free to act as a consultant, refining the knowledge that the children would have taught themselves. The less input the teacher had, the better. Dave had read the research, watched a video where a group of children in rural India had taught themselves biogenetics from scratch and then watched an inspiring TED talk on the same idea; it seemed like perfect material to be seen teaching on a learning walk. However, after letting the class work unimpeded for ten minutes, Dave was beginning to have his doubts that minimal intervention was a good idea. One group had stopped using the laptop entirely and was now just talking.

"So what have you found?" Dave said, walking over. They all looked up at him.

"About what?" one boy said. His mystified look did not bode well for the lesson objective.

"About electricity."

"Oh right, yeah, it's bad," another of the boys said.

"It can kill you," a girl added.

"Okay," Dave said. "And how does the electricity kill you?"

"Well, it's 'lectricity. That's what it does."

"Yes, but how does the electricity actually kill you, what is it doing?"

"It's like. Nrrrrrrgggggh," the girl said, simulating the convulsions of electrocution. A few of the other group members laughed.

"Right, that's what being electrocuted might look like, but why is it making you do that?"

"Dunno," she said and looked around at the others in the group. They all shrugged.

"Okay, so you've found out that electricity *can* kill you: well done. But we now want to find out *how* it kills you." The group looked confused and Dave would usually have done more to support them but the lesson plan suggested that, where possible, he let the magic of their curiosity drive them forward. "A good starting place might be the internet," he said indicating the laptop. He moved onto the second group who, rather suspiciously, all seemed far too engaged with the laptop.

"So what have we found so far?" Dave asked. There was a flurry of keystrokes and the boys all looked up from the screen.

"About what?" one of the boys said.

"About electricity?"

"I dunno." He shrugged. "It's too hard."

"What do you mean it's too hard?"

"I don't get it."

"Well, what about the rest of you?" Dave said, opening the question out to the rest of the group. They all avoided eye contact and shrugged.

"Too much stuff, sir. Didn't make any sense."

"What didn't make any sense?"

"All the stuff. There was loads of it."

"So what exactly did you do?"

"Well we went to google and we typed in: why is electricity dangerous. And it just came up with loads of websites."

Dave paused as he waited for the boy to continue but he had finished. "Listing websites? Yeah, that's kinda Google's thing."

"Yeah, but there were loads of them and none of them made any sense."

"So did you look at any of them?"

"Sort of."

"And what do you mean by sort of?"

"Dunno."

"Well let's have a look at your browser history," Dave said leaning across the group and hitting control and H on the keyboard. Concern registered on their faces. "...now I can help you with some of those sites... so... uh... the first thing you typed in was 'webgames'. Does that sound familiar?"

"Yeah, no that was Neil. That wasn't me," the one sitting at the keyboard said.

"And then you followed a link to a game called Crystal Hunter."

"No, that was an accident; we didn't mean to click on that."

"No, that's easily done," Dave agreed. "But uh, it does look like you then accidentally played it for a further twelve minutes..." None of them made eye contact. "Right, you guys have a new task. Get the pen." One of the boys sheepishly picked up the marker pen. "You are now going to find out what the tragedy of the commons is, okay? Write it down. The tragedy of the commons. Find out what it is. And then tell me how it applies to you and how it relates to whether this class gets to use laptops again."

The third group were admirably engaged in the task however, their engagement seemed confined to images of electrocution scars and burns.

"Look at this one, sir: it looks like a weird tattoo," one of the boys said, stabbing an enthusiastic finger at the screen. Dave agreed that it did look like a weird tattoo, but suggested that it was not really answering the question.

The last group had devolved into three girls gathered around the large sheet of paper and using the different coloured marker pens to colour in the misspelt word "electrcity."

"What are you doing?"

"The lettering," the first girl said, carefully colouring in the tail of the "y".

"The lettering?" Dave repeated.

"Yeah, on our poster."

"Poster? What poster?"

"I thought we were making a poster," the second girl said.

"No. Why would you think that?"

"You said to make a poster on electricity."

Dave looked down at the large misspelt word with each of its letters containing a rainbow of colours. "No, I didn't. And even if that had been the task, you haven't actually done that either. You've just written the word elec-trur-city," he said, trying to pronounce the misspelling. "And then drawn lightning around it."

"Yeah, but we could add more to it next lesson," one of the girls said.

"What next lesson?"

"Are we not finishing this off next lesson?"

"No."

"Ohhh, okay," the three girls said, continuing with their careful colouring-in. "Why did you give us the paper then?"

"To make notes; so that you could tell others what you had found out."

"Oh, Sarah was finding out the information."

"So the three of you have done colouring-in whilst Sarah has looked for the information on the internet?"

"Yeah," the three of them said with the same tone of finality that suggested that this was a completely rational division of labour. Dave took the colouring pens away and gave them a sheet of lined paper so that they would not get confused and draw another poster. After another twenty minutes of strolling around the room, Dave concluded that the lesson fell short of his expectations. Whilst the exam board's specification required the students to learn about electricity and safety, to Dave's trained eye it was almost as though the students weren't interested in learning about these things. Maybe this method of teaching was better suited to teaching students about something that they already wanted to learn. Either way, it was not a lesson he would want to be seen teaching when senior management burst through the door.

By the end of the day, Dave had tried five different techniques and all of them had enjoyed minimal success. He slumped behind his desk and with his left hand plucked a student's book from the pile of marking, opening it at random. Why had all of the lessons gone so badly? He ticked a pencil-drawn diagram and underlined a number that lacked the required units. They had been the most up to date techniques with numerous positive reviews on the teaching websites. He circled some graffiti and scribbled a question mark. Maybe he had lost his touch. He had seen it happen to so many other teachers before him: the old guard steadily becoming less and less relevant, their teaching, calcifying into an inflexible regime of repeated phrases and clunky PowerPoint slides. Dave flicked through a few more pages, ticking the student's replication of the notes he had written on the board. Was this how it started? The gradual erosion of his authority and relevance? He ticked a whole string of numerical answers, scribbled "Great work, complete additional questions for next lesson," and tossed the book into a box off to his right. In a single, fluid movement, he swept his left hand out, picked up another unmarked book and flicked it open onto the desk. He had always assumed that the old teachers were stuck in their ways because they believed the new material to be stupid, but maybe it was because they could no longer make it work. He circled a graffiti penis and wrote "not physics". Maybe the old guard had always wanted to stay up to date, but lacked the ability? He gazed out of the window, did a few more ticks and then looked back down to check them – yeah, they all made sense. He scribbled the mandatory SMART target and tossed the book into the box.

♦ ♦ ♦

Dave dropped his laptop bag onto the staffroom chair, pulled off his microfleece hat and slumped next to Ben Grantham, the department's chemistry teacher. Growler Grantham had been a teacher for forty years and Dave had often wondered whether the young Grantham had started out wearing his trademark tweed jacket with leather elbow patches, or whether this sartorial selection was something he had come to later in life.

"I got a crazy headache," Dave said. Growler snorted disapprovingly but carried on reading The Guardian, his bushy eyebrows pushed together like two caterpillars trying to kiss. "You got anything planned in case you're observed?" Dave inquired. Growler lowered his paper and looked across at Dave.

"Retirement," he said in his low rumbling voice.

Once a teacher had surpassed basic competency in teaching, judgement of their performance often boiled down to the same sort of factors that you might employ to judge say, their dress sense. Whilst these factors were usually defined by the prevailing culture, they could vary greatly between individuals and could often be quite arbitrary. Dave had spent the previous evening in the pub working through the teaching strategies he had downloaded off the TES, trying to wrestle them into a series of workable lessons that he could display to the different members of senior management. However, no matter what topic he chose or which age group he considered, he could not see a way of getting them to produce good physics lessons. He had picked at the salt and vinegar crisps that had gradually turned into his dinner and scowled at his laptop.

The pub was very much Dave's spiritual home. It had the advantage of a free TV and the financial allure of not having to heat your own flat, but the main attraction was the company and the collective wisdom of the regulars. Arthur, the local postal worker had sat with his elbows on the bar and suggested that Dave try something simpler, maybe more student-centred, but as Ian the electrician had wisely pointed out, this was hard to demonstrate in the limited time he would have for a learning walk. The difficulty was not in coming up with an entertaining lesson: that was easy. All you had to do was incorporate chocolate or biscuits and suddenly the lesson would become extremely popular. However, lessons that went down this sugary street always ran the risk of being like a memorable advertising campaign for which no one could recall the product. The point was not to make a lesson memorable because of all the chocolate that had been consumed, but to make some physics concept memorable. Mike the barman had pulled them all another pint and suggested that Dave's best strategy was some kind of augmented assessment that he could apply to a selected learning episode. The others had kicked around a few more ideas, but Dave had eventually settled on Mike's suggestion since it offered the most versatility and, most importantly, the least amount of planning.

Come lesson one, Dave's headache had given up on trying to escape violently from his skull and had muted its attack to a dull thudding. He fired off a few questions about the practical the students had done the previous lesson, gave them a few worked examples of the calculations on the board and then got them to work through questions from the textbook. Usually, he would have walked around the room pointing out correct and incorrect answers, but he decided that this was a good opportunity to try out his new assessment strategy. He uploaded the textbook questions to a website and then encouraged the students to access the answers and provide feedback using their phones.

Historically, schools tended to lag several years behind the technology curve, partly due to limited funds, but mostly because teachers tended to stick with the familiar systems that they knew worked. New technology usually wafted into schools on the breeze of newly qualified teachers. And whilst Dave's uploading of the answers was not an original idea, the relative lack of innovative competition meant that as far as the school was concerned, Dave was a pioneer. The system was far from perfect, not least because phones were ostensibly banned within the school, but as Dave stood at the front watching the whole class using their technological contraband to check their answers, he felt that it was all going rather well. Obviously, before presenting the lesson, he would have to go through the pretence of obtaining some sort of temporary exemption from the phone ban, but Dave was reasonably confident he could structure a convincing argument for the technology. He could throw in a few of the academic references he had googled the previous evening, but there was no rush.

It was at this point that Katarina the headteacher, and Sandra, one of her deputies, entered the laboratory on their learning walk. The two of them looked for several seconds at the room full of students flouting the mobile phone ban and then in unison turned to look at Dave.

One of the skills that Dave felt he had truly mastered in his decade of teaching was the ability to respond to any interruption by completely ignoring it. This was not as simple as just pretending something had not happened, it was far more profound than that. Truly ignoring an interruption was to assert a complete erasure of it, to rewrite the collective experience of the group. It was an expression of such staggering confidence that it actively nullified the interrupter, often forcing them to question whether they had really interrupted in the first place. Thus, Dave actively ignored the Head and continued with his lesson.

His tactic appeared to work for maybe five minutes and then Katarina walked over to where Dave was standing. She pursed her lips as though exerting some self-control and, looking him in the eye, asked to see his lesson plan. Dave winced at the request. In practice, experienced teachers would only produce written lesson plans if they were being specifically observed or applying for a job. A learning walk did not fall into either of these categories and so Katarina's request was not only an expression of condemnation wrapped in the tacit suggestion that his lesson needed structure, but she was asking him for something that in all likelihood he would be unable to provide. Her request was arguably setting him up to fail.

When Dave had begun his training, fourteen years earlier, producing detailed lesson plans had been a routine expectation. Every morning his mentor had demanded that Dave showed them his lesson plans for the day and every morning his mentor would bemoan the lack of detail that they had contained. Dave's response had been to write computer code that did the job for him. He would enter a simple timeline of activities and then the code would produce an expanded more prosaic version, but the code's coup de grâce was its ability to take his class list and the school's database and then populate the lesson plan with massive amounts of student-specific information. It would include all the details concerning their education plans and their individual learning requirements along with all of their previous test results and where they were sitting. It was all information that Dave knew from teaching the students, but for some reason, his mentor had only believed this when he had seen it written down.

Dave now faced a dilemma. He knew that under the school's own policy, he was perfectly within his rights to refuse the Head's request for a lesson plan and that this was the sensible option. However, he had an opportunity to unleash his old code and retaliate against her implicit criticism with the nuclear warhead of excessive detail.

He loaded up the programme and paused, his finger hovering over the mouse. The only problem with unleashing his code was that in truth, his lesson plan was only six lines long and Dave was convinced that an intelligent reader would quickly see through his flimsy attempt to mask minimal content with buckets of spurious detail. He looked up at Katarina who had raised an eyebrow in a somewhat impatient gesture.

Katarina was young for a headteacher, something that the school website displayed prominently on their front page: "One of the youngest headteachers in the country," it said proudly, as though precocity might somehow be an indicator of competence. Fast-tracked into senior management, Katarina had taught business studies for a year and had then hauled her way up the career ladder, rapidly moving from the head of department, through an assistant- and then a deputy headship, before finally reaching the top job after just ten years. By Dave's calculation, Katarina had probably only operated as a full-time classroom teacher for around two years. It was entirely possible that she would be unable to distinguish a good lesson plan from a steaming pile of detail. Dave hit the button.

THE GENESIS OF DAVE

The door closed behind the last group of students as they bounced down the corridor, whooping and shouting victoriously at the slaying of yet another school day. In that moment of departure, the laboratory returned to calm, an island removed from the stream of babbling students beyond. Dave drifted between the benches, collecting the errant pens, scraps of paper and homework sheets left behind. He took all stationery as tribute, offerings that would inevitably be redistributed to those students who seemed permanently bemused by the injunction to write things down. The observation had only been that morning, but three hours of lower-school teaching had distanced the memory. And whilst the lack of feedback was typical for a learning walk, Katarina's request for a lesson plan was sufficiently weird that Dave was expecting repercussions. But this was how he always felt in teaching. Indeed, it seemed to be the dark anxiety that dwelt in the minds of all teachers: the suspicion that perhaps they were failing to do their job properly. Dave had struggled with this anxiety in his first full year. He had immolated himself with hours of additional work until he had realised that the anxiety was not due to any personal deficiency, but rather a reflection of the central tension in teaching: the job was close to impossible.

To plan, teach, assess, modify and then mark a single group's work was easy enough, that was only thirty students. But each week, Dave had twenty-two hours of unique lessons to deliver to twelve completely different teaching groups. In that week, Dave had three hours' preparation time to plan and organise resources for those twenty-two hours of teaching, a total of eight minutes per lesson: that was extremely hard. But to then require detailed marking and feedback of all the work generated by the three-hundred-plus students in those twenty-two hours of teaching: that was almost impossible. The school day ran from eight thirty to three thirty and all of that time was allocated to either teaching, planning or dealing with students. Once the bell had gone, the teacher would have time to deal with routine administrative tasks that had piled up during the day, tasks such as talking with parents on the phone, answering emails, meeting with other teachers to discuss students or sometimes just to grab a few moments to eat a sandwich. These tasks routinely extended the day to beyond five in the evening. Then there were the additional expectations, the afterschool clubs, the help sessions and the detentions, all of which could extend the working day yet further. But even after all this had been done the working day was by no means over, because the work that had been generated by all the students during the day's lessons still needed to be assessed and marked. Marking a set of books could take anywhere between an hour and two hours; with twelve groups that was an additional twelve to twenty-four hours of work a week. When you took all the additional time into account the teaching day would stretch from eight in the morning to ten in the evening, only a third of which was actually teaching. This, of course, was in a week in which there was no coursework to mark, a task that could take anywhere between two and five additional hours for each group.

In his first year, Dave had genuinely tried to fulfil all these requirements along with every whimsical notion senior management had nervously shovelled down the chain of command. He had managed to work sixty- and seventy-hour weeks for two terms and had used all his holiday time to catch up on the planning and marking he had been unable to squeeze in during term time. For Dave, the realisation that he could not do this job had come at a teacher-parent consultation evening. A parent had sat across the desk and had dismissed Dave, and indeed all teachers, as being lazy. "You don't know what hard work is," she had told him. "You get to go home at three thirty every day and you get all these massive holidays. You should try my job: that's hard work." Bleary-eyed from lack of sleep and run-down from the stress of having to provide plans for his lessons, Dave lacked the energy for anger. Instead, he had just stared at her blankly for three minutes and had then stood up and walked out of the school.

The doctor had told Dave to take the whole month off, but Dave had returned after a week. It would not have mattered how long he had taken off: the job would still have been impossible when he had returned. He had figured he might as well enjoy doing a few last lessons before they fired him and so there had seemed little point in keeping up with any of the paperwork or rushing to meet any of the myriad targets that management insisted were vital. It turned out that without all the additional loads, the job was almost fun. The weeks had turned into months and come September, Dave had been surprised to find that somehow he still had a job. After that first year, he had found ways to automate the majority of the admin, writing code that would generate self-marking homework or provide lesson plans at the push of a button, but all the while Dave had held the job lightly, fully aware that his methods were unconventional and that at any moment they would probably fire him. Thus, at the end of the day, when Dave walked into the staff room and learnt that the Head wanted to talk with him, he figured that the moment had finally arrived and it had all caught up with him.

The Head's office was sparsely decorated with a large desk and three uncomfortable chairs. Dave presumed it was to convey a sense of efficiency, but it was always possible Katarina just lacked any sense of interior décor.

"I wanted to talk with you about yesterday's lesson," Katarina said. There was a printout of his nine-page lesson plan on the desk in front of her. Dave nodded, but he remained silent. It was often better to keep quiet until the accusations had been made, that way you had more time to structure your defence. "I notice you've been with the school for some time now. Over ten years." She paused again, but Dave continued to stick with his principle of a silent defence. "Now, you're clearly an experienced teacher, but somehow you've managed to stay under our radar all this time." Dave took a deep breath. This brief retrospective definitely did not sound positive, but in fairness, this talk was probably long overdue. He would have to get his CV sorted, but that would be easy enough; in the meantime, he could work down at the garage as he sometimes did during the summer. That had always been his stand-in for when the inevitable came. The cars and the motorbikes always made a nice change and it would give him the time to figure out a new career. "As you know, Dave, we're a leading-edge school so we expect all of our teachers to hold the highest standards of teaching and learning. Schools from all over the country look to us for our leadership and guidance in how to teach." Dave leaned back in the chair and gave the calm smile of a condemned man. They would be unable to get rid of him immediately – they lacked that power – but he knew where this particular train was heading. First, they would voice their concerns over whether he was meeting the teaching standards and then they would trigger a "support programme", ostensibly to help him. Then, through tripling his workload with reviewed lesson plans and scrutinised marking of books, they would wear him down to an incompetent nub, subject him to a series of formal observations and get the dismissal they sought. He had seen it done before. And whilst it would be easy for him to get a teaching job elsewhere – good physics teachers were a rarity – he had already decided he was ready for a career change ten years ago. He was pretty good at writing computer code and he already did some freelance web design in the holidays, so in many ways he was just waiting for the school to trigger the change. Sure, he would miss the kids and his colleagues but he was ready.

"And your lesson yesterday was, quite frankly..." He held his breath in anticipation of the falling axe, "...exceptional." Dave raised an eyebrow. "We need teachers who are comfortable with technology and can convert those skills into education deliverables." Dave exhaled. This was not what he had expected at all. "It was refreshing to see an established teacher still taking the time to plan out their lessons in such rigorous detail. In fact, I was discussing your lesson with the chair of governors this afternoon and we were wondering how you'd feel about taking on a more influential role in teaching and learning?"

Dave paused as he tried to get his bearings. He had been mentally preparing for a trip to incompetence central but the sudden change of direction had found him unprepared. "Uh, I don't know. What would that entail?" he said cautiously, aware that this detour might wind up in a cul-de-sac of uncomfortable responsibility.

"We see your central role as developing teaching and learning resources within the school, sharing your skills amongst the staff and working alongside IT support to help catalyse the uptake of classroom technologies. You know, showing colleagues how to use the laptops and iPads in their lessons, that sort of thing."

"Mmmh. Okay."

"You'd obviously be delivering teaching and learning sessions on inset days, and we envision you driving the outreach and becoming a local leader in spreading the good practice that we have grown here in the school."

"Mmmh."

"Now obviously we'd pay you for this role."

"Oh. Okay, how much?"

"I think we view this as more of a gateway role. It's an important role, but not one that involves extended responsibilities or managing staff, so that would place you within TLR-three."

"TLR-three? That's up to £2500 a year."

"Yes, *up to* £2500."

"And how much additional work do you see this role taking?"

Katarina looked a little confused by the question. "Well that would depend on a lot of different factors, Dave: how efficient you are, how much you choose to engage with the role..."

"I realise that, but let's say I was to do the job well. How many hours a week, roughly, do you see that taking?"

"I wouldn't want to put some kind of official limit on something like that. It would vary depending on what the demands were in a given week."

"Sure, but as a rough average over the course of a year, are we talking two or three hours a week or twenty-three hours?"

"Well, I'd have thought it's likely to be more around four or five."

Dave nodded as he did some quick mental arithmetic. "Okay. Then it's definitely not worth my time."

Katarina looked at Dave as though he had farted. "What do you mean: it's not worth your time? We'd be paying you."

"I know, but you'd be paying me well below my usual hourly rate."

"Your hourly rate...?"

"Yeah. The school pays me around thirty pounds an hour."

"What are you talking about? The school doesn't pay you by the hour, Dave. You're paid a salary. There isn't an hourly rate."

"Yeah. No, I realise that. It's a theoretical figure. It's my wage divided by the minimum number of school hours I could work. It's not what I actually get, but it basically allows me to assign a monetary value to my free time."

"Where have you got this number from?" Katarina said. She still looked confused."

"I used the 1265 hours of contractual time."

"What?" Katarina's voice took on a menacing tone. "You're saying you don't do any additional work? You just go home at three thirty?"

"No, not at all, I often stay later than that, but in doing so I am actively reducing my hourly rate. But that's something I am consciously choosing to do."

Katarina waved her right hand as though dismissing his numbers. "I really don't understand where you've got these imaginary numbers from. You've obviously picked up this nonsense from somewhere or someone. I don't think it has any actual meaning and to be honest, I don't think that viewing your work in terms of how much you get paid per hour is a particularly helpful way to look at your situation. In fact, I think it's quite divisive."

"Sure I can see why you'd think that. But I happen to think that my time is an incredibly valuable commodity and this is a way of assigning an approximate monetary value to it."

"Of course your time is important, Dave. I'm not suggesting it isn't. Everybody's time is important, but teaching is not about how much you get paid or how much time you put into the job. It's about helping change lives and opening up opportunities for the students. And I'd hope that as an experienced teacher you'd see that."

"I agree, those are definitely important, but they don't invalidate my expertise or somehow render my time worthless."

"I'm not saying your time is worthless, Dave. That's why we'd be paying you on top of your current wage."

"Yeah I get that: you'd be paying me £2500 a year for an additional five hours every week. If I do that the maths that works out at around..." He pulled a mental arithmetic face. "Thirteen pounds an hour."

"Again, I have no idea where you're getting these imaginary numbers from, Dave."

Dave explained his calculation of multiplying up the five hours a week by the number of weeks and then using that to divide the additional money. Katarina made no effort to check the maths but just made the same dismissive hand-waving gesture as before, as though shooing the numbers out the door. "Look, this is a very different role to your normal teaching role, Dave. I don't really think you can expect to be paid at the same rate. There's a very different expectation here."

"I thought the role was *teaching* staff how to use technology in their lessons?"

"But you're not teaching the students, Dave, you're teaching other professionals. You're teaching your colleagues."

"It's still an increase in my workload."

"Look, I'm really struggling to understand what your issue is here. We're talking about a few extra hours a week for an opportunity to advance your career."

"An additional five hours a week? That's umm... a fifteen percent increase on my contracted time."

"Look, Dave, I really don't think this is a helpful way of looking at your time and in fact, it concerns me that you think of your profession in such a cold, mathematical way."

"I thought you taught business studies?"

Katarina paused as she processed this conversational swerve. "I do but I don't see how that's relevant. And in fact, I'm a very good business studies teacher so I know that teaching is about more than just numbers. It's not about how much you get paid or how much your time is worth: it's about inspiring young minds and opening doors."

Dave nodded in agreement. "That is refreshing to hear you say that: I totally agree. So is that how you see this teaching and learning role? As shifting the school away from focussing on exam performance and the cold mathematical analysis of results and us moving more towards inspiring curiosity and a love of knowledge in the students?"

Katarina narrowed her eyes. "No," she said slowly. "And I don't think that those are mutually exclusive. I think if we can inspire the students they will want to do well, but..." she stopped and held her hands up. "Look I'm not going to get dragged into a discussion on the philosophy of teaching. For some reason, you seem to have latched onto these numbers and are using them to justify... I don't know what. I don't understand why you'd turn down this incredible opportunity to progress your career. We're talking a few extra hours a week at most. And you'd be on TLR-three. So, if you want this opportunity to make an impact on the students, then we'd be happy to offer you this role. Otherwise, we'll just find someone else who does want to make a difference."

"Well if you can find someone who's got comparable expertise and is willing to work for thirteen pounds an hour, then I say go for it: that's a bargain."

"So you're not interested?"

"I appreciate you offering me the opportunity, but at thirteen pounds an hour? No."

"I must say I'm a little disappointed in you, Dave."

"That's okay, I'm sure you'll find someone."

Katarina didn't reply to this, but instead got up, opened the office door and thanked Dave for his time. Dave walked out into the low evening sunshine with almost exactly the same sense of impending uncertainty that he had held before the meeting.

THE CHAIR OF GOVERNORS

Dave slid the laptop bag off his shoulder and slumped into his usual chair. He stared at the polystyrene ceiling tiles as he massaged his temples.

"Another late night?" The rumbling comment came from behind the newspaper in the corner. Dave presumed it was Growler.

"Nine thirty? No, not particularly," he said, directing his response to the front page of the Guardian. "You realise you can read that online for free, right?"

Growler Grantham shrugged or rather Dave inferred this from the resulting ripple that ran through the sheet. "Easier to avoid people this way," he said and then after a few moments lowered the paper and looked at Dave. "You're still here?" he observed.

"Uh, I can go if you'd like?" Dave said, indicating the door.

Growler chuckled like distant thunder. "I meant: you still have a job? How'd it go with Katarina?" he asked, resting the paper on his lap.

Dave said he had been surprised at receiving praise for his lesson but the surprise had slipped into caution once Katarina had offered him the teaching and learning post.

"Teaching and learning?" Growler said, turning the words over in his mouth as though trying an unfamiliar food. "What the hell sort of position is that?"

Mary, one of the department's biology teachers, let out a loud "hah!" from where she had been listening on the other side of the staff room. "Sounds like a tick-box position to me," she said, lifting her reading glasses and resting them on top of her head.

Mary had worked in several schools before this one and had even spent four years as a deputy head at a school in Manchester before making the unusual career move of dropping back down to being a classroom teacher. When people asked her about the change she would often say how much she had missed the classroom, or as she often put it, "actually doing something useful." However, when Dave had asked her about her career change at the Christmas meal, she had leaned in close and confessed that the change had been motivated more by loneliness than a desire to return to teaching. "It was tough to find people to talk with. Friends who were classroom teachers never felt comfortable complaining about management around me," she had said, nursing a glass of Malbec. "And management would complain about the staff just as much, but the problem with them was you were never free from the politics. If you offered an opinion or tried to defend someone, you were vulnerable; that'd be used against you. It was always politics." She had adjusted her paper crown and frowned. "And to be honest, they were all a bit weird." Dave had smiled at Mary's tipsy confession as he smiled at her current sober insight. The sudden offer of the teaching and learning position was unlikely to be down to Dave's detailed lesson plan, but rather that management now needed him. In every school, there were certain systems or activities that needed to be in place for the government inspectors to feel that the school was doing a good job. The inspectors would wander around the school ticking off evidence on their checklist and at the end they would point to whatever was missing. Some of the boxes were obvious, like a system of feedback for the students or good exam results, but others were less obvious and the sudden urgency to create a teaching and learning position with its broad technological objectives and community outreach, suggested that some of these more obscure boxes had not been met. The approaching spotlight of an inspection had galvanised management into scrabbling for a solution and that solution had apparently been Dave.

"So did you take the job?" Mary asked. Dave shook his head and explained his hourly rate argument. Mary chuckled. "They won't have liked that."

"Why not? It's a reasoned argument: I'm just assigning a monetary value to my free time."

Mary pulled a pitying face, as though a toddler had just asked her why some people were nasty. "It's very generous of you to imagine that they'll see your reasoning, Dave, but I think they'll just assume that you're lazy."

The day's timetable lumbered forward and barged into lesson one. Dave had planned for his year nine group to find the energy content of different foods by burning them and measuring the resulting temperature rise in water. It was an engaging practical that the students always enjoyed and one that inevitably left the lab smelling like his old student-kitchen. Dave demonstrated the practical at the front, setting fire to a cheesy wotsit and talking through all the safety steps and measurements they would be taking. Enthused by the opportunity to indulge in their pyromania, the year nine group bustled and murmured as they speculated on how much energy was to be obtained from burning the desk, clothes and various friends. However, before they could be set loose on sacrificing their possessions to the flames, Dave harnessed their enthusiasm and directed them into writing their results table and method, as all his experiments required. There was minimal objection since the group was familiar with Dave's lessons, and some had already started. The class laboured in something approaching silence as they drew the experimental setup, a perfect moment for Martin, one of the assistant heads, to walk into the lab.

"Ah there you are," he said, as though Dave's timetabled location had somehow been hitherto a mystery. Martin was a wisp of a man, slender with a questionable goatee beard and a dark-grey suit that made him look like an accountant. He looked around at the class working in silence and gave a little nod of satisfaction. "That's what we like to see," he said as he approached Dave at the front, "the troops all working hard."

Over the years, Martin had developed an affectation wherein he would ignore the conventions of personal space, presumably in the misguided belief that it imparted an air of confidence, and would put his arm around relative strangers or lean in uncomfortably close as though telling them something conspiratorial. Martin moved to within a few feet of Dave and lowered his voice as though wishing to speak into his ear. Dave ignored the cue for him to lower his head and so Martin muttered into Dave's armpit, "Gary Henderson wants to speak with you." He patted Dave on the back. Unfortunately, Martin had failed to recalibrate his tactile dominance for someone as tall as Dave and ended up patting Dave just above his backside. Dave looked down at Martin with a raised eyebrow.

"Who's Gary Henderson?" he said.

"Gary?" Martin said, withdrawing his hand and making a series of exaggerated hand gestures to try to distract Dave from what had just occurred. "How can you not know Gary? Gary Henderson's the chair of governors."

"Uh huh," Dave said and then directed his attention to a student with their hand in the air.

"He's over in Katarina's office."

"Okay, but I'm teaching right now," Dave said, handing a ruler to the student.

"I can cover this," Martin said, waving a hand to indicate the students working in silence.

Dave looked at him doubtfully. "They're going to be doing a burning food practical; I think it'd be a good idea if I was here."

Martin gave a half-laugh, "Dave, I've been teaching for twenty years, I think I can handle a group of year nines. Go have your meeting, it'll be fine."

"Right, but you're a maths teacher."

"Maths and science are essentially the same subjects," Martin said reaching up and placing a hand on Dave's shoulder. "And I'm an assistant head, Dave: I know what I'm doing."

Dave shrugged and gave him a brief description of the experiment, but Martin cut across him again and insisted it was all obvious. "Just go."

Dave left Martin to the year nines and in the late morning sun, wandered over to Katarina's office.

Gary Henderson was a broad man with a large flat face and dyed-blonde hair. Dave had never seen Gary before, but he concluded from the pink shirt, clashing tie and tweed jacket that Gary probably was not all that big on listening to advice.

"You must be Dave," Gary said at a volume that seemed inappropriate for the size of Katarina's office. He stepped forward and crushed Dave's fingers in a combative handshake.

"That's an impressively firm handshake," Dave said extricating his fingers. The observation seemed to disarm Gary. Dave had violated the unwritten rule that a handshake remains undiscussed between opposing parties. "Okay... I'm Gary Henderson: chair of the governors at the school here," he boomed as Dave massaged the blood flow back into his digits. "But obviously that's not my main role: I'm primarily a businessman. And a very successful one." As he said this, Gary hooked his thumbs behind his trouser-suspenders, rocked back onto his heels and gazed out of the window with a Napoleonic stare. "That means I'm a pragmatist. I didn't get to be where I am today by beating around the bush. I'm direct with people and I expect them to be direct with me. I'm not one for all this sugar coating of things; I say it like I see it. I'm a straight talker, you see, I cut right to the chase..." He tapped the desk twice and brought his hand up in a pointing gesture "...so I'm going to get straight down to brass tacks with you, Dave."

Dave enjoyed this preamble, precisely because it was so lacking in self-awareness: direct people rarely employed clichés and they certainly never spent time telling people how direct they were.

"Katarina showed me your lesson plan and told me about your work with the students and I said to her: I want to meet this guy. Now I don't claim to be an expert in teaching, Dave, but I know a good lesson when I see one. And I know a good teacher when I meet one. And you're exactly the sort of teacher we want leading this school."

Dave murmured a cautious thank you, still unsure where this was all heading.

Gary walked over to the window and gestured at the world beyond. "You know what matters out there, Dave?" he asked rhetorically. "Skills. If you've got the skills, you'll do well. If you don't have the skills, then you'll fail. Look at any successful business and you'll see they're successful because they have the right skills." Dave contemplated pointing out the teleology in this false dichotomy but as he watched Gary rock back and forth on his heels, he got the feeling that Gary was unused to learning new things. "Now you've got the right skills, Dave. You've got the technology skills and you've got the teaching skills; that's why we offered you the teaching and learning position. You're the sort of teacher that can make this business a successful business. Now Katarina tells me you turned that position down?"

Dave nodded.

"Now I personally think you're the right candidate for this position, Dave," Gary said, frowning as he looked down at the desk. He paused to inject some dramatic tension and then allowed a smile to break across his face as he said, "So the school is prepared to increase its offer and pay you on

TLR-two!" He nodded as though agreeing with the brilliance of his own suggestion. "What do you say to that?"

"Well, it kind of depends on whereabouts within the TLR-two pay range you were thinking. The bottom end of TLR-two is essentially the same as the top end of TLR-three."

Gary's eyes narrowed and he lifted his chin. "I like you, Dave." He said with a slow, reappraising nod. "You're a strong negotiator and I like that. You remind me a lot of myself." He waved a hand as though wiping away the previous offer. "Okay, here's what we're prepared to do: three large, but you start working on the position straight away."

"Three thousand?" Dave said. Outside of TV, he had never heard someone refer to thousands as "large". "On my current rate of pay that's an additional two and a half hours a week."

Gary shrugged his shoulders, "I'm a businessman, Dave. I don't care how many extra hours you work. It could be two or it could be two hundred: it doesn't matter. What's important in business is the end result. Those are the details that matter. You go to any successful businesses and I guarantee they will know all the details on their key measurables. Because that's how they know that they're a success. I'm not interested in any of this loosey-goosey, airy-fairy stuff, I'm about end results."

"Huh. Okay. So in this particular context of a teaching and learning position, what do you see as constituting 'measurable results'?"

"Well, that's obvious, Dave: better results. I mean this is a school, that's what schools produce."

"It is? Okay, I guess you could argue that's one measure. So are you looking for an improvement in the results of one particular department or were you expecting an improvement from all departments throughout the entire school?"

"Ideally across the entire school, Dave. You've got to set your sights high: this is a school-wide initiative."

Dave raised an eyebrow. "Okay, so let me clarify: when the results come out this summer, if you see any improvement in any results from any department in this school, you're going to attribute that improvement to me?"

"No. Don't be ridiculous, Dave. You couldn't possibly claim that it was just down to you."

"Good, I totally agree: the outcome of a thousand teenagers sitting multiple exams in multiple subjects after two years of study is an extremely complex system with a huge number of contributing factors. It would be totally unreasonable to imagine that one person could be solely responsible for that improvement. So, how do you propose we assess my contribution to those improved results?"

Gary laughed uncomfortably. "Look, Dave, I never claimed to be an expert in teaching, I'm just a businessman. I don't need to be an expert in every area that I deal with. All I need is the big picture and then I can set things in motion. The school will clearly have systems for making measurements on teachers, otherwise how else could you distinguish between good and bad teachers?"

"Well, good and bad teaching is a qualitative judgement; you can do that by simply watching someone teach. But you're asking for a quantitative measure."

"Yeah, in business that's what matters. I'm not interested in people's opinions about how well something is going: I just need the cold, hard data. That's the bottom line."

"Our current system is to take a class of hormone-addled teenagers, make them sit an exam one sunny morning in June and then make that the measure of how well you have taught them over the last two years. I'm unaware of any methodology that can separate out and weight all of the other contributing factors to those results. You know: things like genetic predisposition, culture, economic background, parents, friends and obviously my proposed contribution of marginally increasing their use of iPads. But if there some way of splitting all that out, I totally think we should use it."

Gary leaned forward as if he hadn't heard Dave properly. "What? It seems like you're saying that teachers have no impact. That it doesn't really matter what you do."

"Oh not at all, teachers definitely have an impact on students, I don't doubt that for a moment. But you're the one that wanted to make this role about measurables, Gary. I'm just being a pragmatist. I'm saying there isn't some metric with which you can assess a single teacher's contribution to a child's success or failure."

"You're wrong, Dave. There are systems out there, there must be, otherwise how else could all these schools be operating performance-related pay? They must be using data from somewhere."

"Oh there's no shortage of data, we have plenty of that. But you said you wanted a measurable." A bell rang from outside the office. It was far too early for it to be the end of the lesson and the ringing continued for five or six seconds. It rang just long enough to suggest it needed a response and then it stopped. Gary's brow furrowed as he experienced an uncharacteristic bout of uncertainty. Dave was unsure whether this was due to the bell or his comment on measurable data, but either way, Gary decided to eschew the new sensation and stepped back onto the path of certainty.

"Fine, we'll switch the focus," he said loudly. "Part of this new role is technology, so the school will want to see a definite increase in the uptake of technology in lessons. That's a definite measurable for you. Okay?"

"Sure. Have we got baseline data against which to measure this increase?"

Gary rested his hands on the desk and leaned forward. "Look, Dave, I appreciate that you're a details man, and that's one of the reasons why we want you in this role because you're focussed on all the irrelevant details. However, in business it's often less about the specifics and more about the big picture; that's what's more important. The details can be finalised by other people. At the end of the day what we want from you is some sort of outreach to support our partner schools and a few training sessions on technology in the classroom. So, are you with us?"

In the space of a few minutes, Gary had managed to move the role from having to meet impossibly idealistic specifics to fulfilling a few loose generalities. It suggested that the most important aspect of the teaching and learning position was not what the position could accomplish but simply that the position existed.

"Sure," Dave said. "I'll do it."

"Great!" Gary shook Dave's hand with the same crushing force as before. "Good to have you on board. Just to give you a heads-up: I'm sure you're already aware, but the school is expecting a government inspection in the next few weeks. Now a few of the things they'll possibly want to look at are the school's integration of technology into the curriculum and our wider teaching-and-learning outreach. You know, how we help support our partner schools and things like that."

"Oh right. Do we do that?"

Gary cleared his throat. "Well, the school supports a lot of different projects and we're always looking for new ways to step forward and to engage with new challenges..." Dave took this to mean, no, "...so as the newly appointed teaching and learning director..." Dave raised an eyebrow at the epithet "director". He would have preferred "tsar" but he allowed Gary to continue, "...they will probably want to see evidence of how you're integrating technology into the curriculum and what sort of outreach you're doing to support other schools."

"Well, that would make sense," Dave said, smiling at the adjustments Gary was already making to his language: shifting the emphasis from what the school wanted to achieve, to what Dave should be doing.

"So whatever you decide to implement, it needs to be soon."

This was in some ways the essence of management: the redistribution of responsibility. If the government inspectors didn't feel the teaching and learning position ticked enough boxes, management would now have Dave to blame for the shortfall. On the other hand, if Dave could survive the inspection, management would congratulate themselves on their savvy appointment and then, he hoped, slip back into gently ignoring him.

Dave strolled across the empty playground back to the Science department. The cold air was thick with the blunt scent of decaying leaves and Dave exhaled with a controlled sigh. He had gone into the office convinced that the promotion was nonsense and this had not changed. The money was welcome but a financial supplement of three grand would not come without some additional cost. Maybe he was bored. He knew plenty of people that had taken on extra responsibilities just to do something different with their lives, but he had never thought of himself as being one of them. The more he thought about it, the more he realised that what had really drawn him in, was the absurdity of the situation.

The automatic-door sensor failed to register Dave's existence and thus returned the doors to their humble non-automatic origins. He waved his hand a few times above his head, trying to communicate his presence to the sensor, but the sensor was having none of it. Dave grabbed the handle and wrestled against the door's resistance to being manually operated. The Science corridor was hazy, the far end made grey by the cumulative density of smoke. This was relatively common in Science; many experiments could result in a haze permeating the corridor, but this one seemed particularly bad. As Dave approached his laboratory, the atmosphere grew thicker and the white noise of chaos grew louder. He opened the laboratory door and a cartoonish wall of smoke tumbled out and swirled around his feet. Martin was standing at the front shouting, "No, put that out! I said put it out..." A student ran across the back of the class with their exercise book held aloft, its smouldering corner trailing little swirls like an incense burner. "I'll get angry," Martin threatened. Dave stood in the doorway watching them through the acrid cloud.

The students closest to the door were the first to notice him and murmured "shit" and fell silent, quickly stubbing out the melted ends of their pens on the desk. Dave pulled the handle on the gas cut-off valve by the door and all of the Bunsen burners in the room flickered and died. There was confusion from the more distant students but the silence continued to ripple outwards as more and more of them became aware of Dave's presence. Martin misinterpreted the silence as a response to his threat of getting angry.

"That's much better," he said. "Now I don't want to get angry but I will." The student with the smouldering exercise book seemed confused by the silence but continued to waft it in front of their friend's face. The friend hissed at them to stop and turn around. The student glanced over their shoulder and did a double take as they registered the outline of Dave in the doorway. At this point Martin realised that the sudden turnaround in behaviour was more likely attributable to Dave's return than his own threats.

"Get those windows open," Dave said to the room, his voice no louder than usual, but his tone unequivocal. "You," he said indicating the student with the smouldering book, "outside." He clicked his fingers, the click resolving into a forefinger pointing at the door. The student stubbed out the corner of their book in the sink and slunk out of the room, avoiding Dave's unrelenting glare. Martin folded his arms and nodded at the room, as though somehow backing up Dave's authority. The students all knew that a line had been crossed: the thick cloud of acrid smoke was difficult to deny, and whilst none of them felt they were individually to blame, there was a sense of collective guilt that Dave could now exploit. He took his position at the front of the class and in the same calmly assertive voice said, "All of the equipment: away." Since none of the students wished to be the focus of Dave's attention, they carried out the instruction in eerie silence. Martin cleared his throat of the fumes.

"They were pretty good to start with," he said, "but, uh, I think they started to lose it a little bit at the end there." He gave a little laugh, "you know how they can get before lunch."

"Mmmh," Dave said, refusing to give Martin the absolution he sought.

"Some of this food produces quite a lot of smoke, doesn't it?" He chuckled again.

"Mmmh," Dave said as he leaned over a sink and with his thumb and forefinger plucked out the charred remains of an object that looked to be the unholy union of three biros and a pencil all melted together. The students seated near the sink all seemed extremely busy with their write up, with at least two of them struggling to use the thin flexible core of their former pens.

"You appear to have lost the outside of your biros," Dave observed with mild interest as though commenting on a change in the weather. He continued to hold the melted mass at arm's length. Both students looked shocked, "No sir, they've been like this for ages," they said.

"Uh-huh." Dave walked over to his desk and dropped the monstrosity into the bin. He turned to Martin. "Well, thank you for watching them," Dave said giving only slight emphasis to the passivity of "watching", "I think I can take it from here."

"Absolutely," Martin said with a vigorous nod. "And, uh, if you need any support or extra firepower, just, uh, give me a shout."

"Mmmh," Dave said.

38

The difficulty that Dave had faced for most of his professional life was that the endpoint in teaching was fundamentally abstract. He had once spent an evening explaining this concept to the regulars at the bar, for whom the endpoint of teaching had always seemed entirely self-evident: surely, the kids have to understand whatever concept you are trying to teach them. But this, Dave had tried to explain, is an abstract outcome; it's not always clear if someone's understood an idea and the road to them acquiring that understanding can differ wildly from student to student. How do you know when all thirty students have understood? They all seemed to think it was obvious that you would test them, but Dave had insisted that all this revealed was either how easy or hard you had made the test or how much revision the students had decided to do. If a student did badly on their test because they had been up all night playing Xbox, did that make you a bad teacher or your methods inadequate? Mike the barman had suggested that the measure should be how well the students did in their final exams, but Dave's rebuttal was that by this point it was arguably too late to be finding out you were doing something wrong. Besides, this method was still fraught with the problem of demotivated students. He had gone round the bar and asked each of them how they knew when they had done a good job. Arthur the postal worker had said that he was happy once he had emptied his sack and had then laughed himself into a coughing fit. Ian the electrician had said that he was happy when everything worked safely. A passing contract lawyer had chipped in and had said that she knew she had done a good job when both parties had left the negotiation feeling they had something out of the contract. Mike had just poured Dave a pint and pointed at it. However, for a former perfectionist like Dave, this nebulosity was what had made teaching such a dangerous job. It was always possible to do more. You could always spend more time planning a lesson, more time coming up with a better set of questions, marking another set of books or trying to solve students' personal problems and home lives. No one would ever step in and say, "that's fine. You've done enough for today." After his breakdown, Dave's solution had been to abandon all job-specific perfectionism and instead perfect his optimisation of the work-life balance.

On first consideration, Dave's new teaching and learning role looked like it might suffer from the same nebulosity as the rest of teaching, but the more he thought about it the less concerned he became. He took the river path to the pub. It was slightly longer than the route through town but far more scenic and on this particular evening, he enjoyed how the pale winter-light gave the river a solid, glassy appearance. He realised that his new appointment was really quite specific, all that actually needed to happen was for the government inspectors to like what Dave was doing. And unlike teaching, the only people who would be disadvantaged by him failing in this were those in management and, at a stretch, himself. This relative lack of consequence felt like a luxury. He walked up the old stone steps from the river path and into the warmth of the low-ceilinged bar. A fire crackled in the hearth, the room scented with hot metal and wood smoke. Obviously, he would still have the usual pressure of the possible futures of a hundred or so young adults resting on his classroom teaching, but the new role would not add to that pressure in any way, and that felt liberating. He took off his hat and gloves and walked across the strongly patterned carpet to the table next to the fireplace. A woman with shoulder-length chestnut hair and a well-fitting green woollen sweater stood up to greet him with a brief hug. Despite being some years younger than Dave was, Heather had still accumulated a decade of teaching experience and where Dave had remained in the same school, Heather had worked in several. Dave valued Heather's insights over many of his colleagues because, as he saw it, she had seen a wider range of crazy. He asked Heather how her teaching was going, but Heather was more interested in the details of Dave's new appointment.

"And they've called it teaching and learning kaiser?" she said with a sceptical expression.

"It was something stupid like that," Dave said, opening out a packet of crisps and placing it like a groundsheet in the middle of the circular table. "I'm not entirely sure why I agreed to it though," he picked out a crisp. "It just all seemed so absurd I sort of found myself going 'yeah, why not?'."

Heather sipped her pint as Dave gradually worked his way through the crisps and explained how he had come into his role as "teaching and learning kaiser". She chuckled at his hourly-pay argument and laughed at it being interpreted as a negotiating tactic.

"They obviously really needed someone," she said. Dave agreed. "So what's your plan? What're you going to show the inspectors?"

"Obviously something to do with technology and teaching?" Dave said and opened another packet of crisps.

"Nice. Good plan."

"Thanks. How would *you* go about getting more technology into teaching?"

"That's easy: I'd appoint someone like you, Dave." Dave rolled his eyes and suggested that this was a terrible solution. Heather continued, "I think if you were to take out general technological ignorance, then I'd guess the main obstacle for most teachers is probably a lack of good resources."

Dave extracted his phone from his trouser pocket and gave an encouraging nod. "Yeah, that's good. That's something I can totally work with," he said, swiping the screen a few times as the phone reluctantly emerged from slumber. "I can easily put together a site that pulls together loads of resources and stuff."

"It might be an idea to organise them around the curriculum. That way you could just look up the topic you're teaching and see if there's anything labour saving. Even just links to good YouTube videos would be a start."

Dave nodded and rested his phone on the table so he could type more rapidly. "Yeah, that's easy enough..." he left his sentence hanging as he frantically transferred the idea into the phone. Heather smiled at the stalled conversation and gazed at the fire. Mike had recently added another log and the flames were lazily wending their way across the rough bark, catching the protrusions and smoothing them into embers. A few minutes later Dave looked up and said, "Yeah, I reckon I could get all that online in an evening or two."

"Okay, well that's the tech box ticked," Heather said bringing her attention back to him.

"Yeah, so outreach is a bit harder. Obviously, I'll run some technology training sessions, but I kind of want to do something that stands out as being different. You know, maybe getting other schools involved in something?"

Heather looked puzzled. "What you mean like some sort of academic research?"

"No, but that's not a bad idea," Dave said. "Maybe I could put together some research on how effective certain strategies are?"

Heather sucked air through her teeth, making a sound similar to that of a builder criticising a rival's handiwork. "I dunno, Dave, I don't think research sounds all that feasible. I mean it's a nice idea, but to be honest, I don't think you're going to have enough time. The inspection will be in what? Two weeks? Academic research'll take way longer than that."

"I could do a write-up on just a single lesson. I've seen papers that have done that before." Dave sounded hopeful.

"Yeah, but those are usually by established academics, Dave. They've no idea who you are, they're not going to print the musings of some unknown teacher. They'll reject it out of hand." Dave nodded reluctantly. "And you're going to need something concrete for the inspectors: they're not going to give you a tick for good intentions."

"No, hang on," Dave said shifting on his stool to sit more upright, "I have got some data. In fact, I've got a ton of data."

"About what?"

"You remember that whole seventy-thirty thing, about two years ago?" Dave said.

"Yeah I remember: thirty percent you talking, seventy percent them doing stuff?"

"Yeah that's the one," Dave said. "Well our place didn't think of it so much as a guideline than as a fundamental law. They gave us all stopwatches and told us to start logging our talking time."

Heather opened her eyes wide. "Wow. That is... that is different. I can think of several reasons why that's completely ridiculous."

"Yeah, I know, tell me about it. We even had senior management coming down and checking our logs every Friday."

"They actually checked? Didn't they have anything better to do?"

"Evidently not," Dave said with an accompanying shrug. "I think management tend to panic when they're not actively interfering in stuff."

Heather looked bemused. "But surely you could have just written anything?" She said.

"Yeah I know and I'm pretty sure that that's what everybody did."

"And they just accepted that?"

"Like I said, the whole thing was ridiculous. And..." Dave sighed at the memory and ran a hand through his hair. "Well, at the time it really bugged me. It was all so completely lacking in any kind of critical thought. I felt trapped by the stupidity of it all. Do you ever get that? Like there's this crushing mass of stupidity and you feel like you're the only one that sees it, but you're just completely powerless to do anything about it?"

"Yeah, I call those weekdays."

Dave laughed. "Yeah, I guess it's probably pretty common. Anyway, my solution was to actually take data."

"How'd you mean?"

"That whole seventy-thirty thing was such an arbitrary division of time and yet they were piling all these resources into enforcing it I thought: is it actually possible to measure a difference in student performance based on the amount of time you spend talking? So since we were logging the time anyway, I taught each group with a different prime number ratio of talking to doing."

"Why prime numbers?"

"Oh, you know how it is: people love prime numbers, they seem to think they're magic or something."

"You mean like thirteen herbs and spices, or seven things you must do before you die?"

"Yeah exactly. That's the only thing I can think appealed about seventy thirty: it boiled down to a seven to three ratio. So I decided to take each group and teach each of them with their own exclusive ratio. So one group had a five to three ratio, where I'd only ever teach them by talking for three minutes and they'd work for five, and then the other groups were like eleven to seven and thirteen to five."

Heather laughed. "That's hilarious. How long were you doing that for?"

"Well about six months."

"Six months!"

"Yeah, management eventually got bored with the whole ratio thing and moved onto demanding we all did active group learning or something."

"And did you find anything?"

"No of course not: it was all complete nonsense. But I do have a shed load of data, so I can totally write up some sort of paper on the most effective teaching ratio."

"But you just said the data didn't show anything?"

"Yeah, it didn't, I only ever did the study with classes of thirty, which, if I'd wanted to do some serious academic research would have been statistically meaningless. But for the job of providing a vague conclusion and a faintly academic paper, this data is perfect."

"Unless they pick up on your sample size and reject it before you get a chance to show the inspectors."

"Yeah they may do, but I'm not actually trying to produce some high-calibre research, all I need is something to show the inspectors when they come knocking on my door. The very fact I'll have submitted a research paper is probably going to be impressive enough for them. I mean, how many schools submit research papers?"

"Mmmh," Heather sounded doubtful. "I don't know, Dave. I really don't think it's going to be possible to write a research paper in a week."

Dave finished off his pint and placed it firmly on the table. "Seriously, I'm gonna start on this sucker right now." He reached down to his bag and took out his laptop. "How hard can it be? I mean, I just need something I can submit, it's doesn't actually need to be any good."

"Ah, the indomitable spirit of educational research," Heather said and took out a wad of unmarked tests from her rucksack. She knew Dave well enough to recognise the signs of singular focus and so, true to her usual Friday-night routine, she trawled her way through a pile of marking, red pen in hand. Occasionally Dave would pause from his laptop to take a swig of ale or to paw a handful of crisps into his mouth, but otherwise, he typed tirelessly throughout the evening. Music played from behind the bar and groups of drinkers came and went. Most paid them scarce attention but one young man in a black t-shirt stumbled over and sloshed his pint onto their table. "What you doing? You writing or something?"

"Marking," Heather said. Dave ignored the man completely, his head bowed over his laptop, his fingers a flurry of keystrokes.

"Marking?" Initially, the man seemed confused by this answer but then as he brought his mental processing to bear on the verb he concluded "What? You like a teacher or sommat?"

"Yes."

"Oh right," he said. Then as he searched his mental records for what stereotype this entailed he added with a sneer, "Teaching? That's an easy job that is. Teachers get to go home at half three."

Heather met his unfocused gaze for a few seconds and said, "What time is it now?"

The man fumbled for his phone and peered at the screen. "Uh, half ten," he said.

"Okay, well I haven't been home yet."

The man looked a little confused by this evidence bumping up against his preconception and he made a series of poorly articulated noises as he sought a counter-argument. "Yeah but, you're in the pub."

"Yes, marking."

"Yeah... but, teaching's easy," the man repeated, but this time the certainty had ebbed from his voice. "You get the whole summer off."

Heather returned to her marking. "Well, maybe you should become a teacher then," she said, ticking a student's answer without looking up. "I'm told they get to go home at half three."

By the time Dave had finished the bar was almost empty. Mike the barman was stacking crates of empty bottles by the back door and a man in his fifties with grey stubble was leaning against the wall awaiting a taxi.

"Done," Dave said, twisting his laptop around so that Heather could see his creation. Heather had finished her marking and was now surfing the internet on her phone. She looked up.

"You've finished the whole thing?" She frowned and rested her phone on the table.

"Well, I'm still a bit doubtful about the conclusion, but pretty much."

"That's ridiculous," she said, scrolling down through the pages of his writing. "It actually does read like an academic paper. You've even got graphs."

"Yeah, academics love a graph or two."

"And you did all this, this evening?" Heather looked impressed.

Dave gave a dismissive shrug, "Well, the data was already processed and let's be honest, the writing's not really saying anything all that clever."

"I can't quite believe that I was just sitting here the whole time this was being created."

"I'm still not sure about the conclusion, though."

"Why not?"

"The scientist in me wants to point out that studies like this are unhelpful and the results largely meaningless, but the objective is to get published and the pragmatist in me knows that a catchy headline result is far more likely to get picked up. No-one's interested in null results and a critique of the system."

"So what have you concluded?" Heather said scrolling down to the end of the document. She began reading the last paragraph and chuckled. "Right, so you've suggested that every group of students is unique; I don't think you're going to get much pushback on that." She tapped the down arrow and carried on reading "And then you've somehow managed to conclude that *'every group will thus have its own perfect integer ratio of educating to enacting'*." She sat back and laughed. "I like the phrase *'ratio of educating to enacting'*, that's... that's actually quite catchy."

"You think it's too much?"

"What? That you've concluded something completely unrelated to the data?" Heather laughed again. "As a scientist, I think it's terrible. But, as a work of irony, I think it's genius."

"Well, I doubt anyone's going to actually read it."

INSPECTION

On Monday morning the school was told they would have a government inspection starting on Tuesday. For many teachers, the arrival of government inspectors was a professionally traumatic event. Partly because it held the existential threat of being judged and found wanting, but more importantly, if an inspector were to make an even vaguely negative comment about their lesson it would invariably lead to an indignant management delivering retribution to that teacher and their department over the following months. Teachers frantically updated classroom displays and got students to help clear away the stacks of paperwork that had accumulated at the back of classrooms, their once empty cupboards suddenly overflowing from the flash flood of seldom-used books and test papers.

On Tuesday morning Dave walked into school half an hour earlier than usual, thinking it would be a good idea to spend an extra few minutes tidying his laboratory and was mildly surprised to find the car park completely full. The school was a buzz of activity with teachers rushing around sticking up displays and swearing at the printers and Dave imagined that somewhere in the school a group was frantically shredding piles of incriminating evidence. He had deliberately tried to unplug from the group anxiety by avoiding conversations, planning his lessons for the next three days and ensuring that the majority of his books were marked, but the thrum of nervous activity was difficult to avoid. From his classroom, Dave looked out onto the rear of the school canteen and the waste bins. On this particular morning, Martin and two teaching assistants were bundling the school's most disruptive students into the back of a minibus. The students were all swearing loudly and were slavishly rebelling against the school uniform policy in exactly the same unimaginative way: all without ties, the boys with their white trainers and untucked shirts and the girls with their skirts rolled up to the point where they were arguably more of a belt. They had no idea what was happening to them, but Dave knew. The inspectors were delicate beasts who had to be gently wafted from lesson to lesson to witness dazzling displays of students' work and rows of model citizens eagerly consuming and consolidating perfect learning. This Potemkin village would be unobtainable if the problematic students were allowed to remain and so the school had hastily arranged an exciting series of field trips for them over the next three days. There was something quietly dystopian about bundling disruptive children into the back of a bus and removing them from official scrutiny.

At morning briefing, the government inspectors were introduced to the staff. It was a strange gathering. The inspectors stood at the front, brightly introducing themselves with relaxed smiles and self-deprecating comments as though addressing the village fete.

"We're not here to judge individuals or to look at individual teaching," the lead inspector said with a gentle laugh. "We're not looking for lesson plans and learning objectives. No. In fact, chances are you probably won't even see us." She beamed a smile at the room. The staff sat hunched in silence: pale faces with dark shadows under their eyes, a room of jiggling legs and chewed-on lips. "We just want to get a sense of how the school runs and what it's like for the students here."

After the introduction, John, the head of Science, gathered the department together in his laboratory. He leaned back against the front desk with his arms folded, looking like he was about to attend a funeral in his black suit. "I don't want you to panic about the inspection," John said. "But I would completely ignore what they just told you. They will judge you. And you will see them. So make sure you have full lesson-plans and the objectives on the board."

"But they said they weren't looking at that?" Steve, the newly qualified biology teacher said. He sounded bemused. John gave him a pitying look and explained that this was how all inspections seemed to run: they would say they wanted one thing but really they wanted another.

"But they're not actually assessing us though, right?" Steve said, looking around at the other teachers with an expression of concern. "I thought they didn't grade individual teachers anymore?"

"Well that's true," John said. "But that doesn't mean that you're not being judged. Remember, the inspectors are always going to be accompanied by a member of SLT. So if an inspector submits a report that suggests science lessons are somehow lacking in planning or the students just work from books, they're going to know whose lesson that was." Steve did not look comforted by this information. "Good luck everybody," he said.

Dave watched his colleagues as they filed out. They all looked like poor photocopies of their original selves. Steve stayed behind to speak with John. He had spent the last few months striving to appear relaxed in a bid to challenge the stereotype of the beleaguered newly qualified teacher.

"I really don't see why everyone's getting so worked up about this," Steve said resting against the desk alongside John. "The worst that'll happen is they'll come and observe you, right? But I can't see why that would be a problem? I keep feeling like I'm missing something?"

John raised an eyebrow as he looked at Steve. "Possibly," he said.

"Maybe it's just that I've recently finished my training, so I'm probably quite used to being observed. I must have had hundreds of observations."

"No, I don't think it's that."

"Well, I don't see what else it could be? I don't understand why everyone seems to have gone crazy. It looks like half of them didn't sleep last night?"

"They're not crazy, Steve. They're worried."

"About what? They're just inspectors; they don't have any power."

"People aren't scared of the inspectors, Steve. They're scared of the bad management that follows on the heels of their comments. I've seen management go around and force people out of their job after one of these inspections."

"What? Based on one observation?"

"Not even that. If you're lucky they might stay for twenty minutes, but most only get five."

Steve gave a disbelieving nostril-snort. "They can't fire you based on a five-minute observation! That's nonsense."

"No, no you're right, they can't. But a bad five minutes is a little bit like an accusation of witchcraft. Once it's been made, it can't really be unmade. And management can end up being like villagers with pitchforks: they're not really looking for exonerating evidence, more something to confirm that 'bad sense' that they always had about you."

"But that's really unfair," Steve said. He was no longer leaning on the desk but shifting his weight from foot to foot. "Who are they to judge me? Why is their opinion so important?"

"Well, that is their job."

"It's still unfair."

"Yeah. And now you can see why everybody's worried." John said. Steve left the lab with a similarly anxious expression to the rest of the department.

"You think he'll be okay?" Dave said, walking over to where John was leaning. The two of them were roughly the same height and whilst John was only a few years older, his hair, unlike Dave's, was mostly grey.

John shrugged. "Depends if he gets seen. They sometimes avoid NQTs."

"It's such a messed up way of doing it," Dave said.

"What is?"

"The whole inspections thing. You know, going around judging people."

John shook his head. "No. I don't have a problem with government inspections. I think they're a great idea."

"Really? You surprise me."

"We're all funded out of taxpayers' money; accountability's important."

"I suppose I'd not thought of it like that."

"I think the problem isn't that inspectors are making judgements so much as, how they go about informing those judgements. You see, I'd put money on Science getting a bad report this time around."

Dave looked puzzled. "Why? We got a great report five years ago and we're clearly doing way more now than we did then."

"Yeah, but last year's results were a percentage point down on the year before."

"Sure, but they were three percent up on the year before that. You can't just take a single data point and make it into a trend: that's dumb. Last year's drop was most likely regression to the mean."

"Ah but, Dave, we've had the luxury of a scientific education, so we know what that means. I don't think any of these inspectors are scientists and certainly, no one in SLT is a scientist. So when they see the numbers drop, they don't think, "Ah, that's probably just regression to the mean." They look at that data point and go, "Ooh, that's the start of a downward trend." I think for many people, numbers sort of feel like they're absolute, they don't really see them as belonging to a context. They're more like the oracle at Delphi: they're a mysterious insight into the will of the gods."

"So they're going to say we're failing, even though we're two percentage points up on the results from two years ago?"

"Yes. We're at the start of a downward trend. That's what the results say. All they need now is the supporting evidence for that narrative."

"But that's monumentally stupid."

"That's how these inspections seem to work. I guess it makes sense in its own way."

"Really?"

"Yeah. I think people see results as being hard-data and they think of observations as being soft-data. So if the observations said we were awesome, but the results show we were one percent down on last year, people will just side with the results and view the observations as being aberrant. It's just easier for the inspectors to align their observations with the data."

"But it's not based on anything. Well, I guess it's based on mathematical ignorance."

"Sure. I blame the teachers," John said.

"If only there was some way to improve standards," Dave agreed.

AN OBSERVATION

The door to Dave's lab burst open as though flung wide by the secret police. A portly man in a pinstripe suit marched in brandishing a clipboard. He was closely followed by Martin who seemed to be in some kind of orbit around the inspector. The two of them took up a position at the back of the class and the inspector nodded as though bidding Dave to pretend he wasn't there. Dave did not have a problem with ignoring people, he was after all an expert in this, however, his students were not and so they had all turned round to stare at the inspector as if he was Santa Claus. Dave clicked his fingers a few times to get their attention and when that failed, began using names to turn their heads back one by one. Finally, he was able to resume his explanation of the practical. They would cut out a series of little paper spinners of different sizes and time how long it would take them to flutter to the ground like sycamore seeds. It was a simple and engaging practical for the students, but Dave viewed this more of a bonus since the students were not really the intended audience. The lesson was a bespoke construction for the inspector to witness the current teaching fashions for group work, concept discussions and measurable learning events. Dave talked through the instructions and as he was demonstrating where they should make the cuts on their paper, the inspector walked over and said in a low voice "Sorry, could I just see a copy of your lesson plan please?"

"Uh sure," Dave said, halting in his explanation. He laid down the paper and scissors and walked over to his desk. The students sat in expectant silence as Dave collected a plastic folder containing six pages of dense type and four pages of handouts and diagrams. He handed it to the inspector.

"That's great, carry on like I'm not here," the inspector said, returning to the back of the laboratory as he leafed through the plan. Dave picked up the paper and scissors and once more found he was addressing the backs of everyone's heads. He didn't blame the students: the inspector was fascinating to watch, with his round, protruding belly, expensive city-suit and casual disregard for the conventions of lesson observations. But wrestling back the volatile attention of teenagers was like carefully squeezing compressed springs into a mug: it didn't take much for the whole system to fly apart. It took him a minute to calm them back down and return their itinerant attention to his explanation, at which point the inspector laid the lesson plan down, walked over to one of the smallest girls in the group and asked her in a loud whisper, "So what are you supposed to be doing?"

She looked terrified by the question, partly because a large man in a pinstripe suit was asking her things, but mainly because Dave was still explaining how they would all divide into groups.

"Listening to sir," she said, hoping this was the answer the inspector wanted.

The inspector made a vague "mmmh" sound as though this was not the answer he had wanted. "So how do you know what you're supposed to be doing for the practical?" the inspector said.

The girl looked confused. "Well it's all written on the sheet," she said and held up the handout for him to see.

He flicked through her exercise book and made a satisfied sound at seeing that it was marked. He muttered something about the feedback being good and picked up a second book to which he gave the same praise. He moved on, drifting between the benches like a be-suited dirigible. Dave swiftly wrapped up his explanation and released the students to do the practical, but most of them remained seated, staring at the inspector as he picked up a third book. The inspector's posture became taut and upright. He beckoned Martin to come and look.

"This book wasn't marked for two months," he whispered urgently, flicking the pages with contempt. "And then look at this: he's only marked the last piece of work. Like those are the only pages I'd look at." He shook his head like a disappointed father. He turned to the student. "Is this normal? For your book to go unmarked for months?" The student sniffed anxiously. "It's okay, you won't get into trouble," the inspector vacuously promised. The boy peered at the book.

"Uh, well, someone lost my old book. But it wasn't me."

The inspector tilted his head like a puzzled dog. "What old book?" he said. The boy sniffed and looked around at his friends who were all quietly pretending to ignore the exchange.

"I swear I had it at my dad's." the boy said and wiped his nose on his blazer sleeve. "I'm only there on Tuesdays, but, it might have got thrown out or something, but I didn't lose it, you see. It's not actually my fault." He looked down at the glistening trail of snot and, hoping that no one had noticed, rubbed it onto his trousers.

"So what's this book?" the inspector said, holding up the unmarked book.

"Sir said it didn't matter who'd lost it. I still had to stay and copy up all the notes into a new book. But I swear I didn't lose the old one. It's so unfair."

The inspector wore the expression of a man who felt he had been somehow tricked. He pushed the book back across the desk and, with a scowl, turned to Martin. "Let's move on," he said.

At his point of exit, the inspector had been in the laboratory for a grand total of six minutes and thirty-four seconds and so Dave took this as a sign that the observation had gone well. As he explained to John at break, if the inspector had seen something negative he would surely have stayed to investigate further. Besides, the inspector had probably seen Dave teach for a total of maybe four minutes, two of which were his wrestling the group's attention back after the inspector's disruptions.

THE KING OF WING

The next morning Dave sat in front of his laptop, staring at the list of year ten reports he had yet to complete. Most of his students fell into one of three broad categories, those he wanted to encourage, those he wanted to castigate and those who should just carry on doing what they were doing. Unfortunately, one of the leadership team had recently read an article that suggested positive feedback was highly effective in encouraging beneficial learning outcomes and so management had made positive comments in reports mandatory. He scrolled through the system's prefabricated sentences, desperately seeking something positive with which to describe his most difficult students. He settled on one phrase that suggested the students had good attendance, which was possibly a stretch given they were only present two-thirds of the time, but, Dave reasoned, two-thirds was better than one-third. The only other vaguely applicable comment he could find praised the students for always having their exercise books with them, which was technically true, but less from the organisational skills of the students and more by virtue of Dave not allowing them to take their books home.

The laboratory door opened and Debbie, one of the assistant heads, walked in. Dave stopped typing and said hello, trying not to view her presence with suspicion. This was not because of Debbie, per se, Debbie was arguably one of the more approachable members of the leadership team, but it was highly unusual for any member of management to leave their office and visit staff in their classrooms. In the last five years, Dave's laboratory had been visited on just four occasions and what Dave found unnerving was not the paucity of these visits, but rather that all four had occurred in the last five days.

"Martin said you were seen yesterday," Debbie said, laying a black folder of paperwork on the bench beside him.

Dave lowered the screen on his laptop. "Did he say how it went?"

"Nothing formal," she said. "But I don't think your inspector was all that impressed."

"Oh." Dave tried to read Debbie's body language. She might be here to berate him and warn him that he had better become organized, or she was here to hand him his p45 and then to console him.

"Martin said they felt your lesson was a bit disrupted and fragmentary."

Dave let out an involuntary laugh at the criticism and then covered his mouth, aware that it might appear he was failing to take the situation seriously.

"Yes, it sounded ridiculous to me too," Debbie said with a smile. "From what Martin was saying, it seemed they were only with you for five minutes." She shook her head. "I don't think that's anywhere near enough time: nobody can make a meaningful assessment in five minutes."

Dave nodded as though in agreement. His amusement had not been elicited from the absurdly short amount of time in which the inspector had made their assessment, but rather from their bouncing around his lab like circus performers and then concluding that any disruption they had observed was a product of Dave's teaching. In Dave's mind, it was like walking into a hotel room, spraying silly string everywhere and then phoning up reception to complain that the room was untidy. Debbie continued to tell him how much he shouldn't worry about the observation, but Dave wasn't really listening: the accusation of witchcraft had been made. To some extent, he was now a passenger in a vehicle driven by the perception of others.

"I actually came to talk with you about this morning's meeting," she said picking up the folder she had rested on the bench.

"What meeting?"

"Oh," Debbie said and checked Dave's expression to see if he was joking. "I thought Katarina spoke with you yesterday?"

"Not to my knowledge. Why?"

"Oh. Right, well, today's focus is supposed to be teaching and learning, and so umm..." Debbie paused as she realised quite how absurd this was going to sound. "Well uh, the inspectors wanted to meet with you period one."

Dave nodded slowly as a sense of panic sought to establish itself in his gut. He glanced up at the clock. "Fifteen minutes to prepare for an hour meeting?" he said. "That seems excessively optimistic, even for Katarina."

"I just assumed you knew?" Debbie said. She clutched the black folder to her chest. "I'm not sure if..." She looked up at the clock and then across at the laboratory door. "I don't think there's enough time to reschedule... I'm sorry... I don't know what to do."

Dave closed his eyes and concentrated on balancing his breathing: in through the nose and out through the mouth. Aside from a few good intentions, he had nothing tangible to bring to the meeting. His spurious research paper had been submitted but he had yet to hear anything back from the journals and whilst the website of resources was up and running it had only received twelve views to date, four of which had been him. He opened his eyes and continued to enforce the regular pattern of breathing. The situation was what it was; worrying would not change anything. He pushed the laptop screen open. Debbie was suggesting that the inspectors would probably be sympathetic to Dave's lack of preparation but Dave did not like the sound of that solution. He started taking screenshots of his website and slotting them into a presentation, he didn't need many, just a few to break up the text, although, he had yet to type some text. He glanced up at the clock: ten minutes to go. Debbie had opened up the black folder and was scribbling on the agenda in pencil. She was suggesting that maybe things could be solved by changing the running order but Dave had lowered his head and was typing as much useful information as he could about the aims of the two projects and listing what he had achieved so far. When he had finished typing, he sat back and looked up at the clock: nine minutes to go. He had come up with five bullet points and they just about filled a single slide. The sense of panic nudged him in the stomach again: he did not have enough material to talk for more than a minute, let alone hours. He urgently needed some way of filling the time whilst disguising the scarcity of content.

"I doubt they'll be expecting a presentation," Debbie said, looking over his shoulder at the single slide.

"I know, but I figured my best defence was probably a good offence." They both stared for a few moments at the five bullet points. "Maybe if I spread them out a bit," Dave suggested.

"I'm sure they won't be expecting a presentation," Debbie said again, although she did not sound convinced.

"No I'm sure it'll be fine," Dave said, closing the laptop. "I just need to think of it like teaching a lesson."

"Well, except that you haven't had any time to plan this," Debbie said. Dave checked to see if she was being ironic but Debbie clearly hadn't been a full-time classroom teacher for many years. Full-time teachers rarely had the time to actually plan their lessons.

As Dave entered the conference room, it was immediately clear that there wasn't going to be a conventional meeting or an opportunity for his presentation. The conference room table was covered with folders and stacks of students' books and positioned around the outside of the room were pairings of inspectors with members of the leadership team. The inspectors were scrutinising documents whilst the leadership team all seemed to be in various stages of hand waving or paper shuffling. Katarina steered Dave over to a table where Malcolm Willis, the portly, pinstriped inspector from Dave's observation was poring over a canopy of documents. Katarina introduced Dave as the teaching and learning coordinator and "an up and coming star in the school," to which Malcolm looked up at Dave and gave a nostril snort of derision. Dave ignored this and smiled pleasantly.

"Fine. Tell me about this role then."

"Well..." Dave hesitated. Up until this point, he had quite happily gone around telling everyone that the primary purpose of the teaching and learning role had been to demonstrate to an inspection that there existed a teaching and learning role, but he obviously couldn't now use this justification with the inspector. The hesitation began to stretch into a pause. Dave grabbed a chair and positioned it carefully alongside the table, hoping he could sell the pause as a kind of preparation for a detailed explanation. He sat down and shuffled backwards, finding the chair's most comfortable spot. He still didn't know what to say. Unfortunately, most of the pause had not been spent on thinking of justifications for the teaching and learning role, but rather on coming up with the chair strategy as an explanation for the pause. "...the primary focus of any teaching and learning role has to be the students." Dave said and was surprised to see Malcolm nodding as he continued: "Whatever else is happening in the school, it ultimately all comes down to the students learning and the teaching producing that learning."

Malcolm murmured approvingly at Dave's observation that the verbs 'teaching' and 'learning' both required the concept of students for them to operate. Dave was still frantically seeking a more substantial line and had employed this platitude more as a placeholder for meaning than as an actual justification. It had never occurred to Dave that Malcolm might accept this stalling as sufficient in itself. He decided to continue on this tack of trite platitudes and see how far it could get him.

"We have a duty to ensure that we are providing our students with the highest-quality education and that means we have to be constantly adapting to the needs of our students and striving to raise their performance."

The idea that a school should try to be good rather than bad, seemed to resonate strongly with Malcolm. "I totally agree," he said. "So what have you put in place?"

This was probably as good a time as any to introduce his website but Dave's concern was that as grand educational solutions went, his barely visited website containing other peoples' YouTube videos probably wasn't all that inspiring. However, Malcolm struck him as the type of person who judged ideas not on their conceptual merits, but on the length and weight of the words employed to describe them. Since Dave had witnessed many ill-considered projects sold on the basis of their obfuscating finery, he had some idea how this was done. "Well, as with any organisation," he began. "If we're looking to increase our productivity then it's vital that we implement intelligently-placed, well-structured, targeted support." A more prosaic description would have been, "if we help teachers, they'll do a better job," but this lacked the compound adjectives and long words that made things sound impressive. Dave repeated the idea, but this time with a shot of spurious authority. "There's almost universal consensus amongst leading academics that workplace efficacy can be greatly enhanced by the introduction of a productivity architecture that nurtures and encourages support."

"Yeah, I'd read that," Malcolm murmured. Dave seriously doubted that Malcolm had read this anywhere, but he continued, since Malcolm was responding so positively to the pleonasm.

"Now clearly we're in the business of supporting our learners in the acquisition of knowledge, but we also have to be intelligent about this, we have to look at not just producing the biggest impact but also the most cost-effective impact." Malcolm seemed enthused by Dave's ill-defined double optima and began making notes. "Often a small intervention upstream can have a huge impact downstream and so naturally our support structures will be more effective if they're placed upstream of our learners, rather than downstream." Dave accompanied this with some clarifying hand gestures, moving his right hand to the right for upstream and to the left for downstream. In practical terms, he had no clue what 'downstream of the learners' actually entailed and he suspected it was complete nonsense, but since Malcolm did not seem too concerned with such details, he remained unchallenged. "So we looked at our systems and we quickly realised that our problem wasn't a lack of knowledge, but rather an effective mechanism for the management of that knowledge." Dave said the word "management" with a reverent emphasis as though he was revealing some great truth. "And as any industry leader will tell you, effective knowledge-management is about effective distribution."

"You're absolutely right: I've been saying that for years," Malcolm said and took a minute to explain how he too was really a leader of industry. Dave barely listened, frantically trying to think of a way to describe his webpage of people sharing other people's YouTube videos, as anything but that.

"So what's your solution?" Malcolm asked.

"Obviously there're several components in our strategy, all working in unison to produce a more effective whole," Dave said.

"Of course," Malcolm agreed.

"But the centrepiece is our education portal. There's no point in reinventing the wheel: the wheel's already been invented. So the portal is a gateway into the global village that allows us to aggregate existing multimedia content and position it for effective redistribution and collaborative dissemination."

"That's brilliant. How long did it take you to put it together?"

Dave paused as he considered whether the actual answer of "two hours" was acceptable, but decided that this sounded like he had rushed it. "There was an extended consultancy period prior to the launch," he said. "But we managed to roll the whole thing out in the space of a few weeks. We're extremely proud of it. Ultimately, it allows us to free up our innovative visionaries and facilitates the conversion of game-changing resources into bottom-line deliverables. And I think you'll agree: that's so important in this day and age."

"Oh absolutely, you're absolutely right. I'm always saying it's about bottom-line deliverables. Can I see the portal?"

Dave gave him the address and hoped he would not check anytime soon, he could imagine Malcolm disappointedly clicking down the page and noting that it just seemed to be teachers sharing YouTube videos. Malcolm leaned across to the next table where another inspector was asking Sandra some questions and entering her responses into a tablet. Malcolm asked for a spare tablet, but the inspector shook their head. Malcolm turned back, made a note of the website and thanked Dave for his time. It seemed oddly anticlimactic. All of the preparation and frantic activity of the previous weeks had come down to a mere ten minutes of conversation and now Dave was free to return to his day.

Dave looked at the clock on the wall. There was half an hour of period one remaining but he did not fancy interrupting the cover teacher to pick up the remainder of the lesson. Instead, he wandered over to the Science staff room and made himself a cup of tea. Mary was sitting marking exam papers.

"How'd it go?" she asked without looking up.

"Weird," Dave said and explained the sense of smallness it had all carried.

"You think they'll want you to carry on doing the teaching and learning stuff?"

65

Dave shrugged, "I dunno. I guess so. I can always quit it if they keep asking for stuff." He took a sip of tea. "They see anyone else in Science?"

"Just you, John and Growler."

"They saw Growler?" Dave chuckled as he imagined how that interaction might have played out.

"Yeah. He was doing electrolysis I think. He said it went alright, but you know him: it's not like he's going to be too concerned over what they think."

"He's a great chemist; kids love him."

"Yeah, and he gets them the grades. He ever tell you about his plan B?" Mary said, putting her pen down and smiling.

"Yeah, I'm not sure you can still call it a plan B when it earns more than your plan A."

Most teachers had a plan B of some description: Dave's was to be a mechanic and a web designer. Mary's was to either go back into research or sell her paintings full time. Growler's plan B was antiques, but he was unusual in that his plan B was already making him more at the weekends than his weekly teaching salary. Dave had once asked him why he didn't quit teaching to focus on just the antiques. Growler had momentarily lowered his copy of the Guardian and in his usual rumbling baritone had said, "Antiques are boring: they don't jump when you shout at them." Dave was pretty certain he was being ironic. In his ten years of teaching, Dave had never once heard Growler shout at a student. He had never needed to.

Two weeks later Katarina sent round an email informing the school that they had been graded on the new government system as a four, which on the old system would have been an "outstanding". She helpfully went on to add that the grading had almost been pulled down to a three because of the poor performance in Science, but that the inspectors had graciously allowed the school a four overall because they'd had confidence in the leadership team's intervention proposals to improve the Science department.

"Oh, that'll be fun," Growler said after John had read out the email.

"Wow, they saved us all," Dave said flatly. "Thank you, senior management: you're the real MVP."

"What do you think they proposed?" Mary said.

John leaned back in his chair and stretched his arms above his head. "Who knows? Rearranging the labs? Painting the walls blue? Getting everyone to mark everything continuously? None of it'll make any difference. Year elevens are off in two months. They'll sit their exams. The results will regress to the mean. We'll be up two or three percentage points on last year and everyone'll be happy."

"Yeah, and no doubt management will imagine that their intervention in the last two months of a three-year curriculum made all the difference."

John smiled. "That's how management works, Dave: take credit for success, apportion blame for failure."

PUSHING FROM THE MIDDLE

Dave opened the drawer for the fourth time and gave the red-handled scissors another stir with his hand. He was convinced this was where he had left the mock exam papers, but his apathetic search was revealing nothing new. Clearly, someone had stolen them. He didn't know who, or indeed why someone would want to steal a group of bottom-set year eleven physics papers, but he had plenty of evidence in that the papers weren't in the drawer. Maybe one of the students had sneaked back into the classroom at the end of the day and stolen the tests so that they could find their paper and finish off colouring in all of the O's and closed letter loops without the time pressure of the exam? Or maybe they'd discussed the test with their friends and realised they'd missed a really great opportunity to add a penis to one of the question's diagrams? Both seemed like feasible motives, but Dave knew his students and he doubted that they would do something that involved this much effort. He closed the drawer and scanned his lab in the vague hope that he had been really terrible at looking the previous five times. It was possible that he had left the papers elsewhere. His timetable had placed him in four different rooms during the day so he began retracing his steps, walking over to the English department where he had taught a year ten chemistry lesson and then over to History, where he had taught a year eleven physics lesson. The rooms all contained plenty of paperwork, but no mocks tests. It was possible he had taken them to the morning's year ten tutor briefing, so Dave drifted over to the conference room and without really thinking, opened the door.

Unsurprisingly the conference room was playing host to a meeting. Eight teachers sat in a horseshoe arrangement of desks around Martin, the assistant head. Martin looked over as Dave blundered into the room and rather than responding with confusion or irritation, which Dave would have much preferred, Martin rather worryingly said, "Ah, we wondered when you'd turn up." Dave ran a quick mental check of all the potential meetings he might possibly be missing and came up blank. There weren't any meetings he was missing. He glanced at the teachers to see if they were connected in any kind of clarifying way, like all belonging to the same year group or department, but beyond all being the kind of teachers who sent more than their fair share of annoying whole-school emails, there was nothing that obviously connected them.

"I'm looking for my year eleven mocks. You haven't seen them in here, have you?"

Martin seemed not to hear this information because he continued, "You've missed the first twelve sessions, but I'm sure you'll pick it all up."

"Pick what up?"

"Pushing from the middle," Martin said. Pushing from the middle was the school's homegrown training sessions for "aspiring middle leaders": those teachers who felt drawn to the power and wealth of middle management. Unfortunately, most schools lacked either the budget or the management positions to accommodate the ambitions of all those who would attend such courses and thus in practice the course ended up being little more than a box-ticking exercise for senior management. If an inspection was to ask what was being done to encourage growth and career progression, management could wave vaguely at their pushing-from-the-middle course. The teachers in attendance were mostly young and idealistic with only a few years' experience but sitting in the middle was James, a history teacher in his fifties. James had been attending the aspiring middle leader sessions for the last ten years without ever receiving a promotion. Dave was unsure what this continued attendance said about James, but it certainly said something about the efficacy of the training.

"We've been meeting every Wednesday," Martin continued. "I guess you must have been busy."

"No, I just didn't want to come along to them," Dave said. The others in the room chuckled collectively as if this was a great joke. Dave hung his head in resignation, snubbing the course was one thing, but he didn't really want to highlight the collective misreading of his honesty.

"Have a seat," Martin said. "Julia's just about to give us a presentation on how she would plan a departmental meeting, planning for the year ahead." Dave laughed, thinking this was some sort of management joke, but quickly noticed that he was the only one laughing and so downshifted his amusement to an affirming nod as he took a seat next to a fresh-faced PE teacher.

Julia had clearly spent a lot of time and effort producing the presentation and handed out mock agendas as she talked through a PowerPoint of theoretical PowerPoint slides that she might employ were she to actually have a meeting, planning for an unspecified year ahead. Dave was bemused at how earnestly everyone seemed to be receiving this meta-presentation and the questions at the end managed to sustain the surreal supposition that something meaningful was really being discussed. A young geography teacher asked whether or not Julia had considered placing imaginary item three of the agenda ahead of purely hypothetical item two because purely hypothetical item two felt like it was more in tune with fictitious item four. There were a few nods, as though this had also occurred to everyone else. Dave put his hand up, unsure whether he had understood the premise of what was happening:

"Can I ask: is this a meeting that's actually going to happen?"

"Oh no, it's a model meeting only, it's so we can safely explore the ideas."

"Yes, you certainly wouldn't want a badly planned department meeting to actually happen," Dave said with a chuckle and was surprised to see everyone nodding sombrely as though they'd once lost a lot of good men to a badly planned departmental meeting. "Well, it's a nice presentation," Dave said diplomatically. "How long did you spend on it?"

"Probably only four or five hours, I'd have spent some more time but unfortunately my three-year-old son needed me at his birthday party," Julia said with a sigh.

This, Dave realised, was probably the true utility of the sessions: identifying those individuals who were willing to spend large amounts of additional time doing meaningless work for no extra pay. The school had plenty of positions that fitted those criteria.

Martin stood back up and pointed at the geography teacher. "Neil, you were telling me about something you implemented in your department this week, why don't you share it with the group?"

Neil gave a nod and cleared his throat. "I came up with the idea of a brainbox," he said. "It's um, a cardboard box with the word 'Brainbox' written on it."

"Brilliant," Martin murmured.

"Yeah, it's there so that if anyone in the department comes up with a good idea, they can write it down on a piece of paper and put it in the box."

"Brilliant," Martin repeated. "Does everyone see where the genius in this lies?" Everybody nodded apart from Dave. "Dave?" Martin said, noticing his reluctance.

"Yeah?"

"Do you see why this is so smart?"

"I don't know? I guess any system is going to be more robust if there's a mechanism for constructive feedback. And... I guess I can see the utility in it being anonymous, especially if your head of department is tyrannical and averse to criticism..."

Martin shook his head like a disappointed parent. "No Dave. No. The genius here is in calling it a 'brainbox'. You see it's all about making something catchy and memorable and 'brainbox' works on so many different levels. You see, a brainbox is a clever person but in this case, the box is not just a physical cardboard box, but where people are actually putting their ideas, as though it was a real brain. Do you see?"

Dave took a moment to recategorise Martin as a much bigger idiot that he had previously thought. "Wow, I completely missed all of that," he said flatly.

"Ahh, you see good management is often about looking beyond the surface, Dave." He turned to Neil. "Have you had any good suggestions yet?"

Neil shook his head. "No. No one's put anything in the box yet."

"Give it time," Martin said. "Give it time. It's a great idea. Marsha, you were telling me about your vision for the library. Why don't you share that with the group?"

A young woman on the far side stood up. "We really wanted to make the library a purposeful learning environment," she said.

Martin nodded and murmured, "Good, good."

Marsha continued, "So we put up signs telling all of the students that from now on, the library was going to be a purposeful learning environment and then we told the tutors to make sure that they told their students that the library was to be a purposeful learning environment. And then obviously we reminded staff that the library was a purposeful learning environment and that if they caught any students who weren't helping maintain that purposeful learning environment, that they should eject those students from the library. You know, so that we kept it as a... well, a purposeful learning environment."

"Brilliant," Martin said. "Remember people, in management, it's so important to keep a clear sense of what we are trying to achieve. If we can say something enough times to other people, then what you are saying becomes a reality." The others in the room nodded in agreement. Dave raised an eyebrow. "If we want to make our vision into a reality, we just need to say it enough times and with enough conviction, to enough people."

"I'm pretty certain that's not true," Dave said.

"Ah, but it is true, Dave."

"No. No, it isn't. Do you actually believe that?"

"That's the brilliant thing about it, Dave. It is if you want it to be and that's what makes a good manager: that self-belief."

"But by your own argument if I assert that you're wrong to enough people, enough times, then my statement will magically become true, at which point your statement will become untrue."

"But in doing that, you would be proving that I'm right."

"And thus wrong."

"I'm not sure I follow you, Dave."

"No, I realise that."

Martin put out his hand as if to quell Dave's continued questioning. "The secret to good management is having a vision. If you have a vision, then you can make that vision come true."

"What if your vision is wrong?" Dave said.

Martin looked confused, partly by the question, but mostly because his outstretched hand appeared to have failed in stopping the questions. "Why would your vision be wrong?"

"I don't know? I might be an idiot."

"But we don't employ idiots in management, Dave."

"No, I realise that's not a selection criterion for management, but that doesn't actually stop people coming up with idiotic ideas. They might have great intentions and wholeheartedly believe that their ideas are going to be super helpful, but what if they're not? What if your vision is actually counterproductive? How would you know? What do managers do to check that their vision isn't completely insane?"

"Well, I imagine the people around them would say something?"

"And run the risk of getting fired?"

"Look, Dave, it's not the sort of situation that's ever likely to occur. Think about it. Why would a manager ever come up with a vision that they think is insane? Eh? They wouldn't, would they?" Martin looked smug, as though imaging his logic was unassailable. Dave sighed heavily and allowed Martin to move onto his next activity, encouraging everyone to come up with new ideas and projects that the school could use when they joined the new multi-area partnership. "It's going to be an extremely exciting time for us all!" Martin enthused.

A few of the teachers asked Martin what joining the MAP would actually entail, but Martin's responses were characteristically vague. "It's going to be much better," he said. "And don't worry, nothing's going to change."

The group began writing their ideas in marker pens on index cards but Ed, the sandy-haired PE teacher next to Dave, was unsure what a multi-area partnership was, let alone how they might come up with ideas to improve it. Dave gave him a brief history of education policy, describing how governments often seemed to come into power with firm beliefs on education whilst rarely seeming to check whether these beliefs had any evidential basis. The most recent ministers seemed to have acquired the belief that schools would do much better if they operated like successful businesses.

"I guess that makes sense," Ed said.

"It does?"

"Yeah. I mean, if you look around at how many successful businesses there are it obviously works in the private sector, so it only makes sense that it would work in the public sector too."

Dave looked closely at Ed, searching his big blue eyes for hints of subversion, but it seemed he was being genuine.

"Well, I'm not an expert, but your observation that businesses are mostly successful could also be explained by survivor bias." Ed looked blank so Dave continued, "You're only seeing a world of successful businesses because all of the countless crappy businesses have failed and disappeared."

"Right, I can totally see that. Yeah, so the idea is that the bad academies will close and we'll only be left with the good ones."

Dave paused as he tried to see how Ed could have arrived at this conclusion. "Uh, well I imagine some people might have hoped that would happen," Dave said. "But we've had five or six years of academies and I still feel like many of those predicted improvements have yet to materialise."

"Oh right, okay, so you're saying it works but it'll just take more time. Yeah, I can see that. But I guess if they're being run like a business, then they're going to be much more efficient than before."

"Again, I'm sure that was the intention and maybe some of them are more efficient, it's difficult to know how efficient they were under the old system. But there are increasing numbers of academies who have accrued huge debts, either through mismanagement or through misfortune."

"That's terrible. So what do they do with them? Sack them?"

"Basically, yes. They fire the old management and send in a team of experts to cut any unnecessary costs."

"That sounds positive."

"Sure, if you're on a cost-cutting team I imagine it's a great gig," Dave said. "They essentially treat the academy like it's a bloated business."

"That makes sense. A business has to operate within its budget: that's just basic, good business practice."

"Clearly," Dave said, avoiding the temptation to start naming companies historically bailed out by various governments and investors. "It's a ruthlessly efficient system. First, the cost-cutters fire all of the expensive, experienced teachers and bring in much cheaper newly qualified teachers and then they restrict all of the unnecessary photocopying of worksheets, halt the purchase of new textbooks and educational resources and slash ICT expenditure on unnecessary hardware, like laptops for teachers. It works brilliantly: within a few months, they can bring an academy's expenditure back in line with their budget. Bizarrely though, there doesn't seem to be a commensurate improvement in results?"

"Oh right, was that something they were expecting?"

"I don't know, I think it was something ministers were hoping would happen. For some reason, it just seems that schools staffed by under-resourced, inexperienced teachers don't seem to produce good results for their students. But I guess the important thing is they operate within their budget, which is what schools are for."

The PE teacher paused. "No that's not what schools are for," he said, looking concerned. "Schools are there to give the students an education. If they can't manage to do that within their budget they should just close that school."

"I think some people have certainly tried doing that, but it turns out that that those academies can be 'bad' for a whole raft of reasons and simply closing them doesn't always seem to solve any of the underlying social problems that may have contributed to their original difficulties. Plus, you still need to educate all of the academy's disrupted students somewhere else. And that's when they came up with the idea of MAPs or multi-area partnerships. The government is encouraging all of the institutes in a geographical area to kind of club together and help each other out, sharing their resources and good business practices in a giant cooperative, communistic way, but all the while operating under a central authority called the MAP."

"Oh right, so like a sort of parent company coming in and buying up a smaller business."

"Exactly. Or like a local education authority."

"That sounds like a great idea," Ed said and picked up a pen to write down his ideas. Martin came round and collected all of the cards in, noting with disappointment that Dave had produced nothing.

"Right, one of the most important managerial skills you can acquire is how to organise other people's ideas," Martin said holding up his handful of cards. "So let's go round and see what we've learned from previous sessions. How would you arrange these ideas?" He began pointing at each teacher in turn and with each point of his finger, someone would shout out a noun or a verb that corresponded to some previous session.

"Washing line!" Julia shouted. Martin nodded.

"Pyramid!" Again, Martin gave a satisfied nod.

"Composting," another shouted.

Dave turned and mouthed, "Composting?" but everyone else seemed to be having too much fun.

"Wagon wheel!" Ed said.

Martin turned to Dave. "Dave? Have you got any management techniques?"

Dave was amused that Martin would consider that these exercises constituted management techniques, but since Dave rarely paid attention to the exercises routinely foisted upon staff at meetings, he could not think of anything new. "Uh? I guess you could diamond-nine them?" Dave said.

Martin shook his head. "Pushing from the middle is all about innovation, Dave. We could all come up with diamond nine: that's an old idea."

"Uh, okay..." Dave said and wracked his brains for some other nonsense he could substitute for arranging meaningless cards into an equally meaningless shape.

"Maybe you could... trapezoid-twelve them?" There was a moment of silence as those around the room took a moment to absorb this shiny new concept. "I'm sure you all know trapezoid twelve?" Dave said, cementing the lie with a spurious origin, "I think it started at uh, Google, am I right?"

There were a few nods and murmurings of "Yeah, yeah Google."

Dave noted who his fellow blaggers were and then continued. "The idea's simple: it's like a diamond nine, only three better."

There were some approving murmurings of, "Ooh. Three better!"

"That's great, Dave." Martin said and smoothly inducted himself into the bullshit hall of fame with "We were due to do trapezoid-twelving next week, but it's great that you've introduced it today. Good work."

PERFORMANCE MANAGEMENT

When trying to describe what the world of teaching was like for most teachers, Dave often employed an analogy to freediving. It wasn't necessarily a great analogy, because the pub regulars he was explaining it to had often done as much freediving as they'd done teaching, but it helped him communicate the asymmetry of a teacher's year. He explained that in August you take a long glorious look at the sun-soaked landscape, attach a large weight to your feet and then at the start of September you jump into a deep, dark hole. At the beginning of your descent you can still see things, you can still go out in the evenings, you can still see friends and family but with each passing week the pressure builds and the light dwindles until at Christmas everything is dark. You don't have time for friends because the pressure is everywhere, you are planning and you are marking. You are swimming, kicking your legs in the void but you cannot discern your motion because everything is dark. You are setting work, delivering work and marking work, but it does nothing. You cannot see beyond the current week. As you kick through the winter months and into March, the pressure is still everywhere but now it is gradually becoming less. Your year elevens are starting to finish their courses and you and all of your colleagues are impressing upon them the importance of their exams. If you're lucky enough to be in a good school, the students start to do more work. You are still kicking, aching from the months without oxygen but now the water is growing lighter and you can see the world around you. You know now that you can make it, you're setting more revision lessons and you can see the circle of blue above you. As you enter May, the water becomes warmer and the job gradually becomes that thing you enjoy. And as the year eleven and thirteens depart on study leave, you suddenly have a reasonable timetable. You break the surface and take great gulps of free time. Now you paddle around and do your job properly. You have the time to deal with six months of emails, you can plan school trips, you can improve the schemes of work, you can engage with your colleagues and you can even start to have a life outside of work.

This was when Dave and everyone else in the department became their most productive. Two or three teachers would often wind up chatting in an empty classroom when they would have had year eleven, talking about their year, comparing practical lessons and sharing new ideas over a cup of tea. These were some of the most useful conversations that Dave and his colleagues could have, but this was not a sentiment shared by the senior leadership team. Each year Martin would send round an email that effectively forbade teachers from using their gained time for, "sitting around drinking tea and chatting." His justification being, "This is not a productive use of your time." Dave loved this annual statement and took it to be a wonderful insight into Martin's own conversations, from which presumably nothing useful ever arose. Fortunately for the school, the majority of teachers ignored his tea-and-talking injunction and communication and creativity continued to flourish.

The year tens bounced out of Dave's laboratory with several of them thanking him for the lesson and at least three expressing surprise at having enjoyed learning. Dave smiled as they left. It was not a lesson that Dave would have marked out as being an obvious hit, but they'd all loved it. An ordinary lesson on terminal velocity had triggered a question about how fast you could fall and then as Dave had begun to answer them and show them a few clarifying videos, there had been more questions and Dave had provided more answers and more videos until steadily the whole group had become swept up with an enthusiastic curiosity about Newton's laws, feathers and hammers, coins dropping off skyscrapers and animals with survivable terminal velocities. By the end, the whole group had drawn their own comic strips of a skydiver and correctly labelled the forces at the different stages of descent. Dave walked across the corridor to Growler's lab. He was taking down the Perspex blast shields at the back and stopped to listen as Dave recounted his lesson.

"Good work," he said with a smile. "S'good feeling."

"Yeah, it's rare, but it does make it feel like it's all worthwhile."

"I know what you mean. If you can get one or two of those in a year, it's been a good year."

"It's weird though. I wouldn't have pegged terminal velocity as the topic that would have engaged them."

Growler chuckled. "Yup. I just did a lesson on explosions. On paper, you'd have thought that'd rank as their favourite lesson ever."

"And it wasn't?"

Growler shrugged. "They were okay with it, but I guess for a fourteen-year-old, any lesson on explosions that ends with the lab still intact is going to be a major disappointment."

"And you finished the lesson with all your limbs."

"I know. What was I thinking?" Growler said, closing up the cupboards and strolling back to his desk at the front. Dave was still pleased that his lesson had gone well and so he continued down the corridor, looking for more colleagues with whom he could share his esoteric experience. Mary was sitting writing university references and she smiled in recognition of the sensation as Dave stood describing his lesson.

"It's just a shame it doesn't happen more often really," she said. Dave agreed. "Hey, did you hear that Debbie had resigned?"

"Debbie? Assistant head, Debbie?" Dave shook his head. "No. When did that happen?"

"Last week apparently."

"Why? She get another job?"

"Don't think so. I just heard she handed in her notice."

Dave raised an eyebrow. "Didn't we officially join the MAP last week?"

"Yeah."

"You think they're connected?" Dave asked.

Mary looked at him with disdain. "You think they're not? You realise that Gary Henderson is the chairman of the MAP, right?"

"Sure, but I don't know if Henderson would be drastic enough to start pushing people out from day one. I mean, it was only six months ago that the school got the equivalent of an 'outstanding' from the inspectors. Clearly, we're doing something right."

"You've met Gary Henderson," Mary said. "Did he strike you as a rational human being?"

"Well, I wouldn't say rational as such. But it's not like he has any reason to start changing things around?"

"You're joking. He's an arrogant narcissist who imagines that his extremely limited experience makes him an expert on absolutely everything. He's exactly the sort of person who wades into an unfamiliar environment and starts making random changes. You think it's a coincidence that it's the most rational member of the leadership team who resigned?"

"Yeah, that is a bit worrying," Dave admitted.

"I imagine she questioned one of his crazy ideas and he gave her an ultimatum: his way or the highway."

"We don't know that's what happened."

"No, we just know Debbie would rather be unemployed than working for Henderson," Mary said and explained that at her last school the headteacher had pushed out everyone who opposed her and then micromanaged the school into failure. "Building up a good school takes years and years of hard work with an intelligent head, a good leadership team and a strong core of experienced subject teachers behind them. On the other hand, a well-placed idiot can single-handedly destroy a school inside a year."

Dave was still thinking about what Mary had said when after lunch he went to his performance management meeting with John. Twice a year John would look through Dave's targets, make some comment about how pleased they were with his work, sign the paperwork and the two of them would then leave to get some work done. Today, however, Sandra the deputy head was sitting in John's office too. Dave generally tried to avoid Sandra, partly because his default position was just to avoid all senior management, but mostly because Sandra seemed way more intense than everyone else on the leadership team. She had long, dark-brown hair, wore navy-blue power suits, heavy jewellery and far too much perfume. When addressing the staff during briefings she would often pound her fist on the desk to emphasise her points. Once she had hammered the desk so hard she had managed to bounce a mug of coffee off the edge and it had shattered on the floor. She had carried on hammering the desk, ignoring both the crash and the spreading pool of liquid until someone had moved to clear up the puddle, at which point she had barked at them to, "leave it!" And had then resumed explaining how important school-uniform checks were.

"Have a seat, Dave," she said softly. Dave looked across at John to try and get a read on what was happening, but John's expression was impressively neutral. "As I'm sure you know, Dave, the school has become a part of the MAP. This means there are going to be some changes across the entire school, but I think one of the most obvious changes is to the performance management cycle."

Dave sat down. "Oh right. Okay."

"Gary's very keen to bring schools in line with industry practice and I'm here to ensure that things get implemented correctly."

"Oh right. Were they not being?"

"No, it's that performance management is far more important now that the pay policy's changed."

"I didn't realise it had changed. Shouldn't there have been some sort of consultation or something?"

"There was," Sandra said. "As part of the MAP, we automatically fall under the pay and conditions of the MAP. We obviously consulted with your union rep but they were quite happy with the new conditions."

"I have a union rep? Who's my union rep?"

"Martin."

Dave paused. "Martin? As in, Assistant Head, Martin?"

"Yes."

Dave looked at John who raised an eyebrow as if to say 'I know!'

"Isn't that a conflict of interest or something?"

"No," Sandra said firmly. "There's nothing to prevent Martin from being the rep and besides, he was the only one who volunteered for the role." Dave silently cursed the apathy of his colleagues but then realised that this equally included himself. "So we're modernising the school by introducing performance-related pay. Gary was keen to bring the school up to date with the majority of industry." Sandra said.

Dave nodded slowly. "So like paying a car salesman based on how many cars they've sold? That sort of performance?"

"Yes, but obviously it's about how well you teach the students. Now, the idea is we have a look through your data from the past few years and then have a talk about how you've performed. We can look at how your past performance might have affected your past pay had we been operating the current policy back then."

"Wow, you can assess my performance from the data?"

"Yes," Sandra said, as though this was obvious. "We have data for all the teachers."

Dave was not opposed to performance-related pay in principle, he had just always assumed that teaching was such a vastly complex and nuanced role that incorporated so many intangible variables, that it was essentially impossible to judge the performance of a teacher. "I'm genuinely impressed," he said, viewing Sandra with a renewed respect. "I mean the emotional support, the social development, the wider, extra-curricular activities, the moral encouragement, the broader cultural education..." Dave shook his head. "I wouldn't know how to even begin measuring those, but if you've managed to combine and weight all those manifold variables into a single metric, that's really impressive."

"A what?" Sandra looked confused by Dave's sentence. "No, it's much simpler than any of that. Like in your analogy, a good car salesperson is one who sells a lot of cars. A good teacher is one who gets the kids good grades."

"Grades?" Dave repeated the word slowly as he realised he had misunderstood Sandra. "How can you possibly assess a teacher on just grades? Isn't basing a teacher's performance on how well the kids do, a bit like basing the car salesman's performance on how well the customers drive their cars home?"

"No, those are different systems, Dave. You can't compare them like that."

"Oh right. So you're not judging me on the performance of the students?"

"No, we are. We calculate the value added for all your groups and for those with a positive value added, we'll pay you a bonus and for those with a negative value added, we'll deduct from your bonus. If you consistently produce a negative value added then we will move you back down the pay scale."

Dave nodded slowly, unsure whether Sandra's scheme sounded as stupid as it did because she had not explained it properly or because it was just fundamentally stupid. "Forgive me," he said smiling apologetically. "But how do you actually calculate the value added for a student?"

Sandra narrowed her eyes at him. "I would hope that as an experienced teacher you're already familiar with this, Dave?" Dave smiled but did not say anything to stop her continuing. "Last year your top set had a value added of..." Sandra paused to look at the data in front of her. "Minus 0.3. That means they were on average achieving a third of a grade below the grade predicted from their key-stage-two results."

"Right. I get that bit; I guess what I'm really asking is how do you actually arrive at that predicted grade for each student? So, on my class list, it might say that we're expecting Tommy Tomkins to get a 4. How do we actually know that Tommy Tomkins should be getting a 4?"

Sandra looked mildly appalled at Dave's ignorance and turned to John. "It looks like your department might need some additional training in the basics of data analysis," she said and added, "I'm actually finding it hard to believe that an experienced teacher has managed to get this far without understanding the concept of value added."

Dave leaned forward to interrupt her exchange with John. "It's not so much that I don't understand it as I'm just looking for some clarity. You're essentially making my final pay contingent upon that predicted grade. I'm just curious to know what data you're using to inform that prediction."

"It's calculated from looking at past students from across the whole country," Sandra said her bracelets chiming as she swept her right hand through the air. "We look at their key-stage-two results and then see what GCSE grades those students went on to get. You can look it up on the department of education website." She brought her hand back down to the desk and squared the paper in front of her. "Now if we have a look at your top set..."

"Oh right," Dave said, interrupting her. "So it's for a past year group from across the entire country?"

Sandra kept her head looking at the paper but flicked her eyes up. "Yes."

"So if I was teaching the entire country, those would be the grades I could expect them to get?"

"Yes."

"But I'm not teaching the entire country? I'm only teaching thirty kids."

Sandra paused and leaned back from the sheet of paper. "I feel like you're trying to make some sort of a point here, Dave, but to be honest I'm not entirely sure what it is? Of course, you're only teaching thirty students: you're a classroom teacher. But we can still take those predictions and apply them to your groups."

"No, actually I'm not sure you can do that. I mean, I'm sure you understand this system far better than I do, I'm just a physicist, but what you're describing sounds a lot like the ecological fallacy?"

"You're right, Dave. I understand this system much better than you do and I've no idea what you're talking about. Now, I'm sure you think you're being very clever, but the bottom line is, value added has been used in schools for decades and it is very reliable."

"But you're inferring the results of individuals based on the results that you're expecting their group to get."

"Yes, that's what value added is. That's how statistics work, Dave. Honestly, I'd have thought a physicist like you would understand this."

"But that's exactly what the ecological fallacy is. You're taking an aggregate data set – that is the whole of the country – and calculating a predicted grade for the group of students that got a particular key-stage-two result, which is fine. But then you're taking that predicted grade and applying it to a completely different data set – that is my set of thirty students – and from that deducing an increase or decrease in my performance. That's employing a fallacy. Normally, that wouldn't really be an issue, but when you're freighting that single number with such meaning, it becomes far more problematic."

Sandra sighed heavily. "No, I really don't think you understand, Dave. Value added is a standard tool for assessing teacher performance. The government produces the prediction matrix and schools calculate how well their students are doing from that. It's not that difficult to understand. Are you trying to tell me that you're somehow smarter than all of the teachers in hundreds of schools all over the country?"

"No, I'm not saying I'm smarter, I'm just questioning the flawed methodology of over-interpretation."

"It's not a flawed methodology, Dave. Look, I suggest you go and look up how to calculate value added so that next time you don't embarrass yourself as much as you are right now." With a percussive jangle, she tapped the piece of paper with a finger. "Now, when we look at your current top set year eleven group, their mock results suggest that your value added should turn out to be slightly positive."

"Oh right, those guys. Yeah, I've only taught them this year: they were taught the majority of the GCSE course by someone else in years nine and ten. I mean whose pay are their results going to affect?"

"Well, Dave. Since you were the last teacher to teach them, they're your responsibility."

"So even though I'm a terrible teacher I'll get paid for the excellent work of my predecessor? How is that fair?"

Sandra took a deep breath and brought her fingers together into a little steeple. "I see your point, Dave, and clearly there are some issues that might need refining, but overall the effect of your teaching should emerge from the data. We're not expecting the system to be accurate for every single child, but overall it should paint a fair picture."

"Okay, but what if John decides he really doesn't like me any more: maybe I insult his suit one morning." John nodded as though this was something that might transpire. "What's to stop him as head of department from consistently giving me crappy year eleven groups who have spent two years being taught by non-specialists? Their results are likely to be lower, but you're now going to punish me by paying me less every year and then reward the non-specialists who get my brilliant students. What's my incentive to do well then?"

"Dave, it strikes me that you're being deliberately unhelpful," Sandra said, her tone shifting from one of patience to one of emerging frustration. "Your example is ridiculous. Why would a head of department undermine a good teacher?"

"I don't know, maybe they're weak and insecure? The point is that my performance can easily be skewed by my head of department."

"Well if you feel like your head of department is bullying you, then you can file a complaint, Dave. Just like normal. That hasn't changed. But by holding teachers accountable to the grades of their students, coasting teachers can no longer get a free ride. Now when I look at last year's results, your year eleven group was down 0.3 on their predicted grades. So if..."

"Hang on. What are the confidence levels on that figure?"

"What?" Sandra said, bristling with indignation at being interrupted. "Confidence levels? I'll tell you how confident we are, Dave, we're extremely confident. We've been tracking the performance of teachers for years, Dave, that's how we know. We know exactly which teachers are underperforming..."

"No, no, that's not what I meant. Any statistical prediction will have an associated uncertainty, the smaller the group, the bigger the uncertainty. If you quote a number without the uncertainty levels, it's pretty much meaningless."

"What? What are you talking about, Dave? Honestly, you're worse than the students." Sandra said, her voice straining with irritation. "How many times do I have to explain this to you? Value added is extremely simple." She began to slap the palm of her hand on the desk with each emphasised word, "Take the *actual* grade. Subtract it from the *predicted* grade. If it's *positive*, we pay you *more*. If it's *negative,* we pay you *less.* It's that simple. There's nothing clever about it. There are no tricks. You can't hide from the data, Dave. It tells us exactly how good you are."

Dave was unruffled by the desk-slapping. "I understand it's possible to subtract two numbers from each other, but the predicted grade isn't a number: it's a range of numbers. And even then, for physics, the baseline confidence levels will probably be an underestimate. There was that government commissioned 2014 paper? Was it, Benton and Sutch?" Sandra bit her lip and sucked air through her teeth as though controlling her temper. "That one where they looked at whether key-stage-two data was correlated with GCSE results? I can't remember all of the conclusions, but I'm pretty sure that the predicted grade was only really meaningful for maths and English. I think for physics there was a much weaker correlation, something around 0.5? I mean, obviously it was far worse for languages, so I don't know what system you're planning to use there?"

Sandra brought both hands down on the desk. "Right. That's enough. I'm not interested in your theories or some nonsense you've read on the internet. Value added works. That's been proven."

"Really? Where?"

"Schools all over the country are using it, Dave."

"That's not actually proof..."

"Yes... it ... is. It's all the proof I need. The school will use value added. And we will assess your performance using it. End of discussion."

"I don't think you've understood..."

Sandra snorted loudly and muttered, "I don't understand?"

"...I don't have a problem with value added in itself."

"Oh my god! Then why are you wasting my time with this?"

"Because there are four obvious flaws with your performance metric: firstly, only maths and English would be reasonably correlated with the predictions it generates. Secondly, there's no fair way of establishing who has had what educational impact on groups taught by more than one teacher. Thirdly you're quoting figures without confidence levels and that pretty much makes them meaningless. And finally, your entire system is predicated on the statistical fallacy of applying national predictions to small unrepresentative datasets. Although, you could possibly encode that into the confidence levels, I don't know. I'm not a statistician."

Sandra sat glowering at Dave for a few seconds. "Are you done?"

"Yeah."

Sandra spoke softly. "Your performance is going to be assessed using this metric, Dave. You can't do anything about that."

Dave shrugged. "Okay, sure."

Sandra clamped her lips tightly together and narrowed her eyes. "You seem to have very strong feelings about not having your pay linked to your performance, Dave." She said, opening the performance management folder.

"I don't actually have a problem with performance-related pay as an idea," Dave said. "It's more your metric and the assumption that it's capable of assessing performance."

"So last year I see you were down 0.3, Dave," Sandra said, ignoring him. "I have to say that's not good." She flicked over the page. "Shall we carry on and see how your pay would have fared in the past?"

"Uh, sure, if you want to."

Sandra read the data for the previous year and grunted with disappointment. Then she turned the page to read the year before that and grunted again. Dave knew that she would be going back over ten years of data and only finding positive value-added figures that were averaging between one and two grades above the national average. He scratched behind his ear as he waited for Sandra to finish. She closed the folder. The three of them sat in silence for a few seconds.

"Still. Last year was a negative value added, Dave. Perhaps we're seeing the start of a trend?"

John, who had been sitting in complete silence up until then leaned forward and murmured apologetically: "Uh, actually Sandra, can I just interrupt there." She looked irritated. "Uh, strictly speaking, that group wasn't really Dave's group. Tilley went on, uh, maternity leave after Christmas and Dave kindly agreed to cover them for the final few months before their exams. So, I'm not sure we can really say that Dave properly taught that group."

Sandra gave a frustrated nostril-snort and turned to Dave. "So you didn't teach that group?" Dave shook his head. "Then why are you letting me waste my time with this information if it's not even relevant?" she said accusingly.

"I assumed your metric would take that into account."

Sandra shook her head as she looked back at the data. "I don't understand why you, of all people, would have such a problem with this system?" she said and then without further explanation moved onto discussing his performance targets. "We're not just looking at the data here: we're looking at your performance as a whole. We get it. We understand that teaching is about more than just the numbers. These targets are an opportunity for you to demonstrate your wider contributions and to be rewarded accordingly."

"That sounds positive," Dave said. "So if I made running an afterschool club one of my targets, would that be taken into account if my grades were below average?"

"No. If your grades go down you would lose your performance bonus."

"So what's the purpose of the target?"

"The targets are there for teachers to demonstrate the broader impact they're having within the school and obviously we can use that as a part of assessing your overall performance."

"So, do I get a bonus for achieving my targets?"

"No, there's no pay mechanism related to personal targets, they're there for you to demonstrate your broader impact on the school, which is extremely important."

"No doubt. So what would happen if I fell short of one of my targets?"

"Of a performance target?" Sandra shook her head slowly. "Well, hopefully, you'd work hard enough to avoid that, but if you missed a target then I don't think that it would be unreasonable for us to judge that you've had a failure in performance."

"And so I'd lose pay?"

"Yes. That's what performance-related pay means, Dave. It's related to your performance."

Under their old system, staff had been encouraged to view the performance management process as an opportunity for self-improvement and urged to select targets that were appropriately aspirational. It now seemed to Dave that such target setting would be extremely naïve. The targets appeared to have a distinct one-way bias: a failed target could always reduce your pay, whereas all a successful target could manage was the implication that you might not be incompetent.

"Okay, so this year I'll set my target as an average student-approval rating of ninety percent for my year ten group." Dave said.

Sandra looked suitably impressed. "That's a good ambitious target, Dave. That's what we like to see: teachers aiming high. And your whole-school-development target?"

Dave paused for a moment and then remembered. "Well, I am the teaching and learning coordinator?"

"Oh yes, I'd forgotten you did that," Sandra said, writing something on the paper. Dave silently cursed himself for reminding management of this role. "We also need to assign you a career target."

"A what?"

"A career target: Gary is keen for all his employees to become as resilient as the rest of his industry and he believes he can instil that resilience by giving you all a sense of personal agency. You're responsible for where you end up in your career, Dave. If you're still on the bottom rung after several years, that's because you haven't worked hard enough. So, Gary wants everyone to stretch themselves."

"And what does that mean?"

"Well, you need to apply for stretch roles."

"Stretch roles? What the heck is a stretch role?"

"You need to be applying for roles beyond that of just a teacher, Dave. You need to start applying for other roles: head of department, head of key stage three, those kinds of things."

"But I don't want to do any of those."

Sandra made a disappointed tutting sound. "That's because you lack ambition, Dave. And unless you have ambition you can't improve."

"No, it's just that I don't want to do any of those jobs."

"It doesn't matter, Dave. You need the interview practice: that's your career target. Get out there and be something."

"I already am something. I'm a teacher who's quite happy being a teacher and doesn't want a senior position."

"That doesn't matter, Dave," Sandra said, ignoring his protestations and writing down his targets. "This is to help you grow."

SOCKLESS LEARNING

With a pint of ale in one hand and three packets of crisps in the other, Dave made his way down the pub steps to a mezzanine terrace overlooking the river. Heather was sitting at one of the wooden picnic tables, one hand resting beside her pint glass, the other, holding open a book. She was wearing white trousers and a floral-patterned blouse that flared out around the hem. Heather always managed to look effortlessly stylish and in the three years he had known her, Dave could not recall ever seeing her wear the same combination of clothes twice, although mathematically he reckoned it must have occurred at some point. She looked up at Dave as he sat down opposite her.

"Whatcha reading?" he said, dumping the crisps into the centre of the table.

"It's a good book." Heather twisted her wrist so Dave could read the cover. "It's about how money and debt operate in the economy."

"Economics?" Dave said with an exaggerated expression of surprise. "But, I don't understand? You're not an economics teacher?" Heather laughed. She had previously complained about her friends' shock at her reading books outside of her subject.

"No, I know. What was I thinking?" she tucked her bar receipt between the pages and laid the book down. "Don't tell anyone, but I was reading a history book last week." Dave laughed and took a long drink of his ale, gazing out across the river at the early-evening light as it filtered through the trees and sparkled off the water. "So I hear your place has joined a MAP?" Heather said. Dave nodded and held his hand out to feel the wall beside the table. It was still warm from the heat of the day. "Noticed any changes?"

"Not really, I mean, it's still quite early. I don't imagine they'll try and change any of the day-to-day stuff but there've been a few changes."

"Like what?"

"Performance-related pay," Dave said and mentioned his meeting with Sandra. "I think the real danger is that once you start collapsing the job down to a few numbers, you end up distorting the whole thing. The success metric you employ inevitably becomes the hoop through which everyone has to jump."

"But management would presumably see that as a positive thing," Heather said. "By tying your pay to the grades they get, they're hoping to end up getting better grades out of the students."

"Then why bother engaging with the students' emotional needs? Or running afterschool clubs?" Dave said. "None of that pays."

"Well, it does in that those are all a part of you being a professional. The assumption is that you continue to do your basic job but then you get paid an additional amount for getting the good grades," Heather said. "You can't argue that because one aspect of your performance now has a pay-related component, that all aspects do."

Dave shifted on the bench as he considered Heather's point. "Yeah, I suppose so," he said reluctantly. "But kids can get good grades for all sorts of reasons."

"Oh, I'm not disagreeing with that, I'm just saying that your previous line of argument was spurious. Especially when you consider all the questionable assumptions you could go after," Heather said picking up a crisp from the open packet and dipping it into her beer. "Like, do financial incentives for teachers actually improve grades for the students? And if so, in what context? I've read that for complex tasks, financial incentives tend to degrade performance, so it's probably worth the government investigating how strongly teachers respond to monetary incentives. I mean if you think about it, you've got graduates with highly sought after degrees like maths, chemistry and physics opting to go into teaching when you'd have thought if they were financially driven, they'd have already gone into industry or finance."

Dave nodded. "I'd not thought of it like that."

Heather let out a long sigh. "And I'm not even sure what problem it's trying to solve?" She said. "It's not like there's a problem in motivating teachers to work: most of them are already working fifty- to sixty-hour weeks on the fixed paycheques they get. If you read the research on poor outcomes, it's rarely the teachers that are the primary component in that shortfall. It's usually wider family and social issues."

"Yeah, student performance is not necessarily teacher performance."

"But I can totally see how if you were outside of teaching, you might look at performance-related pay and think it was a good idea."

"Really?" Dave sounded surprised.

"Yeah, absolutely. If you're outside the system, I imagine it looks like an obvious solution. Teach the kids well, get them good grades and get rewarded."

"You can't just lean into a completely unfamiliar industry and imagine your ignorance qualifies you to come up with a solution."

"Teaching's a bit different though," Heather said. "The majority of people have been through a school themselves and so they can remember their own good and bad teachers, so they have a sense that they know how the system works. They won't think of themselves as being ignorant. If anything, they'll think of themselves as an expert in their own experience."

"But that's like me arguing that I understand international banking because I have a bank account," Dave said, wafting away an inquisitive wasp with a beer mat. "Just because you've passed through a system, doesn't mean you know how best to operate it."

"Oh, I bet you have a great time at parent-teacher confrontation evenings," Heather said leaning back as the wasp investigated her ale. "I think when parents show an interest in the national structure of education that's great. But often that interest is really just centred upon their own child. Which is fine, there's nothing wrong with wanting the best for your kids, but meeting the needs of an individual is a long way from meeting the needs of a nation." Dave watched Heather as she spoke, the graceful movement of her hands, the way she leaned in and held his gaze with her light-brown eyes. When Dave had first met Heather he had tried flirting with her a few times, working into their early conversations how much he enjoyed her company and how delightfully infectious he found her optimistic outlook. On another occasion, he had praised the sharpness of her wit. And after a few more meetings, how much her outfits had suited her and how stylish she always looked. Heather had thanked him and then proceeded to talk about her boyfriend, which Dave had taken to be a gentle but unequivocally firm rejection.

"So what were the poorly correlated numbers they linked to your performance?"

Dave took a drink and recounted the details of his performance management meeting with Sandra.

"I don't' think we use value added," Heather said once Dave had finished. "We're on progress eight?"

"Yeah, that's still a value-added system," Dave said. "I mean, don't misunderstand, there's nothing inherently wrong with making predictions off the key-stage-two data. The problem, as with all statistical tools, is the danger of over-interpretation. You can't quote a child's predicted grade without also quoting the confidence levels. It's meaningless."

"I don't think anyone in our SLT would know what that meant. What are they supposed to be using? Two sigma?"

Dave nodded. "Yeah, I think so."

"So what did she say?"

"What? About the value added?"

"Yeah?"

"Well, nothing. She just ignored me."

Heather laughed. "I guess that's one way of dealing with uncertainty. What were your other targets?"

"I figured since she seemed to love numbers without really understanding them, I'd go for a ninety percent approval rating from my year ten group."

Heather chuckled. "Nice. SLT love all that student-voice stuff. What're you going to do? A week of fun lessons?"

Dave popped a couple of crisps into his mouth and nodded whilst munching. "Yup. Chocolates as prizes. Give 'em the survey. They usually just rate their last few lessons."

"Ninety percent is still quite high though? I mean, aren't you running the risk of falling short?"

"Not really," Dave said shaking his head and grabbing another handful of crisps. "I've done them before. The survey only has five options and three of them count as being satisfied. If you do three or four fun lessons you typically get dictator-like approval ratings."

Heather smiled. "I might try that."

"Has your place got career targets?"

"I don't think so. I'm not even sure what those are?"

Dave shrugged. "I dunno either. It's the first time I've come across them. Seems to be a thing that Henderson's come up with. Apparently, mine is to apply for senior positions."

"Like what? As in head of department?"

"I guess so. She wasn't really all that clear. She just said I needed to have interview practice."

"For what?"

"Oh you know, for all those jobs I don't want."

"That's such a weird target," Heather said. "And there's a lot of potential for that to go wrong."

"In that, I might end up with a position I really don't want?" Dave said. "Yeah, that's what I thought."

"You might end up as a teaching and learning tsar."

"Exactly," Dave said with a laugh and then added with regret, "Unfortunately I had to remind her I did that. I think they'd actually forgotten."

Heather rested her pint glass back on the table. "You know what you need to do," she said with a mischievous grin. "You need to apply for a position that you're in no way qualified to hold."

"There're plenty of those," Dave said and then paused to consider the brilliance of this idea. His career target was simple, he merely had to apply for a senior position but there was no requirement for him to do well in the interview. "We had an assistant head resign this week," he said thoughtfully.

Heather's grin broadened. "And here you are with absolutely no management experience whatsoever. You'd be perfect for that job."

"I might even get that career target ticked off before the end of term," he said.

"Well, here's to badly constructed targets," Heather said raising her glass. The two of them took a drink. "Oh, you could have so much fun with this," she said. "Have you read the R-N Paradigm?" Dave shook his head. "Oh, you should totally reference it. It's a spoof management guide. I'll lend you my copy."

"What? Reference it in the interview?"

"Absolutely. Apply for a management position and cite a spoof management guide as your inspiration: you'd totally get a position at my place."

"Yeah?"

"Yeah, the bar's set quite low," Heather said. "We've had a week of sockless learning."

Dave spluttered into his beer as he unsuccessfully tried to combine both drinking and laughing. "What the hell's sockless learning?"

"Do you really need to ask? Surely the name says it all."

"No. That's not a thing," Dave said, convinced she was winding him up.

"No, I'm serious. Our school paid a £1000 to some self-deluded imbecile to come in and talk to us all about the wonders of sockless learning."

"You're serious?"

"Oh yes. Apparently, there's 'research'," Heather said holding up her fingers to indicate air quotes. "Nothing more specific than that though, just 'research'. Occasionally the sockless guru upped the stakes by adding that the research was scientific, but he didn't mention in what way."

"So what's he saying? That kids learn better without socks?"

"You got it."

"That's insane. How can you possibly think that?"

"Apparently the 'scientific research' shows that students are more connected with their environment when they're not wearing socks."

"In that, they have colder feet?"

"Quite possibly. He had some crazy atavistic argument about how our ancestors didn't wear socks."

Dave laughed loudly. "That's a terrible argument," he said. "For a start, all our ancestors are dead, which I can only presume is through a lack of socks."

Heather shook her head. "None of us could believe it. Apparently, there are loads of benefits. He spent ten minutes listing them all."

"Like what? Students have an increased aversion to walking on gravel?"

"No, apparently students are far less likely to get involved in a conflict when they're not wearing socks."

"Well, that's probably because they're scared by all the weird adults requiring them to take off their socks. I mean, who's going to kick off in that environment?"

"I guess it also makes it harder for them to run away," Heather added.

"Which is the same justification that you would use for chaining them to the floor."

"The whole training session was unbelievable. Seriously, Dave, you'd have loved it: we were all sitting there whilst this grown man passionately enthused about taking away kids' socks. It was so surreal."

"And the school paid him?"

"Yeah, which is ridiculous in itself, but even more ridiculous is how seriously the school's taking the whole thing," Heather said leaning forward. "They've made it compulsory for students to take their socks off during lessons."

"Think of all the conflict that's not going to happen."

"And if any of them refuse, we're supposed to phone home about it."

Dave sat there with his mouth open for a few seconds. "That's awesome," he said laughing loudly. "I'd love to see both sides of that conversation. Hi, we've sent your son home because he refuses to not wear socks."

"Yeah, so once all those kids stormed out, surprisingly the ones compliant enough to sit and work without socks did so without much conflict."

"I don't know who this man is, but he's a genius," Dave said shaking his head in disbelief. "I mean, seriously, that whole scenario is almost exactly what I'd have come up with if I was trying to write a spoof about dumb management being suckered in by a con man."

"I know!" Heather said. "So you can imagine my delight when the fire alarm went off on Wednesday." Dave began laughing even before Heather had managed to describe the chaos of all the students tip-toeing across the asphalt in the rain and one of them stepping on a piece of metal. "And I imagine the deputy who hired this charlatan will probably end up with a five-star performance review."

"Getting paid £1000 to tell people to take off their socks?" Dave shook his head. "Man, I am in the wrong business."

DYNAMIC ENACTING RATIOS

The corridors and playgrounds were silent, the classrooms eerily devoid of children. It was a training day and so the school, bereft of students, had become a hollow replica, an infrastructure devoid of vitality. Dave collected a cup of coffee from the echoing canteen and made his way to the theatre where the teachers were gathered. Sometimes training days were useful and everyone would agree it had been time well spent, but more often than not, the day would devolve into a pedagogic fashion show, a forum for educational entrepreneurs to disseminate their latest teaching and management ideas. An entire industry had grown up around these educational philosophies and to Dave, it often seemed that the only consistent feature in each new method was that it was different from its predecessor. The school would hire a speaker who would tout the virtues of their new 'game changer' in some area like lesson delivery and whilst the older teachers would largely ignore their claims, the younger teachers would eagerly adopt the new method and possibly spend the next few years trying to develop resources to incorporate it into their subject. The following year there would be a speaker describing a new classroom management technique, the year after there would be some new method of student assessment and finally, it would emerge that the 'game changer' lesson delivery from three or four years ago was ineffective, and potentially damaging. Fortunately, there was always a new technique to replace it and thus the process would start over. The seemingly endless recurrence of these cycles was not through a lack of decent research. There were plenty of established techniques that were demonstrably effective for a great number of students, but these were often too expensive, requiring subject specialists, smaller class sizes or bespoke interventions. Or they were just seen as being a bit boring. Schools, it seemed, were willing to pay any number of itinerant speakers in the hope of hitting upon the cold fusion of teaching, the miracle breakthrough that would solve all their attainment and financial problems in one fell swoop.

The man at the front was wearing a shirt but no tie. Such non-threatening attire suggested that the talk would be on some trendy, new assessment or pedagogical technique. If the speaker had worn a suit, then they could have likely expected something on management or educational theory. The man swished together the long red curtains that hung down from the theatre's ceiling and in the half-light, walked back to the stage. A long, low note emanated from the theatre's sound system. "For thousands of years, mankind has struggled to make sense of the world," he said in a tone of voice more suited to a movie trailer than a training day. A picture of Galileo appeared on the large projection screen behind him. "We moved from a world described by superstition to a world described by data." The picture shifted to a photograph of a yellow manuscript with columns of numbers and a geometric diagram of a circle with some triangles. "It is through observation and data that we developed... science." The low note resolved into a major chord as he said the word science. "And it is through science that we have achieved the wonders of modern technology." The music continued with some triumphal fifths and the image on the screen transitioned to a stock photo of a woman in a white coat and safety specs bending down to look along the length of a green laser beam. Dave chuckled: the spurious goggles would have been useless at protecting her eyes from the laser, being, as they were, transparent. He glanced around at his colleagues, but no one else seemed to have noticed this error. "Teaching should be no different," the man at the front continued. The music transitioned into a melodic sweep of strings, the image to that of a young woman in front of a whiteboard and a group of students with raised hands. "But for too long we have assumed that because each class is different, we cannot develop a scientific way of teaching them. But now, for the first time, research has given teachers access to science." The strings swelled with the emotional intensity of a death scene. "For the first time, science can tailor your teaching style to the individual needs of your classes."

Sitting next to Dave, Mary muttered: "I don't think science means what he thinks it means."

"Today I am proud to introduce the future of teaching..." The music fell away to a single sustained note as the man moved onto a new slide. It had three letters arranged vertically on the left-hand side: DER. Dave gave a soft chuckle. DER were the same three letters that he had used for the acronym in his spurious academic paper, only he had chosen them because they sounded like someone saying "duh". "D...E...R," the man spelt out. "Or duh, because it's that easy to implement." There was a ripple of polite laughter across the theatre. "The D stands for dynamic," he said, the word appearing after the initial letter. Dave narrowed his eyes. It was probably just coincidence that the acronym and the first word were the same as in his nonsensical dynamic enacting ratios. "Dynamic because the system is able to change and adapt to each of your classes." He clicked the slide. "Enacting," the man said. "The system is one that you actively employ in your lessons to enhance your academic outcomes." Dave glanced around the room to see if people were watching for his reaction, convinced that this must be some sort of a wind-up. But the theatre of teachers seemed focussed on the man at the front. "And ratios," the man concluded.

Dave frowned. Clearly, some scurrilous academic had read Dave's fake research paper and stolen the only thing of value within. "That's my acronym," he whispered to Mary.

She nodded. "Yeah, it looks familiar."

"This is the key to academic success," the man at the front continued. "Finding the correct ratio for your group and then enacting that ratio. Now, of course, you're wondering, what does this man mean by ratio?" There was a murmur as a few people felt it was necessary to confirm that: yes, this was what they were thinking. "Well this is the good news, it's something you're already familiar with." The slide changed to show a pie chart with an unequal division, one marked 'talking' the other, 'doing'. "Seventy, thirty," the man said and explained the idea of splitting a lesson into the time spent by the teacher talking and the time for the students working.

"Oh you are kidding," Dave said as it became increasingly apparent that the model being described was the same as the one that he had fabricated for publication. Some academic must have stolen not just his acronym, but his entire idea.

"Now this scientific model has taken the educational world by storm," the man said. "There have been several follow up papers, but the original research was conducted by an academic practitioner who works in the classroom."

"Oh my God," Dave said. Projected on the screen was an excerpt from Dave's own academic paper, a graph with error bars the size of the y-axis. The man at the front was referring to it as, "a convincing piece of evidence".

"Isn't that your paper?" Mary asked, leaning over and speaking in a low voice.

"Uh, yeah."

"I thought you made all that up?"

"I did."

Mary smiled. "Well, that's an interesting position for you." She said. Dave sighed heavily as he considered his options. He could go full ostrich and eschew all responsibility for the paper, keeping his head down for the duration of the training, but this felt selfish, especially when he knew the whole concept was nonsense. It would be wasting the time of his colleagues. However, if he stood up to denounce his own work, he might save the theatre from a wasted morning but then he would have to explain why he had cynically submitted such nonsense to an academic journal in the first place. He doubted he would receive much sympathy from explaining that his paper had been the quickest and easiest way to tick a box on his teaching and learning position. The simplified, take-home narrative would be that Dave was irresponsible and lazy and this was not an image that he wished to cultivate.

The man at the front showed another of Dave's graphs, this one had a broad scatter of about ten data points that looked more like a star field than a graph. There was no discernible pattern and yet a best-fit line confidently cut through them at forty-five degrees. For Dave, the inclusion of such a meaningless best-fit line had seemed like a good way of signalling to the reviewers that the paper was a joke. However, the man at the front was not party to this joke and was thus enthusiastically describing the line as showing a clear trend. It suddenly dawned on Dave that denouncing his own work might be ineffective. The man at the front was heavily invested in the model being true and so Dave was unlikely to get much traction by loudly announcing to the room that the model was nonsense and thus all who followed it, fools. In all likelihood, the man would just dismiss Dave's claims to authority and carry on with his presentation. There was nothing to be gained from a public showdown and so Dave resigned himself to watching his fiction being applauded by a stranger.

The man at the front described a case study in which Dave's technique had improved students' performance by twelve percent. Dave furrowed his brow as the second hand of the theatre clock swept out the wasted time. Maybe there was a third way? If he could avoid confessing to the paper being a cynical, self-serving shortcut then maybe he could avoid the accusation of being lazy. Dave smiled. The solution was to impose some retrospective continuity and claim that the paper had always been a deliberate hoax. This was not a new idea: in the nineties, Alan Sokal had submitted a fake paper on postmodern cultural studies to highlight the lack of intellectual rigour in the field. The difference, however, was that Sokal had come clean the moment the paper had been published whereas, for Dave, that ship had somewhat sailed. Maybe he could argue that he had been waiting to see who would start circulating the fake paper? Then he could claim that his issue was with the educational opportunists who monetarised flimsy ideas and sold them to financially struggling schools. However, there was no need for a confrontation with the man at the front. Dave could write a press release over the summer and denounce both the paper and the opportunists, later. Dave leaned back in his chair.

Sitting on the front row, Katarina raised her hand. "Who did you say the author was?"

"Dave Winger," the man said. Katarina, the leadership team and all the orbiting, aspirational middle managers turned in their seats to look at Dave.

"Is this your paper?" Katarina asked, directing her question to Dave.

"Yeah, Dave, is this your paper?" Mary echoed, smiling.

Dave squirmed in his seat and scowled at Mary. The man on the stage took a step forward and peered into the audience. Dave was obvious in that he was the only person not looking around at Dave. "Are you Dave Winger?" he asked with what Dave felt to be an uncomfortable amount of awe.

Dave slumped a little lower. "Uh, yeah. I guess so." He said with the reluctance and resignation of a student agreeing to a detention.

"That's incredible," the man said and jumped down off the stage and approached Dave. "I can't believe you're actually Dave Winger." Dave looked up at the man's outstretched hand and, when it became obvious it wasn't going to go away, reluctantly reached up to shake it. "It's an honour to meet you, sir," the man said. Dave slumped a little lower in his chair. "Why didn't you say something at the start?"

"Ummm..." Dave glanced around the room as he tried to come up with a reasonable explanation. "I'm a very modest person?" he said speculatively.

The man seemed to accept this and nodded. "So your data was all taken from students at this school?"

"Uh, yes."

"That's amazing," the man said, although Dave had no idea why he would find this amazing. "How long did it take you?"

Dave sighed heavily and made a series of vague hand gestures that suggested some length of time. Fortunately, Katarina interrupted them: "So this paper's had a big impact?" she asked from the front row.

"Oh yes," the man said, taking a step back so he could face Katarina. "I've been in educational theory for the last ten years but this is the first system that's really excited me: it's just got so much potential." He looked back down at Dave and indicated the stage with his right hand. "I really feel like you should be up there explaining your model, not me."

Dave shook his head. "No, it's okay, honestly."

John had turned in his seat and was smiling broadly. "Oh, I think you should go up there, Dave," he said. "I for one have got a question about those error bars."

"Yes. I'm sure you do."

"They seem quite big."

Dave rested his hand on his forehead like a sun visor. "Yes. Yes, they are," he muttered, gradually lowering his palm so that the rest of the room disappeared from view.

"It would be an honour to hear you talk about your research," the man said.

Dave kept his head and his hand lowered. "No, it's okay," he said. "I'd just get in the way. You carry on. You're doing a great job explaining it."

"Wow, that's really kind of you," the man said with a beaming smile that Dave avoided. "That's made my day." He walked back up to the stage and continued his presentation, only this time he did so whilst continually nodding and smiling in Dave's direction.

John moved so that he was sitting alongside Dave. "So, this is what happened to your paper?" he said.

"Uh huh," Dave said trying to avoid eye contact. John was clearly enjoying Dave's discomfort.

"Tell me if this sounds familiar: a man shoots the side of a barn and then goes over and paints targets over the bullet holes. You ever heard that story before?"

Dave sighed and looked at John's grinning face. "Yes, I'm well aware of the sharpshooter fallacy."

"So these enacting ratios that you describe for each of the classes, you got those numbers by giving them a different test at the end of each lesson and then looked to see which ratio gave the best results. Explain to me how that's not painting a target?"

"John, you and I both know from looking at my incredibly flawed data..." he waved a hand at the numbers projected onto the stage screen. "That I've basically p-hacked my way to a series of significant results."

"Yeah, but don't worry, Dave, I don't think anyone else has noticed."

Mary leaned in. "I noticed," she whispered.

"Apart from Mary," John said. "And probably Growler. Although..." he looked over at the slumped figure of Growler in the corner. "He might actually be asleep."

"In my defence, I was planning on revealing how flawed the whole system was," Dave said.

"Oh right, is that due straight after this?"

Dave sighed. "No, I'm not even sure how I can go about doing it now anyway. Look at this guy." The man at the front grinned at Dave and gave him a thumbs-up. The slide moved onto one entitled 'Practical Workshop'. "I can't stand up and denounce the whole thing with this guy here: it'd be like kicking a puppy in the face."

John chuckled. "I think that's going to be the least of your complicated problems."

"How'd you mean?"

"Are you kidding? Katarina will be all over this. There's no way that by the end of today there isn't something on the school webpage about us having a 'Leading educational researcher' on staff."

Dave's shoulders slumped and he rested his forehead against the palm of his hand. "Oh god, I hadn't even thought of that."

"She's all about the optics, Dave. I guarantee by the end of the week you'll be doing interviews for the local paper."

Dave looked into John's face. "But it's complete nonsense," he said. "What's going to happen when I denounce the whole thing as a hoax?"

John shrugged. "I dunno. It'll be entertaining though."

"Yeah, entertaining for you, maybe."

"I wouldn't worry about it," John said. "It'll be like when a newspaper apologises for a front page slander by printing a retraction in eight-point type on page thirty-seven. No one will pay any attention. Your paper is simple and easy to grasp, people will prefer that story over a complex truth of how statistics were misused."

"Is that supposed to make me feel better?"

The rest of the theatre had dissolved into a white noise of chatter as people moved around to get into workshop groups. A young, blonde-haired teacher approached the three of them and introduced herself as Natalie. She smiled at Dave and asked if she could join his group. "I'm not sure that our group is going to be all that useful," Dave said, bemused as to why a newly qualified geography-teacher he had never spoken with would specifically want to join his group. "I don't even know what we're supposed to be doing." She laughed as though this was a funny joke. Mary raised an eyebrow and suppressed a smile.

"Shall I read the instructions?" Natalie asked and then proceeded to read the handout to the three of them. There was some example data from which they had to decide what the group's enacting ratio would be. Natalie seemed excited by the task and spent the next five minutes poring over the data, narrating her thought process as she went along.

"Your problem isn't going to be so much that the rest of the world won't listen," Mary said, ignoring the background murmur of Natalie's narration. "It's going to be how you square the truth with SLT. None of them has any kind of scientific or mathematical training, so to them, this paper is going to look like bona fide research."

"And I guarantee, they'll use it to promote the school," John added.

"Exactly," Mary continued. "They're not going to want to look stupid when you reveal the whole thing's nonsense. You'll need to come up with some way of protecting them from embarrassment or they'll just take it out on you."

Natalie interrupted them with her enthusiastic prediction for the enacting ratio and handed the data to Dave for his opinion. Dave glanced at the data for no more than half a second and then placed it on the empty chair behind him. "Sure, sounds about right," he said.

"Wow, that took me ages compared to you," she said, misinterpreting Dave's disinterest for brilliance.

"Yeah, really impressive, Dave," John said.

The man at the front went through the solutions and gave the groups a new task. "Each of you has a series of cards with different ways you can change your teaching. You've got five minutes to trapezoid-twelve them into which are the most effective."

Dave flinched at the phrase 'trapezoid twelve'. "Trapezoid twelve!" he exclaimed. "I came up with that like, two months ago."

Mary looked sceptical. "Yeah, whatever, Dave."

"I did!"

"I think you'll find trapezoid-twelve came from a think tank at Google."

"No. No, it didn't, that's what I made up. I made that up. I said it came from Google to make it sound more legitimate, but it didn't, I just made it up in a middle-management meeting."

Mary shook her head and sighed. "You don't get to come up with everything, Dave."

THE
INTERVIEWS

D
ave sat in the school theatre whilst a man with white hair and a blue tie jabbed a finger at the teachers in front of him and explained how he would fire anybody who fell below his extremely high standards. He was one of the candidates applying for the role of assistant head and he seemed keen to communicate how little popularity mattered to him. Gary Henderson, the chair of the MAP, had decided that the interview process should start with the candidates delivering a presentation to an audience of staff and management. The candidate's presentation would describe their personal suitability and explain their vision for the school and whilst Dave could see the logic of the forum for assessing public-speaking ability, he was unsure whether Gary needed to have made it into quite such a circus. Dave sat on the front row along with the other candidates. In line with his career target, Dave had dutifully applied for the position of assistant head and a few days later had received a successful application letter, not from the school, but from Henderson Managerial Services, the organisation running the MAP. Since the entire purpose of applying had been simply to apply, Dave had reasoned that he need not make any further preparations. He didn't want the position and so the quicker

he could get eliminated the better, but Dave was also aware that there was a fine balance to be struck: if he came across as completely incompetent, then questions might be raised over his classroom teaching and as usual, Dave wished to avoid as much contact with SLT as possible.

The evening before, Dave had decided to ask the regulars at the bar how they would approach this process. Ian the electrician had suggested that Dave's school vision be the Finnish educational model, this, he assured Dave, would make him seem both competent and yet unsuited to a senior position. Competent, in that the Finnish model produced excellent educational outcomes, unsuited, in that his proposal would make him seem like a dangerous leftie. Mike the barman had pulled a pint and suggested that the outcomes of the Finnish model might have had more to do with the country's more cohesive community structures and so they might not be as effective in the UK. Davina the florist had agreed and suggested that Dave make his position a much broader one of raising standards by instigating a system of community support. A stockbroker, who had been passing through the town, had pointed out that Dave was not running for elected office but applying for an assistant headship, and that a broader social stance might make him seem delusional. She had then pointed out that Davina's idea was problematic in that it assumed poor educational outcomes were somehow a measure of community dysfunction. Davina had clarified that she thought the connection was more correlation than causation, but that a programme of support would still have utility. Arthur the postman, had brought the conversation back to Dave's original problem of wanting to be refused the senior position by suggesting that he turn up to the interview naked. Dave had nodded as though considering Arthur's suggestion and pointed out that whilst this would certainly lose him the job interview it also ran the significant risk of losing him his current teaching job. Those sitting at the bar had nodded in agreement. Arthur had acknowledged that this was a possible drawback and had modified his suggestion to merely turning up in Lycra.

Dave had chosen to ignore Arthur's advice and was thus sitting in the theatre wearing his suit. It was lunchtime and there were about forty teachers, presumably figuring that this would be a more entertaining accompaniment to their sandwiches than marking. With a strangely theatrical flourish, the candidate in the blue tie moved the slide onto a flowchart which bore the heading: The Carson Method. "This will soon be standard in schools," he said with authority. The slide contained vaguely threatening steps like 'weed out weakness' and 'enforce overtime' along with nebulous inputs like 'raise standards' and 'encourage growth'. For Dave, the most entertaining aspect was how all of the different routes had no choice but to converge upon a box marked 'success', and he was doubtful that something so poorly constructed and obviously flawed would become a school standard. Dave leaned over and whispered to the woman next to him. "What was this guy's name?"

"Mel Carson," she replied.

"Ohhh," Dave said, suddenly realising why he had never come across the Carson Method before.

"My background is in business, so I know about effective management." Mel Carson said, delivering another slide change with a flourish of the hand. "Now this is standard wisdom in business," he said indicating the slide behind him. It contained an equation that read:

Experienced staff + effective management + timely solutions = business success

"Now if we rearrange this equation," he said progressing the slide. "We get this."

The new slide read:

Effective management = business success – timely solutions – experienced staff.

"Now, we can clearly see from this, that the key to effective management is to remove time pressures and to fire the experienced staff, many of whom are the most expensive individuals in an organisation. And this is what the business equation clearly shows us: effective management has the power to compensate for the loss of their experience. A business is a bit like an army, you just need a good leader at the top and for the men below to follow their orders. The troops don't need to be geniuses: they just need to follow orders. Now, this..." he indicated the equation behind him, "this isn't just my opinion: this is maths."

Dave sat biting his lip to stop himself from laughing out loud. There were so many things wrong with Mel's logic it was difficult to know where to start. He leaned over to the woman sitting next to him and said, "Can you believe this guy?"

She nodded. "I know. It's incredible. I can't believe I didn't know any of this," she said. Dave took a moment to process her response, scanning her tone for sarcasm, but it was worryingly absent. He went back to watching Mel, who was now fulminating against all forms of expertise and railing against experience as an overrated attribute. Dave figured this was all part of some bold strategy wherein Mel would conclude that his own ignorance was a virtue, but he was wrong. Mel transitioned smoothly into describing his own extensive expertise and experience in management and concluded that this made him perfect for the job. It was like he hadn't heard his own presentation. Or perhaps the part of his brain that had written the conclusion just hadn't consulted with the part that had written the central argument. Dave looked around at the other teachers, quite a few of whom looked as confused as he was.

"Any questions?" Mel said to the theatre. Dave was surprised: there had been no requirement for the candidates to take questions and yet Mel was inviting them during a presentation that had raised so many.

The woman next to Dave lifted her hand: "I have a question about the Carson Method," she said. Dave smiled as he anticipated a nuclear strike on the woefully flawed flowchart but was disappointed when she asked: "Is it available in a book or something?"

"Yes, I'm glad you asked. It's available as an E-book. You can purchase it from Amazon," Mel said.

Dave wasn't sure which was the more disturbing, the fact that this woman wanted to read more about the Carson Method or that Mel had put the time and effort into producing a book of this nonsense.

"I have a question," Katarina said. Mel nodded at her. "Your business equation that you showed..." Once again, Dave grinned, anticipating the logical evisceration of Mel's management system. "...how do you propose to take away that time pressure from management? We obviously have certain immovable deadlines like exams."

"Excellent question, I'm glad you asked." Mel said and began describing how some time pressures were "motivating pressures" whilst others were "resistance pressures". He used the phrases with the confidence of someone employing generally accepted terms.

Dave glanced around the room. It didn't look like anyone else wanted to ask a question so he raised his hand. Mel nodded at him.

"Could we just go back to your equation for a moment?" Dave asked. Mel obliged by clicking back to his original slide. "Through your own method of reassembling motivational word equations to create new meaning, can't you just rearrange that equation to conclude the irrelevance of management?

Experienced staff + timely solutions = business success − effective management?"

Mel looked at the equation for a few seconds and then shook his head. "No, it doesn't work like that."

"Well, why not? That's exactly what you just did."

"No, you can't do that," Mel repeated with dismissive authority. "It has to still make sense."

"Well that's my point: none of them makes sense. That whole thing's not a mathematical expression: it's a motivational slogan."

Mel took another look at the equation and then turned back to Dave. "No, you're actually wrong," Mel said. "If you had as much experience as I do, then you'd understand. Any more questions?" He paused for half a beat and then thanked everybody. There was a smattering of polite applause.

Dave took the stage and smiled at the assembled staff. Public speaking had always felt like a natural extension of teaching, the skills of reading the mood of a classroom, thinking on his feet and projecting his voice had always felt highly applicable when addressing a room full of adults. He rested a hand on the lectern and introduced himself. "Hi, I'm Dave. And I'm a physicist." He spoke with the same intonation that one might use at a support group. There were one or two chuckles of amusement. Dave had concluded that his safest strategy for failing the job interview whilst avoiding accusations of incompetence was to be as bland as possible. He would minimise the engagement of his audience by avoiding the use of slides and the only information he would offer would be simple statements about what teachers and management did. That should be bland enough. He already had the distinct advantage of lacking any experience. All he had to do was avoid saying anything that could be construed as interesting and then he could sit back and let that total inexperience do all of the hard work.

"As a physicist I try to inform my opinions and beliefs through the available data." This, he figured, was probably enough to satisfy the 'tell us a bit about yourself' section. He glanced along the front row. It was primarily composed of the senior leadership team, all of whom were sitting with their arms folded and their expressions ones of stony disapproval. Next to Katarina was Gary Henderson. As usual, he was wearing a clashing tie and occasionally he would lean over and whisper loudly to her.

"I've met this guy before," Gary hissed. Katarina nodded, trapped by the social awkwardness of having to respond to her boss and yet wishing to avoid a conversation amongst an otherwise silent audience.

"A lot of people might imagine that the students are the most important part of a school, and in some ways they are. But if you have a good school, you won't have any difficulty finding kids to fill it. For me, the most important people in a school are the teachers." In a room full of teachers, Dave figured this statement was unlikely to get much pushback. "You can spend as much money as you want on the most amazing classrooms and the most up to date software, but if you don't have good teachers, you won't have a good school." There were several nods of agreement, although none of them came from management. Gary leaned across and in a theatrical whisper said, "That's not right. In business, it's always infrastructure first, staff second."

"So in many ways, the teachers are the primary infrastructure," Dave said, seamlessly responding to Gary's criticism without breaking his rhythm. "A classroom without a teacher is just a room full of kids. If we want to be an excellent school, then we need excellent teachers."

"He's saying the school needs better teachers," Gary hissed, correctly summarising Dave's whole school vision. Katarina's jaw tightened and she nodded again.

"For me, the role of the teacher is to teach the students. But in order to do this, they need a safe and productive learning environment. I think it is the role of management to support teachers in constructing that safe and productive environment." Again, the room of teachers muttered their approval although this time senior management also agreed, presumably thinking that they did this already.

"It is the job of the teacher to try and improve the students' grades. It is management's role to provide the resources and support that teachers need to focus on their job. In doing this, I would try to ignore my own preconceptions. I realise that what I would need as a teacher is not necessarily what you would need." As Dave said this Martin turned to Sandra and anxiously whispered, "Don't we already do this? I already do this."

Sandra nodded. "I know, so do I. You can ask anyone."

Dave continued: "We all have different styles of teaching and that diversity is an important component of what makes a robust learning-environment. I would try and maintain that by listening to what you say you need." Dave paused in response to a murmur of approval and then without thinking followed it up with a joke: "As my grandma used to say: there's more than one way to skin a cat but whichever method you choose, a groundsheet's a really good idea." This statement completely threw Martin, who turned to Sandra and asked: "Why would you need a groundsheet?" Gary Henderson gave a loud laugh of approval and then clarified what his laugh meant by whispering loudly to Katarina: "That's funny."

"In conclusion," Dave said. "I will strive at all times to maintain an optimal level of competence. Thank you."

There was a ripple of applause, most of it gratefully acknowledging the brevity of Dave's presentation. Gary Henderson whispered to Katarina: "An optimal level of competence. That's good. No one else is promising that."

As Dave sat down, the woman in the chair next to him stood up and took the stage. She introduced herself as Anne-Marie Klein and then spent almost as long as Dave's entire talk looking for her presentation file. The room watched as she tentatively moved the mouse pointer from one side of the screen to the other. Occasionally she would click on something, it would open and then she would herd the cursor up to the top right and close the window again. Eventually one of the ICT teachers went up to help her, finding and opening the file in under ten seconds. Anne-Marie began by describing the farm on which she lived. On the screen behind her, she projected a picture of a horse.

"This is one of my horses," she turned to smile at the picture. "This is Annabelle," she said it as though she was introducing the horse to the room. "Annabelle is the youngest in the stables and she's been through a lot." Dave assumed that Anne-Marie was going to use her horse as an elaborate pastoral metaphor and as she recounted how Annabelle had started out as a nervous foal, had grown in confidence and could now jump fences, Dave scanned her story for symbolic meaning. He guessed she would probably draw the narrative threads together and talk about caring for the students or supporting the teachers. Anne-Marie clicked onto the next slide. The image was of an organisational flowchart for what looked like a media company. There was a head of marketing, a demographics analyst and a production team. Anne-Marie however, was describing how Annabelle was currently receiving antibiotics for an infection in her leg. Dave looked around the room to see if he was the only one troubled by how non-sequitur this was. Most of the teachers looked like they were peering at the flowchart and desperately trying to construct some meaning out of it. After a minute of describing the antibiotics, Anne-Marie moved onto the next slide, a picture of an Indian woman in a sari, laughing along with an eight- or nine-year-old child who was playing with a hosepipe.

"The thing that's so different about riding a horse is that it's really a partnership. There are two of you. You both have your personalities and you have to remember that a horse is really just like a person." Dave squinted. Maybe she was making a point about how teaching was done through relationships? The picture was arguably of two people sharing a moment and building a relationship together and so it was kind of re-enforcing what she was saying. "And sometimes if I go away for a few weeks and I don't see Annabelle, she'll be really annoyed with me. She'll not come over to see me. She'll be deliberately distant." Dave nodded: he could see a kind of emerging coherence, maybe something about attendance being important because of the relationship you're building with the students. The projected slide changed. The picture was replaced by two headings. The first read 'The Attributes of Successful People' and underneath were twenty words that were all tediously positive. The second heading read 'The Attributes of Failure' and had a list of characteristics that nobody would ever use to describe themselves, such as: 'small minded' and 'petty'.

"So anyway, that's a little bit about who I am," she said. "So let me tell you about my vision for the school."

Dave's mouth hung open as he realised that all of the elaborate, symbolic meaning he had been reading into her story was purely of his own creation. The whole story of Annabelle the horse had been devoid of all higher meaning. It had truly been just a synopsis of a horse called Annabelle. The pictures in the presentation had presumably been there to just give everybody something to look at whilst they sat and listened to how much a specific horse enjoyed cheese-and-onion flavoured crisps. Anne-Marie's vision for the school turned out to be as long as it was incoherent. Her central idea was probably something about working together, but it was difficult to tell because part-way through she seemed to get distracted by an anecdote about a man she had once worked with who'd changed jobs after becoming depressed. Again, her slides seemed to have either come from someone else's presentation, or she was using them more for their impressionistic qualities than for the information they contained. She seemed to be embarking upon another anecdote when she suddenly caught the audience off guard by uttering: "thank you," and then walking back to her chair. There were five seconds of silence as the room collectively processed that she had just finished, followed by the patter of sympathetic applause. "I think that went rather well," she said to Dave as she sat down.

◆ ◆ ◆

Anne-Marie Klein emerged from Katarina's office with a scowl and without acknowledging anyone in the reception area strode straight out of the front of school and slammed the main door behind her. The receptionist scrambled to his feet and called after her in a bid to recover the visitor pass around her neck. Dave did not consider himself an expert in reading the emotions of others, but he was reasonably confident that her reaction was a negative one. Katarina emerged in her office doorway and told Dave they were ready to speak with him. As Dave closed the door behind him, he could hear the receptionist scuttling after Anne-Marie and calling her name along with the word 'lanyard'.

The last time Dave had sat in Katarina's office was during his teaching and learning interview. The pot plant in the corner was marginally more dead than it had been before, but otherwise, the office had remained as plain and as boring as always. To Katarina's left was her deputy, Sandra and to her right, the Chairman of Governors and head of the MAP, Gary Henderson. Their large cushioned chairs were positioned on one side of the central desk and on the other sat a generic moulded-plastic chair recruited from the theatre. Dave looked at the chair and then at the three of them. He had deduced the failure of the other two candidates from their subtle responses: Anne-Marie Klein through storming out the main entrance and Mel Carson through collecting his jacket from reception and then announcing loudly to no one in particular, "You're all idiots." It seemed logical that Katarina would tell Dave the bad news and simply re-advertise the position to gain someone appropriately qualified. Sitting down and listening to five or ten minutes of feedback on why Dave had failed to get the position seemed like an unnecessary chore for both of them. Dave could have written his own feedback. He had absolutely no management experience, he had offered no coherent plan or vision for what he thought the role should entail and in all of the interview activities he had taken a decidedly passive role, stoically sitting back and letting the other two candidates boss each other around. There was no way he had the job.

Katarina smiled. "Dave, we have a few final questions for you."

Dave raised an eyebrow. Final questions? There shouldn't have been any questions, let alone a 'few final questions'. He should have been dismissed as a viable candidate long before even getting through to this stage.

"What do you think makes you the best candidate for this role?"

He froze. They were taking the time to ask him proper interview questions. This suggested he was in real danger of actually getting the position: there would have been no point asking such questions of a candidate you knew to be completely unsuited to the role. Somehow the three of them had concluded that his lack of vision, absent experience and total disengagement with the interview process, were all desirable qualities in a senior manager.

"I don't think I am: I don't have any management experience and I don't really have any new ideas to bring to it. I think there are plenty of people better qualified than me." Dave said, hoping to both remind them of his obvious shortcomings and come across as someone radically insecure.

The three of them wore the same confused expression, as though trying to work out a plot twist.

"So... why did you apply?" Katarina asked.

Dave toyed with the idea of telling the truth, explaining that this job application was the easiest way to tick a box on his performance management whilst avoiding the extra responsibility of a new role. It was a terrible reason to apply for a job and it should have immediately disqualified him, but Dave was concerned that his obvious lack of experience had not already disqualified him. If he came clean about his cynical approach there was a dangerous possibility that they might conclude he was impressively pragmatic or maybe, refreshingly honest. He had to come up with an explanation that made him seem stupid without compromising his competence.

"I read the Richmond-Nillesen Paradigm recently," Dave said, referencing the management-guide parody that Heather had lent him. "I liked it. I felt like I finally understood how management worked. It said that in order to succeed you have to have either speed or aggression. So I thought, well I don't really want to be aggressive, so I'll act fast instead. So I just applied for the first promotion that came up." He smiled, hoping to come across as impossibly naïve, a man with the knowledge of a scientist, but the common sense of a child, stumbling into a world they did not understand by eagerly confusing a parody for a genuine guide. Unfortunately, instead of looking confused or smugly amused at Dave's stupidity, Gary now looked impressed.

"I like your drive and ambition," he said. "Richmond-Nillesen's a great management guide. I learnt a lot from reading that one too."

"Really?" Dave said, unable to hide his surprise.

"Sure, it's a classic."

Dave wondered if maybe there was a serious guide out there with the same name. "The one about speed and aggression? With the woodland creature parables?"

"Yeah, those parables really helped me get a proper understanding of the whole paradigm," Gary said.

Dave realised two things: firstly, Gary was a bigger idiot than he had previously given him credit for, and secondly, if he was going to fail this job interview he was going to have to be far more drastic. However, there was still an upper bound to how drastic he could be. Whilst punching one or all of them in the face or stripping naked, standing on the chair and singing the national anthem would clearly succeed in failing the job interview, it would also fail to keep him his current job as a teacher.

"What would you say your vision for the school was, Dave?" Katarina asked.

Dave swiftly considered the various scenarios that might sensibly lead to his failing the interview and concluded that being annoyingly disagreeable was probably his safest option. If he could insistently disagree with them, he would come across as the sort of difficult person you would avoid having on your team.

"Well, I actually think the school is heading in the wrong direction," Dave said with a slow shake of his head. "I disagree with the entire principle behind the MAP and I don't think schools should be run like they're a business."

Katarina tilted her head to one side. "But Dave, schools are businesses. That's not a direction we've chosen, that's just the reality in which we live."

"Okay, so as a business, what do we produce?"

"We produce results."

"So who buys those results?"

"What? No. Nobody buys the results, Dave, that's not how it works." Katarina looked irritated by Dave's assertion, which Dave took as a positive sign.

"So what determines our income?"

"Well, we have a number of sources of income, Dave, but the school is primarily paid through the number of students we recruit."

"So we're not paid for the results, just for the number of students we can attract."

"Yes," Katarina said and looked at Gary with an expression that suggested they should possibly reconsider. Again, Dave took this as positive. "But since the number of students we can recruit is determined by our results," she continued. "In a sense our income is also dependent upon those results."

"But the school has a limited capacity, right? We're limited by the number of classrooms we have and by the number of staff we have to teach classes?"

"Yes of course, but we still need to get good results."

"But if we're a business, those results just need to be good enough for us to reach capacity each year. We don't need to invest additional resources in attaining good results."

Katarina paused as though Dave might be trying to trap her into saying something stupid. "No," she said slowly. "We still have to get the students the best results."

"But why? From a business perspective, the student's results don't have a monetary value. Once we've reached capacity, an additional improvement in results has no marginal utility for us: they're irrelevant."

Katarina shifted in her chair and took a deep breath. "But we're a school, Dave. An improvement in any student's grades has a huge marginal utility for that student."

"But again, as a business, those improved grades cost resources whilst providing no benefit."

Gary nodded approvingly, which Dave found disconcerting since he was deliberately adopting an extreme position to make the opposite point. Katarina closed her eyes as she paused. Sandra leaned in, her jewellery clattering on the desk as she tapped the surface.

"So you don't care what grades the students get? So long as we've filled enough places?" Sandra said with a shake of her head. "That's not what schools are about, Dave. Schools should be run for the students."

Dave nodded. "Yes, I completely agree with you, which is why I'm saying we *shouldn't* run state schools like they're businesses."

Sandra took a deep breath to attack Dave's point and then realised he had just agreed with her; she had just made his argument for him. Robbed of its momentum, her outrage settled into a smouldering resentment.

Gary shook his head disapprovingly. "No. You don't understand how business works," he proclaimed. "I can give you thousands of examples that prove you wrong. Just look at private schools, they make huge profits and they've been running for hundreds of years."

Dave was relieved: here was something on which he could clearly disagree. "Private schools?" he said with exaggerated confusion. "But private schools have a completely different revenue model. Their income isn't fixed for them by the state, they charge their own fees. They have to invest in getting the grades because they're competing with other private schools, and more importantly, free state-schools."

"Exactly," Gary said seemingly unaware that Dave's statement wasn't agreeing with him. "Competition drives up excellence. That's just a fact. That's how the whole of the economy works. Businesses with great ideas succeed and then other businesses come along and improve on those ideas. That's why it's vital that schools become more like businesses."

"Right, but that's not actually an argument for why schools should be made into businesses. All you've really said is that successful things are good."

"Well, they are."

"But what makes a business successful isn't necessarily what makes a school successful."

"Exactly," Gary said as though responding to a completely different conversation. "Once schools start competing with each other, standards will go up."

Dave paused, temporarily thrown by Gary's apparent deafness. "What do you mean competing with each other? Competing for what?"

"The invisible hand of the market raises all ships," Gary said with the conviction and tone of a wise man surrounded by his acolytes.

Whilst Dave enjoyed the mixed metaphor, he was unsure how successful he was being at disagreeing with Gary: it seemed as though Gary was unaware of any disagreement. "What makes you think that the free market is even compatible with schools?"

"Of course it is," Gary said. "The free market is the perfect solution to the education crisis. It allows the successful schools to thrive and grow and then other schools can see the best way to do things."

"Is it?" Dave said, refusing to give up on his campaign. "The free market is great at optimising the distribution of resources, but it does that through a process of wastage."

"What's wrong with that? A bad manager loses money and their business closes. The market punishes bad decisions and rewards good decisions."

"Right, but when you apply that model to education, the wastage optimising the system is essentially the lives of the students. If you bankrupt the school, you get to dust yourself off and try a different approach. Unfortunately, the students from that failed school now have, at best a disrupted education and at worst, no education."

"Sure, nobody wants kids to suffer," Gary said with the offhand rapidity of someone who had never really witnessed suffering, "but sometimes you have to consider the bigger picture and in this case, the bigger picture is that the system as a whole is stronger, Dave. That's how business works. Sometimes, you have to make the tough decisions. Sometimes I have to lay people off so the business as a whole will get stronger. But I'm a successful businessman, and as a successful businessman, that's what you have to do."

"So your argument is that we have to deprive some kids of an education, but as long as a few really smart kids benefit from that, society as a whole gets smarter?"

"No, just that we don't need everybody to be smart. It's the way things have always been. The smart people are successful in life and they end up running things. And let's be honest, the rest are probably better off not being smart. They're happy, they've got TV..."

Katarina cleared her throat to cut across Gary. "Either way, it doesn't really matter," she said. "The role of assistant head doesn't have the power to change something as fundamental as this in the running of the school."

Dave spoke rapidly, realising that his whole argument might have been too abstract to disqualify him from their favour. "It is a flawed premise to say that some have to suffer in order for others to flourish. And handing over education to a market model devoid of direction and protection is just plain irresponsible."

Gary nodded. "Well, I think the reason I understand the free market so well is because I'm a successful businessman." He said. "I know that competition drives excellence. So if there's competition, then everyone strives to be more excellent and so standards improve."

Katarina inhaled as though about to interject, but Dave rushed in, smiling with the smugness of a chess master delivering a winning move. "So explain to me how pulling together all the local schools into this new multi-area partnership, encourages competition?" he said. He felt like he had manoeuvred Gary into facing his own ideological contradiction, establishing that his business beliefs were at odds with the communistic vision of the multi-area partnership. Gary would have to reconcile the two and the embarrassment would force Dave's rejection.

"Well obviously collaboration also drives up standards," Gary said confidently.

"Wait, what?" Dave said. "How can collaboration also drive up standards? I thought competition drove up standards?"

"Yeah, they both do."

Dave looked puzzled. "Aren't they like, the opposites of each other?"

"Business is complicated, Dave," Gary said. "But I like your drive and I like that you're thinking about things. That's really important in business."

Katarina cut in, saying, "Yes, that's excellent, Dave. We've all been very impressed with your educational research and what you've shown today is that you're clearly passionate about education and making a difference. That's exactly that sort of passion and drive that we need in leading our school." She stood up from behind her desk and reached out her hand. Dave closed his eyes and let out a long sigh. "Welcome to the senior leadership team, Dave."

PUB CRICKET

Under a blue vaulted sky, the hot Sunday sun shone down on the village green and the drone of distant insects merged into the sigh of the perimeter trees. The cricket ball tore through the day like a rifle bullet, the only clue to its passage a puff of fine sandy earth. Dave was still waiting for the delivery when a sharp jolt travelled up his wrist to his elbow. The ball ricocheted randomly off the bat and bounced along the grass to his right where a man in white ran to collect it, stooping as he approached. There was a smattering of polite applause as those sitting on the wooden benches around the village ground misinterpreted Dave's lack of movement as a fine defensive stance. Usually, the pub team bowlers would puff and wheeze their way up to the crease and then release the ball like it was a dove. This year, however, the team from the Red Lion had clearly managed to find a professional fast-arm bowler. From the other end of the pitch, Mike the barman gave Dave a thumbs-up gesture presumably because Dave had survived the first ball. The Drovers' Inn had fielded a pub cricket team for the last five years and they were proud of their remarkably consistent performance of placing last each season. Their secret, which no one had ever asked after, was shunning the accepted wisdom of practising, preferring instead to turn up on the day and just seeing how things turned out.

The Red Lion bowler started his run somewhere near the boundary about twice as far away as the usual bowlers did. He had a long, lolloping stride that made him look like he was running in slow motion and then it was over. There was another puff of earth, a dull thwack and an exuberant cheer from the Red Lion supporters as the wicket detonated into five separate pieces behind him. Dave frowned as though the bat's solidity had somehow let him down. He walked back across the cricket green and held his bat aloft as the Drovers' Inn team cheered his score of zero. Heather was sitting with them wearing white shorts and a red blouse, her long hair tied back in a ponytail beneath a large hat. She smiled as he approached.

"I got you a beer," she said sliding a pint of pale ale across the table to him. Dave finished giving high fives to the team and rested his padded gloves on the table.

"Weren't you worried it might get too warm?" he asked. "I mean, I might have been out there for hours."

Heather laughed and then pulled a deliberately straight face. "No you're right, it was a calculated risk." She said as Dave took a long sip of the amber liquid. He watched as Heather tried to keep the straight face.

"I can tell you're dying to ask me about it," Dave said. He would usually meet up with Heather two or three times a month, but she had been away on a series of school trips and so for the last few weeks she had been unable to ask Dave in person about his appointment to assistant head.

"I thought the plan was to avoid getting promoted?" she said shaking her head. "Did you forget?"

Dave let out a heavy sigh. "Apparently getting a senior leadership position is much easier than I had expected," he said and described the interview process along with his strategy of maintaining a minimal level of competence so that he could remain employed. "Unfortunately the other two candidates didn't seem to even meet the minimal competence you'd need to be a teacher, let alone an assistant head. So in comparison, I guess I must have appeared awesome."

Heather bit her lip as she tried not to laugh. "So why didn't you just turn the position down?"

"I thought about it," he said straightening up and taking another sip of his ale. "And right now it sounds like that would have been the easiest thing in the world to say, but, when you're sitting in a tiny office with them all congratulating you on getting this stupid position, well... it just felt really awkward."

Heather nodded sympathetically. "Turning it down would probably have come across as a bit insulting."

"Exactly, and involve far more questions and complexity than I was looking for. No, going along with the whole thing just seemed way easier."

"So you accepted the promotion out of apathy."

Dave considered her analysis for a few seconds as he watched another wicket explode and the replacement batsman swing wildly at the empty air. "Well, apathy and not wanting to offend people, sure. I guess so."

"So how's it been?"

Dave rubbed his forehead. "I want to say busy, but it's not really busy. Not in the same way that teaching a full day is busy. This is..." He paused. His timetable of lessons had been largely replaced with meetings and briefings, but unlike his lessons, the conversations at these meetings carried so little information that they had left him feeling as though he was floating through space. "I suppose you could describe it as full," he conceded. "You're always somewhere having someone talk at you, but it's all got such a low meaning-density that you could drift off and not really miss anything." The Drovers' Inn team cheered another successful score of zero and sent their third batsman out to face the fast-arm bowler.

"And how are they dealing with your complete lack of experience?"

"Oddly that doesn't seem to have posed any kind of a problem so far."

Martin had been assigned the task of orientating Dave to his new position, because he, like Dave, was an assistant head. However, in practice, the majority of Martin's orientation had been given over to telling Dave how difficult each task was going to be, or how difficult Martin's own job was. "Assistant head is probably one of the hardest jobs in the whole school," Martin had said at the start of their first meeting. "I think from the outside it might look like an easy job, but it's not. It's hard. It's like when an Olympic weightlifter makes something look really light but it's not: it's actually really heavy." Dave had just nodded politely, hoping that there was a natural limit to how long Martin could talk about himself. "I think the problem is, I make this job look easy," Martin had continued. "I mean you're a classroom teacher, Dave, so you probably think teaching's quite hard, but I have to say, compared to this job, I think teaching is actually quite easy." Again, Dave had just nodded. Martin believed teaching to be easy in the same way a toddler believes painting to be easy, but he kept this to himself. Each morning Martin had embarked upon a new story of how his elite management skills had averted disaster and each morning, Dave had sat listening with about one percent of his mental capacity whilst the remainder carried on sending emails, organising calendars and completing paperwork.

At the start of the first week, Martin had assigned Dave a series of tasks, the largest and most important of which was for Dave to construct the school's timetable for the following year. Martin had taken great pleasure in recounting his own past difficulties as though the timetable were one of the twelve tasks of Hercules. "Honestly, every year I had to lock myself away for five full days," Martin had said, shaking his head. He had described how it would always seem like the task was almost complete but then it would all fall to pieces and he would have to start over. He had gleefully described how friends and family would assume he had gone missing because of how much time he had spent on the timetable. "And that was me working with the benefit of years of experience." Martin had added with a somewhat sadistic grin.

Heather frowned as Dave described the conversation with Martin. "Was he being serious?" she asked.

"What about the time it would take to complete?" Heather nodded. "Yeah, I think so," Dave said and explained how complicated a task the timetable was. Dave had to ensure that each student in each year group had the requisite number of subject lessons spread over a two-week period. The difficulty was that different subjects required different amounts of time and that in any one period there were not enough teachers for an entire year group to all be doing the same subject. To Dave, this seemed like exactly the sort of problem that computers were excellent at solving but Martin had explained that the timetabling software could not handle the unique complexities of the school. The only way, he had assured Dave, was to write out every single lesson on index cards and then connect them with pieces of coloured string. There were no shortcuts.

"Cards and string? Are you joking?" Heather said. "That sounds like the methodology of a complete maniac. Was he expecting you to do that too?"

"Well, he dug out the string to help me, so I guess so."

"So what did you do? You didn't use it did you?"

Dave explained how he had taken the timetabling software to the pub with him after school, but after an evening of failing to get the software working, he had been forced to conclude that Martin had been correct. However, Dave had been reluctant to employ the coloured-string solution, and so the following morning he had phoned the software company to see if they could fix their programme for him.

"You actually phoned the company?" Heather said. Dave nodded. "That's a bit of a long shot, don't you think?"

"Maybe. The thing was, in some ways their software was really close to working. It just needed to handle the data in a slightly different way."

Heather laughed and shook her head. "I love that your solution to avoiding this really tedious, complicated timetable task is to try and get the software company to improve their software. That would just never occur to me as a potential solution."

"I don't like card and string," Dave said.

"Yeah, evidently. So what did they say?"

"Who? The software company?" Heather nodded. "They were pretty cool about it actually," Dave said. "I got bounced around a bit to start with, but I eventually got through to the lead programmer."

"You spoke with the guy that wrote it?"

"The woman, yeah. It was a really productive conversation."

"So what, they fixed it?"

"Well not immediately, it took us a bit of time to work stuff out," Dave said and took another drink. Behind him, the Drovers' Inn team was enjoying a surge in their score as the bowler had been replaced by someone normal.

"Wait, you helped them fix it?"

Dave wiped the condensation off the bottom of his glass with his finger. "Yeah, after we'd talked about what wasn't working, she thought it would probably be easier if I just helped them straighten out those sections."

"So you helped them rewrite their programme?"

"Yeah."

"That sounds like you're kind of doing their job for them. Shouldn't they have paid you or something?"

Dave turned to watch as the Red Lion team caught out yet another member of the Drovers team. "Yeah, they did," he said, applauding the catch. "They were really good about it. They paid me a consultancy fee, but I wasn't really doing it for the money. I just didn't want to use bits of string. And once you've solved the programming problem, you don't ever have to use string again."

Heather laughed and repositioned her hat to sit further back on her head. "You started out trying to come up with a school timetable, but you ended up getting paid by a software company to help them fix their code?"

"I really enjoyed doing it. You know how it goes: you start on something and you just get pulled into it."

Heather nodded. "How do you even have the time to do that? I mean you're still teaching, right?"

"Barely," he said. "My timetable has gone from forty-six lessons a fortnight to something like eighteen. It's ridiculous."

"Oh wow. That's quite a reduction," Heather said and then added. "But aren't you the school's only physics teacher?"

"Yup. Although, Katarina thinks four of my groups can be covered by increasing the teaching load of the other science teachers."

Heather's brow creased in confusion. "How does that help things? Making their jobs harder isn't going to turn them into physicists."

"No, I agree, but they're a lot better than her solution for the other four groups."

"Which is?"

"A newly qualified PE teacher."

Heather raised an eyebrow. "A PE teacher?"

"Yup."

"Not a maths teacher or another science teacher?"

"Nope."

"How does she think that's going to work?"

"I asked Katarina that same question," he said.

"And?"

"She said that when they advertised the position they didn't get any applicants. So they re-advertised the role for a PE teacher with additional timetable responsibilities. They just went with an NQT as the cheapest option."

"Wow," Heather said and then shifted her tone to something gentler. "That sounds like a really difficult situation for her."

Dave continued in an irritated tone, "Promoting me makes absolutely no sense. You can't just replace a physicist with a PE teacher and pretend they're the same thing. They might start with the same letter, but I'm not sure that's enough."

"Well, I'm sure they'd rather have got an actual physicist, Dave."

"Well, according to Katarina, the core skills of teaching are the important thing, the subject knowledge can always be supplemented later. So once you can teach one subject, you can essentially teach all subjects."

"That sounds more like a convenient belief system for when all you can hire are non-specialist teachers," Heather said and recounted her own school's difficulties with trying to hire science and maths teachers. In her department she was the only science teacher with a science degree, the rest were geographers and historians who had attended conversion courses. "I'm not saying they can't disseminate the material," she said. "I'm sure they can and I'm sure some of them will turn out to be brilliant teachers. But they usually struggle to answer any question that falls beyond the next lesson."

Dave nodded. "Any non-specialist is like a low-resolution image," he added. "They can give you an overall picture, but if you want them to zoom in, there's no detail there."

"Right, but the problem is much larger than just your lessons, Dave. If you think of it from the perspective of the country, physics, chemistry and maths are vital if you want to remain competitive," Heather pushed her drink to one side so she could emphasise her point with her hands more clearly. "But because they're so useful and their uptake so low, their graduates end up being highly employable."

"Which is great if you're a graduate."

"Right, but much harder if you're a government trying to convince those graduates that teaching is a viable career and that rather than working in an interesting industry earning good pay, they should spend their intellectual capital on cultivating the next generation of physicists or chemists."

Dave nodded and swirled the last centimetre of his drink. "Pretty much everyone I graduated with either went into research, industry or finance," he said. "I don't think any of them bothered with education."

"And that's the supply spiral. If the government cuts educational funding, then science and maths teaching gets stuck with fewer returning graduates to train the next generation and then the shortfall has to be filled with non-specialists like your PE teacher."

"Which is why it makes no sense to promote a physics teacher," Dave said, bringing the conversation back to his current bugbear. Heather sighed and took a drink from her glass. "I'm serious," Dave said. "It's a terrible mismanagement of the school's resources."

"I dunno, Dave. I think Katarina might be smarter than you're giving her credit for."

"How so?"

"Well, she's just hired you as an assistant head: that seems pretty smart to me."

Dave laughed derisively. "How is that smart? She's just moved the school's only physicist into a job that any that idiot could do."

"You say any idiot could do the job, but you've already saved the school thousands of pounds."

"How'd you figure that?"

"You fixed the timetabling software. The school no longer needs an expensive member of SLT spending a week each year messing around with bits of string. *That* was a waste of resources, but now you can just give the timetabling to admin."

Dave nodded sullenly. "Maybe," he conceded. "I think that was more luck than anything."

Heather looked disapproving. "You're a physicist citing luck as a causal mechanism?" she said with a slow shake of the head. "I think Katarina may have been right to reduce your teaching load."

Dave chuckled. Heather had always been good at making him laugh whilst holding him to a higher standard, picking up on his implicit assumptions and throwing them back at him. Time spent with Heather always seemed brighter and more meaningful than the rest of his week. He sometimes wondered whether he should try flirting with her again. After all, she did spend a lot of time with him so he suspected that she enjoyed his company. But her initial rejection of him had made Dave cautious. He felt like their relationship was built on the implicit assumption that he wouldn't flirt with her. Whenever their gentle closeness felt like it was straying into a romantic tension, Dave was reminded that this romantic closeness might be entirely contingent upon there being no possibility of that romance. If Dave were to start expressing a physical interest, it would disrupt that, like turning up the light to catch the shadows. And so Dave chose to remain in the dark, acutely aware of how attractive Heather was, but unwilling to shine a light for fear of losing what they had together.

Mike the barman interrupted them. "We're on," he said with a grin. Dave turned to read the scoreboard. Twenty-five all out was not considered a strong score in cricket. "There's still everything to play for," Mike said, more from habitual optimism than through an expression of the reality.

A NEW
ACADEMIC YEAR

September slammed into the rear end of the holidays and jolted Dave out of his summer reverie. Senior management returned to work a day earlier than the rest of the staff and so Dave wandered down a deserted corridor towards the conference room. He wore dark-blue jeans and a casual shirt that, with the addition of a tie, could step up if the meeting's dress code turned out to be more formal than he had anticipated. It was a minor concern that had never bothered him as a classroom teacher, but his worry about becoming a part of management was that inadvertently flaunting some dress code might be seen as deliberately antagonistic. The job was going to be difficult enough without kicking the whole thing up into hard mode by alienating himself from the rest of the leadership team.

The smell of fresh coffee blared down the corridor, its deep, earthy bass notes and acidic treble buzzing the back of Dave's nose. He paused outside the open door. The familiar sense of being an imposter that had accompanied the majority of his teaching career had now matured into the full anticipation that he would be fired in the next few days. The four weeks of induction he had done at the end of the last term had only served to highlight how little experience he had to offer the leadership team and how ill-suited his teaching skills were likely to be in the role. The kudos that he assumed Katarina was receiving from having a renowned education researcher on her staff would be short-lived once it became evident that his academic paper was more of a hoax than a paradigm. Dave took the inevitability of this fall to be something of a comfort: he was going to lose the job irrespective of his performance and so he could probably relax and see what being an assistant head really entailed.

Katarina was sitting half way along the conference room's lozenge-shaped table and Martin was pouring a mug of coffee next to the machine with Sandra. The three of them, in shorts, skirts and sandals, looked like they had just decamped from the beach. Dave untucked his shirt and walked into the room. They smiled and welcomed him to the meeting with the usual small talk exchanged between colleagues: inoffensive questions about holidays and comments about the weather. Given the extent to which Dave had previously avoided senior management, the vagueness of the conversation allowed him to hide how little he knew about them. At some indistinct point, the conversations morphed into the meeting and Katarina started handing out sheets of A4 with the summer's exam results for each subject. She gave them a few minutes to look at the data and then said, "There are some great successes to be celebrated here. Our intervention in science looks like it worked wonders: they're up three points." Martin and Sandra smiled and there followed a brief description of how wonderfully effective this last-minute intervention had been.

"I dread to think what the results would have been like if we hadn't intervened," Sandra said, discounting three years of science teaching in favour of their ad-hoc injunction to mark some books.

Katarina continued: "But obviously the big concern we'll come to shortly is the decline in the English results." Martin frowned as though the English results were a personal affront. "Now, I think it's important that we also celebrate our other successes and I think it's fair to say that the school's biggest success has been Sandra's Jumpstart Initiative." Sandra gave a self-effacing nod. Jumpstart was Sandra's big project from the previous year, a programme in which she and other senior staff had dragged children with low predicted grades out of their lessons and given them one-on-one support in English. Dave had few doubts that such direct interventions would improve the grades of those selected students, but he had serious reservations about the efficacy of taking the most highly paid members of staff and investing their time on a single student. He suspected there was probably a more cost-effective way of achieving a similar outcome, but Katarina's proclamation that the initiative had been a shining success, suggested that she was not looking for improvements. "The five students we targeted all got at least one grade above their target grades, so I don't think anyone could argue that it wasn't an unqualified success." Dave stared intently at his laptop screen.

"If only the English teachers could manage these levels of improvement, we wouldn't have to deal with this results shortfall," Martin said.

This struck Dave as a monumentally stupid statement. Comparing the gain made by one intensely tutored student to those of an entire class, suggested that Martin had entirely forgotten what classroom teaching was. "So you think we should expand the Jumpstart programme?" Dave said.

"Absolutely," Martin said. "An initiative like this could give us exactly the sort of situational leverage we need over the results disparity."

"Although, whilst we're at it, why restrict your hourly sessions to just one student?" Dave said. "If you spent that hour with thirty students, you'd massively increase your leverage."

Martin paused as he tried to process Dave's suggestion. "But that would be like teaching a normal class?"

"Yes, it would," Dave said. "But, wasn't that your point? That the English teachers should be emulating your achievement with their classes of thirty students?"

Sandra interrupted. "No, I don't think you've understood, Dave. That wouldn't be an intervention. That would just be a normal class."

Dave let out an exaggerated "Oh," of realisation.

Sandra continued, "It wouldn't work in the same way: you need to have small numbers for interventions to be effective."

"So what was Martin's point about the English teachers then?"

"Well, I was just saying that if the English teachers could manage the same levels of improvement..."

"...with their classes of thirty?" Dave interjected.

"Yeah, with their classes," Martin said, the conviction in his voice eroding like a sandcastle in a rising tide.

"As opposed to your class of one?"

"Uh, yeah."

Katarina spoke across the continuation of Martin's confusion, "I think what Dave's saying is, you can't really compare a single Jumpstart student to an entire class."

Sandra agreed with Katarina. "Jumpstart isn't meant to replace teachers," she said earnestly. "It's designed to support them and those students who need that extra support. Of course, if we had the staff, we would teach all the students individually."

Martin shrugged off the confusion as an aberration and bolstered his certainty with buzzword sandbags. "What I'm saying is Jumpstart is a turnkey initiative. It gives us elevated leverage over our value extraction and provides measurable outcomes. I think as educational visionaries we should be pushing for these kinds of pedagogic revolutions."

"No of course," Katarina said. "And you're right. English is the big worry. I spoke with Gary yesterday and he was particularly keen for us to identify where this decline has come from. And he made it very clear that he wants a solution." Dave looked down at the results and then used his laptop to look back through the historical trends. The standard measure of a subject's performance was the percentage of students achieving a grade 4 or higher and whilst the national average for English language had risen gradually from just under sixty percent to just over, the school's percentage had increased far more substantially. The moving average had risen from fifty to seventy percent in the space of ten years and had then risen more slowly over the last five years. The drop in results that Katarina was now lamenting was a single percentage point decrease. In Dave's experience, such a small drop was as likely to be attributable to noisy data as it was to an actual decline in standards. However, as Dave emerged from his data analysis and stumbled back into their discussion, the leadership team seemed less interested in understanding the data than in apportioning blame.

"I'm not one to spread rumours," Sandra said, clearly indicating that she was about to perpetuate a rumour, "But I walked past one of her lessons at the end of last term and... well, it just seemed chaotic to me. It's not what I would expect from a strong teacher."

"Yeah, I've never really got a good vibe from her," Martin agreed. "She had another parental complaint just before we broke up."

"Yeah?"

"From Mrs Jackson again. She said there was a complete lack of control during her daughter's English lessons. I managed to implement an escalated resolution, but to be honest there wasn't much I could say. I basically agree with her. I think there comes a point when we have to start asking some of the difficult drill-down questions about the effectiveness of certain members of staff."

Sandra shook her head in disappointed agreement. "I had an almost identical conversation at the consultation evening where Mrs Jackson said she wasn't happy with the progress that Matilda was making. You're right though, we have to start looking at the bigger picture and thinking about what's best for the students."

Dave blinked in confusion, partly at the personal nature of their criticism but mostly because he could not think whom they were discussing: none of the English teachers he knew fitted their descriptions. "Who are we talking about?"

Sandra exhaled derisively through her nose as though the answer should have been self-evident. "Maria," she said.

Maria was an English teacher in her late fifties who had been teaching at the school far longer than Dave had. He would not have described her as a close colleague, but then it was unusual for any teacher to see staff from outside their own department during the day. The only occasions when Science really came into contact with the English department was on staff training days or at the Christmas party. One year, Dave had struck up a conversation with Maria. He had been sitting at the hotel bar in his suit and bowtie, with tinsel draped around his shoulders like a festive, feather boa. On some level, Dave had always struggled with the absurdity of school: the central premise of the job was a nebulous and unachievable ideal penetrated by constantly shifting targets fired off by a management beset with existential anxiety. He had never understood how Maria, like the rest of the English department, could routinely arrive to work at seven in the morning and go home when they closed the school at seven in the evening. "Do you not feel like management are taking advantage of you?" he had asked. "I mean, you get paid the same as everybody else, but you work twice as hard?" English, in Dave's mind, was a much harder subject to teach than physics, not because the concepts were any more difficult, but because English required vastly more marking. Physics exams often had clear, well-defined answers, whereas English essays usually employed vague, subjective criteria that took a lot longer to assess. Maria had disagreed, pointing out that whilst they both taught the same number of lessons a fortnight, her lessons were spread over fewer groups, whereas Dave taught almost twice as many students.

"That means you've got twice the marking," she had said with a grin.

"So why are you routinely doing twelve and thirteen hour days?" Dave had asked.

Maria had smiled and explained how much she loved English. How her Grandmother had given her a book of Auden's poetry when she was twelve and how from then on, throughout her life, poetry had always given her great solace. "I'm lucky enough to have a job where I get to talk about the subject I love pretty much every day." She had said. "Showing someone how expressive, how comforting and how transformative poetry can be? How beautiful a gift is that? If I have to spend a few extra hours marking essays to have that opportunity, I'd say it was worth it."

Maria was a teacher guided by an ideal and whilst Dave admired the honesty of her motivation, he believed it would make her vulnerable to an anxious management style that desperately sought to give the impression of constantly doing something. In teaching, it was always possible to do more for the students and Dave's response to the system's absurdity had been to see how slowly he could commit professional suicide. Maria's response, however, was seemingly to ignore the absurdity and to work as hard as she could. It was like a negotiated erasure of her own importance. All she wanted to do was teach and so she was a soft target with whom management felt free either to make increasingly absurd demands on her time or to assign her the burden of blame without fear of reprisal.

"So what's she done?"

Martin scowled as though Dave was intolerably slow. "As we've just been saying, there are quite a few problems. There are complaints about her teaching style, her lack of classroom management, not stretching the students: there's a whole catalogue of them."

"Are these complaints from a range of different parents or just from Mrs Jackson?"

Martin seemed irritated by the idea that there was a difference. "In a way, it doesn't really matter, Dave. There are a disproportionate number of parental complaints showing concern over the education of their children."

"But you know what kids are like. It's always possible for one or two of them to dislike a perfectly good teacher."

"But that's not the case here," Martin said with a dismissive wave of his hand. "When it comes to educational deliverables, Maria is not hitting her targets. We know that for a fact, you just have to look at this year's results. And we know for a fact that the department's results have declined. Now it doesn't take a genius to put two and two together and realise where the problem lies."

Sandra joined in with Martin's condemnation. "You only have to walk past her classroom to get a sense of what her lessons are like. The students are all talking and she's just walking around the class like she doesn't care."

Martin seemed energised by Sandra's support and began to stumble over his words. "It's the noise levels! The noise levels are evidence. They're the evidence that she doesn't have control over her classes."

Dave looked doubtful. "I'm sure we've all taught lessons that haven't gone as well as we'd have hoped. I'm not sure we can assume that any one moment is representative of the whole."

"Why not?" Sandra asked. "I think a snapshot like that can often give you all the information you need to build up a representative picture. Have you read Blink? It says that your first impressions are often really accurate and that spending extra time getting additional evidence is usually unnecessary."

"I'm not sure that was its conclusion, but let's take an example," Dave said, indicating Martin with an open-handed gesture. "Martin took my year nine lesson a few months back. Now we all know that Martin will have had that class working in absolute silence for forty minutes. But unfortunately, on the exact moment of my return, a student suddenly leapt up from their hard work, set fire to a friends' book, ran around the lab laughing and the whole class dissolved into incoherent shouting."

"That's completely different," Martin said vigorously shaking his head. "Harry Walters is a known troublemaker. He's done far worse than that in other teachers' lessons, you can't just take that one isolated incident. That could have happened to absolutely anyone."

"I totally agree," Dave said. "But someone walking past might have erroneously thought you were incompetent."

"I very much doubt it. I had that situation under control the whole time." Martin said, although this assertion was presumably for his own benefit.

Sandra cut across them. "We get that students can be disruptive: that can happen to anybody. But look, we're not here to point fingers and to play the blame game," she said. "The difference with Maria's lessons is that whenever you walk past her door, the lessons, they often feel...you know? There's just this sense that they're not quite in control?"

"Exactly," Martin said. "You keep walking past the same classroom day after day and you're seeing the same problems time and time again: I think you can start to say that you've got evidence. And when you couple that information with the parental complaints... Well, you know what they say? There's no smoke without fire."

Dave winced at the cliché. "Of course you can have smoke without fire," he said. "What do you think smouldering is?"

"That's still fire," Martin snapped.

Dave raised an eyebrow at both the force and the absurdity of the claim. "Even if it is, smoke without fire is a terrible philosophy. You're essentially saying that any circumstantial accusation, no matter how absurd, must have some truth behind it."

"No, I'm saying tons of evidence means we know what we're talking about. We've been doing this a long time, Dave. We know what incompetence looks like."

"Oh, I'm sure you do," Dave said.

Martin continued: "I think it's difficult for a classroom teacher to appreciate how comprehensive an overview management really has. We get so much information from so many different sources. We're like the generals sitting on top of the ridge looking down on the troops. We get to see the bigger picture in a way that the troops really can't grasp. We can see which units are fighting hard and which are just going through the motions. We know what's going on."

Dave found this martial analogy both unhelpful and slightly disturbing: who were the teachers supposed to be fighting? The students? If so, did this make the students the enemy? And did Martin really want to characterise management as sitting around on top of a hill whilst classroom teachers sacrificed their lives?

"I'm obviously coming at this as a relative outsider," Dave said. "So I don't know the history of the complaints, or about any of the formal observations that you've made."

"No, we appreciate that you're new," Martin said condescendingly. "You're trying to understand how these things work."

"And likewise I don't know about all the hard work you guys have done in supporting Maria, like all the support structures that you've put in place to assist her and her line manager. Or all the efforts that you've made to help lighten her workload so that she can be a more effective teacher for the students. You know all those avenues of support that managers can initiate."

There was an awkward silence. Katarina cleared her throat. "We should probably make it clear, Dave, that Maria hasn't done anything wrong. She's not the target here."

"Really?"

"We're just discussing the English results and trying to ascertain probable causes for the decline. Now I agree with you, if Maria was on capability, then yes, we'd have put support in place. But she's not on capability. She's not done anything wrong."

"So Maria's not on any kind of support programme?"

"No, Dave, Maria's not the focus of this discussion. We're talking about the drop in the English results."

"Martin just said you had tons of evidence. So at the very least, Maria should be on some sort of support programme, if not on capability."

"No, Maria hasn't done anything wrong," Katarina repeated, this time more firmly. "Martin was just saying we need to look at her performance, along with everyone else in the English department, from a purely professional standpoint."

"That's not what Martin said," Dave said flatly.

Katarina's tone hardened as she reasserted that Martin was not being personal and so Dave let it go. Martin then took Katarina's cue and began describing the decline in more general terms. He suggested that the English department had begun to foster a 'permissive culture' in which students were being left unchallenged and standards were being allowed to drop. Maria's poor individual performance, he suggested, was just symptomatic of this larger problem. Sandra then took on Martin's permissive-culture theory and built on it by suggesting that this culture had arisen through a lack of oversight. She claimed that management had entrusted the English department with too much autonomy and that this had backfired. Dave listened patiently as they painted a dark picture of a rogue department shot through with incompetence and corruption, and when it seemed like they had done, he asked, "And what does the data say?"

There was a pause. "We know what the data says, Dave. The results have declined. That's the whole point of this conversation," Martin said and gave a shake of the head to the other two as if to say: this guy is slow.

"The results show a fluctuation of one percent," Dave corrected. "I don't think we can go as far as to characterise that as a decline in performance."

"Oh, not this again," Sandra said with an exasperated exhalation. "You can't argue with the numbers, Dave. This year's English results are lower than last year's. You can't get around that fact. Or are you trying to tell me that seventy-seventy percent is somehow higher than seventy-eight?" She tilted her head to one side and raised an eyebrow, as though delivering a fatal blow to any future argument.

"Well, yes actually, in a way I am," Dave said.

Katarina looked appalled. "What? I don't understand you, Dave? Are you trying to be deliberately provocative or something?"

"No."

"In that case, you're just being ridiculous. We're trying to have a sensible discussion about the results and you're here arguing that seven is bigger than eight. What's wrong with you?"

"You have to look at the absolute data. This year, English got a higher number of students above a grade 4."

Martin clamped his hands to the side of his head in a physical display of his disbelief. "No, they didn't!" He fumed. "We're not stupid, Dave. We understand how maths works. You're not going to convince us that a somehow a smaller number is bigger than a bigger number. We're not idiots."

Dave ignored the theatrics and continued to talk calmly. "If you look at the absolute data, this year, English got ninety-three students above a grade 4 whilst last year, it was only ninety-one."

"What are you talking about?" Martin said hammering the air either side of his head with open hands. "This year's percentage is lower. It's a smaller number. The results are worse."

"The difference in the percentages comes from the difference in the number of students entered for the exams. This year's cohort was 121 students, whereas last year's was 117. Hence, the relative drop in the percentage. But don't just take my word for it. Here. Do the maths," Dave said, loading up the calculator app and pushing his phone across the table to the three of them. "Last year was ninety-*one* divided by a hundred and seventeen."

Martin's mouth hung open as he struggled to decide which was the more absurd: Dave giving them some idiotic maths exercise or Sandra entertaining him by typing in the numbers.

"Seventy-seven point seven percent," she said. "So seventy-eight percent."

"And now this year's results: Ninety-*three* students divided by a hundred and twenty-one."

Sandra typed the numbers into the phone and paused.

"Which is?"

"Seventy-six point eight," she murmured slowly, as though trying to figure out the trick behind a street magician's scam.

Dave leaned across to recover his phone. "So, I'm not sure that the data really supports this idea that the English results have declined," he said. "You could certainly argue that they've gone up slightly or stayed roughly the same."

"Well obviously the cohort size changes the percentage," Martin said dismissively and without missing a beat, reframed the new interpretation to fit the original problem. "The point is, the results have stagnated, and that's because there's this permissive culture of accepting failure within the department."

At this point Katarina could have disagreed with Martin, arguing that the English results were evidence of a department consolidating their incredible achievement of outcomes well above the national average, but she chose to agree with him. The permissive culture that Martin had used to explain the drop in results was now the explanation for some imagined future decline. The solution, which in many ways felt like the entire point of the exercise, was to have Sandra monitoring the English staff far more closely. And so, despite the absence of any evidence, the three of them had collectively created an imaginary explanation for a fictitious problem that only they could solve.

Katarina continued with some vague calls for increased accountability and then her tone shifted as she moved onto describing the school's finances. The government had proudly told parliament that it was maintaining its commitment to education and that they would guarantee the same level of education funding as the previous year. Whilst this might have sounded good to the average voter, it was terrible news for the schools. Costs had risen over the year and by freezing school incomes, many would now be running a deficit. Katarina described their financial predicament quietly, her voice thin with worry. They had spent the last three years cutting support staff and reducing the number of subjects available for the students, but this was not enough. There would have to be further cuts from somewhere or the school would spiral into debt and face restructuring. There was silence around the table. Their previous disagreement over the English results seemed oddly parochial when placed next to the existential threat posed by the funding shortfall. Dave had always been dimly aware of the financial pressures facing the school, but being a classroom teacher he had just focussed on doing his job. This was no longer an option. Now, the burden was partially his to bear.

"I don't think we have any choice," she said. "The government's forced this position onto us; we're going to have to cut even more of the teaching assistants." Katarina began detailing the numbers, talking in terms of the school deficit and, however regrettable it may seem, the loss of each teaching assistant would help save the school £12,000 a year.

Teaching assistants were vital to the support of the students: some were there to aid those with muscular dystrophy or to help those in wheelchairs to move around the school; others were there to help support the literacy and numeracy of students, some of whom could be several years behind their peers. And always the teaching assistants were there to provide an adult who would listen to the concerns of the students. Losing teaching assistants would have a huge impact on the both the students and the teachers, but Dave understood that Katarina would not have made this decision lightly. Things had to be bad if they were resorting to this.

Katarina sombrely reminded them that in these times of austerity, everyone had to tighten their belts. Sandra and Martin bowed their heads, as though considering the lives of those affected; this had been a common refrain through the last decade of staff meetings and Dave no longer thought of the phrase as conveying meaning. Katarina paused as she looked over her agenda items.

"On a more positive note," she said, "the governors were very impressed with the school's overall exam results this year and they wanted to thank all of you for your exemplary leadership." Martin and Sandra nodded in agreement: they too, felt they had been exemplary leaders. "And both the governors and the finance committee have agreed to the ten percent pay rise for senior management."

Dave looked horrified. Sandra and Martin looked happy.

WOODEN POLE

Summer was fading into autumn, but this particular October afternoon had obviously not got the memo and felt oddly warm and out of place for being so. Dave walked back from the canteen along the top of the school field, the sun warm on the back of his neck. The school's finance officer, Bob, had latched onto Dave in the canteen and had followed him out into the sunshine. Bob was an emotional raincloud. Not an interesting raincloud, like a thundercloud or a mass of swirling storm clouds but one of those flat, monotonous-grey clouds that replaces the whole sky and rains on everything. Bob delighted in complaining, taking a perverse joy in reframing his every experience as negative and dragging his audience down with him into a sodden bog of misery. Today, Bob's monologue was how the multi-area partnership was little more than a corrupt value-extraction tool for the board of directors and how nobody seemed to care but him.

"The school's run as a trust so there's absolutely no money to be made in running a school. Any profit is just fed straight back into infrastructure. But the partnership? That's where they start making the money. Did you know the MAP charge us eight hundred quid just to turn up to a meeting? Can you believe that? Eight hundred. Imagine if we started doing that. And it's not like we have a choice. These are meetings we have to have." Bob said, waving a sandwich in his right hand. Dave agreed that it sounded corrupt but Bob didn't seem to notice the affirmation. "And you know what really gets me? The service contractor. You know who owns that? Henderson. Henderson can't make a dime directly off the schools, but there's nothing to stop him getting all the schools to get all their admin services through his own private company. And none of us had a choice over that," Bob said, pausing yet again in his sandwich consumption. He had been eating the same sandwich for the past ten minutes. "They do all our admin and payroll stuff and we pay them, 200,000 a year, but we could hire all the same people for less than 120,000." He took a bite from his sandwich and continued. "Mf mwas me, ah'd scrap mh whole damn mfing."

Dave half listened to Bob's diatribe as they walked along the top of the field. The freshly mown grass stretched out like the baize of a snooker table, the lunchtime students either sunning themselves or chasing after various balls. By the school's perimeter fence, a group of four boys had managed to find an eight-foot-long wooden pole, presumably from someone's garden trellis, and one of them was now swinging it around his head like a two-handed sword. Over the years, Dave had developed a sphere of awareness, the radius of which would vary in accordance with the level of behaviour that the students displayed. Small, low-level disruptions like shoving or swearing would have to take place within two or three metres for Dave to register them. If they occurred outside this radius, Dave would walk by as though preoccupied and slightly deaf. However, as the levels of misbehaviour increased, so did the accompanying radius of awareness. Thus, a child wielding a wooden pole like a medieval weapon had a very large radius of awareness and despite being over two hundred metres away, Dave felt obliged to intervene.

"I probably need to go sort that out," he said tilting his head in the direction of the swinging pole. Bob looked terrified at the prospect of disciplining students and took another mouthful of sandwich. "M've got mwurk m'do manymay," he mumbled and sloped off to the main building. Dave walked steadily across the field, pleased that he had stumbled upon a new strategy for escaping Bob's negativity. As he grew closer, he could hear the mandatory sound of light-sabre noises accompanying each ungainly swing of the pole. The four boys quickly registered the inexorable approach of Dave as he strolled towards them, however, given the hugely obvious nature of the pole and the hugely open nature of the field, there was very little they could do. There was a brief flurry of activity as they ran through various iterations of hiding the pole and acting normally before concluding that this strategy was unlikely to work. By the time Dave arrived at the group a minute later, the main boy was standing holding the pole as though it was a giant staff, leaning against it in a relaxed fashion.

"Hello sir," he said cheerfully. "Lovely day, isn't it?"

"Yes, yes, it is, a lovely day." Dave agreed. "How are you chaps doing?"

There was a chorus of, "Good thanks, yeah."

"I couldn't help but notice..." Dave left his sentence hanging and he simply pointed at the wooden pole.

"Oh, this?" The boy said as though surprised that Dave would bother to mention it. "Oh, I just found it," he added, presumably wishing to clear up the outlandish possibility that it was his and he had deliberately brought it into school.

"Evidently. Whereabouts?"

All four boys pointed vaguely at the fence. "Just over there."

"Just over there?" Dave said, sounding sceptical. "You found an eight-foot-long wooden pole, just lying by the fence?" The boys all nodded and suggested that they too were surprised at this situation. Dave took a moment to peer over the fence but there was no obvious source. Besides, he was reluctant to demonstrate his caber-tossing skills by hurling an eight-foot pole into a stranger's garden. "Before you decapitate one of your friends, I think I might take that off you," Dave said.

"Oh yeah, of course, sir." The boy rested the pole into Dave's hand.

"You understand why I'm taking this away?" Dave asked. The group correctly surmised that it was because they would probably hurt themselves. Dave finished the exchange with a brief safety rundown and the suggestion that next time they found something dangerous, they tell a member of staff. The point wasn't to crush the curiosity and playfulness from them with punishment, but rather to safely remove a potential hazard.

Martin looked up from his laptop screen with an expression that was consistent with watching a colleague drag an eight-foot wooden pole into a small, shared office.

"Where did you get that from?" he asked.

Dave shifted a chair out of the way with his foot and balanced the pole in one corner of the room. He turned around. "Get what from?"

"The pole?"

"Oh, that," Dave said turning to look back round at the pole. "Yeah. Oh, I just found it."

"Yeah, but from where?"

"Oh, it was somewhere out there," Dave said, vaguely waving at everything outside of the office.

Martin's curiosity was remarkably short-lived because this seemed more than enough explanation for him. With a satisfied nod, he shuffled through a neat stack of paper on his desk and fished out a letter.

"I found another good one for you," he said, waving it in Dave's direction. "It's a council initiative to support students without internet."

Dave sat down and focussed on the waving sheet of paper. "What does that entail?"

"Ah, if I told you that, it wouldn't be training," Martin said, as though the master was teaching the student a profound lesson.

Dave raised an eyebrow. "So how does that make training any different to just doing the job?"

"Learning that is a part of the training too," Martin said. Dave mouthed the word 'oh' and did an exaggerated smile-nod combination as though Martin had availed him of an incredible insight. What Martin really meant was that he had no idea what this initiative entailed, nor did he have any idea how to deal with it beyond delegating it to Dave. After one month, it had become apparent that this was Martin's modus operandi. Whenever tasks were too tedious or complicated, Martin would just shift them to Dave under the guise of training and, as it turned out, there was an awful lot that Martin found difficult. "I had a meeting with Katarina earlier," he continued. Dave took the council initiative document and placed it next to his laptop. "We've decided it would be a good idea to get Malcolm Willis back in."

"Malcolm Willis? I don't know who that is."

"He's one of the government inspectors. We thought it would be a really good idea to have him come in and have a good look round at the English department. You know, in an advisory role."

"Why would you think that?"

"He's got a lot of experience of seeing how other schools do things and we think he could be a big help in structuring our support strategy."

"What support strategy? I thought we'd established that the English results were fine?"

"No, it's the optics of the situation, Dave. It's about getting a fresh pair of eyes on the situation. Malcolm's much better placed to think outside the box. And we need to demonstrate that we're being proactive in dealing with this decline in the results, for the sake of the students. Now, I know you're going to say it wasn't a decline..."

"Well, it wasn't. That's just maths."

"I know, but Katarina had a meeting with the sponsors and they didn't really go for the whole maths-argument, they were more concerned about the optics of a school that they are sponsoring, struggling to maintain their standards in a core subject. So they're putting a lot of pressure on us to do something about the results."

"By the sponsors, do you mean, Gary?"

"No, it's not Gary, it's the Henderson Educational Consortium. They're a distinct business entity."

"Distinct? As in their CEO is Gary."

"Look, the consortium operates as our sponsor. Now, the fact that Gary's also our chair of governors is separate. If anything, that just shows how invested he is in the school. He's a world-class businessman with a lot of connections and I think we're lucky to have him as an integral part of our team. However, you can't just ignore that the sponsors have committed a lot of money to the school, and so they have a lot of sway. Now, I realise that you're new to this, Dave, but getting a handle on this high-level politics is a big part of being on the leadership team. You've got to realise that there's a whole new set of outside pressures that, before now, you had no idea about. As a classroom teacher, we shield you from all these really big pressures. You're just focused on whether your board pens work and whether your kids are doing well. But now you're playing hardball with the big boys, Dave, it's a different game."

Dave stifled a laugh at Martin's assertion that being an assistant head in a rural secondary school was 'playing hardball' and that Gary presumably constituted, 'the big boys'.

"So, you're saying it's political."

"It's always political, Dave. When you're operating at this level, it's all about politics."

"Let me just get this straight in my head. We're going to pay Martin Willis to come and look at the English department because we wish to appear proactive in addressing an imaginary problem that's being generated by our sponsor refusing to acknowledge basic maths?"

"No, now you're just being flippant, Dave. The reality of the situation is far more complicated. Our sponsor has committed a lot of money to the school. And whether you like it or not, that comes with certain realities and one of those realities is that we need to keep that sponsor happy. Now if hiring a government inspector to come and look over the school is what it takes to reassure them, then that's what we do."

"You say they've committed money, but there's no requirement for them to follow through with actual payments. The government only requires that a sponsor *pledges* money and as you keep saying, that's just an exercise in optics."

"No, no, no. I don't think you understand how this works at all, Dave. The sponsors aren't about optics. The sponsor puts the money into a trust, and that then becomes the capital generator that powers the school. It's harnessing the power of the free market to drive education forward."

"But pledging money isn't the same as donating money. The government doesn't have any requirement or time limit for the sponsor to fulfil their pledge. Over the last six years, Gary's consortium has pledged a total of ten million to five schools. And you know how much of that has actually materialised into donations?"

"Look, I don't think the actual numbers are important, Dave, it's the principle that you should be focussing on. Moving education towards a free-market model is essential. The free market has consistently been shown to be the best method for solving everything."

"£200,000."

Martin paused as he considered the information. "Well, that's still a lot of money," he said.

"That's £40,000 for each school, Martin. Over those six years, that's less than £7,000 a year. That barely covers the school's photocopying bill, let alone producing a magical, money-spewing trust."

"I'm sure that's not true, Dave. There's a lot of negative press out there from the left-wing papers and the unions and a lot of it just doesn't stand up when you actually get a look at the real figures. They're so keen for the government's strategy to fail they'll jump on any rumour they can. You have to ask yourself, where are they getting these numbers from?"

"Oh, it wasn't from an article. I was in a meeting with some of the other schools in the MAP. They were all telling me about their financial problems. If their experience is anything to go by, we won't receive anything for at least six years and maybe never at all."

"Look, as I said, the numbers aren't what's important here, Dave. I'm telling you about the political reality, and the reality is if we want to hang on to that sponsorship, we have to jump through certain hoops. And one of those hoops is improving the English results. We are going to show that we are committed to improvement by using Malcolm in an advisory role. That will make us look innovative."

"But I've just told you that the sponsorship money is probably an illusion. So you're responding to an incentive that in all likelihood doesn't exist."

"So what? You're suggesting we just ignore our primary source of revenue?"

"No, I'm saying that pledged money should not be considered as a revenue source and that our actions should be in the service of the school and the students, not the sponsors."

"So you're suggesting we just ignore the two million pounds? I don't think the governors would agree with your assessment, Dave."

"Given that Gary's the chair of the governors, I think you might be right."

"Gary's a successful businessman, Dave. You don't get to be as successful as he is by pretending to have money."

"Do you really believe his businesses produce enough surplus capital to donate another two million on top of the ten million he's already pledged?"

Martin shifted uncomfortably in his chair. "Look, I don't know about the finances of his company. For all I know he could be making hundreds of millions. But either way, why would he lie about how much money he was going to donate? Nobody's forcing him to donate that money, it's voluntary. What would he gain from lying? Eh?"

"You mean, apart from his annual five-hundred-K salary and the fact that we have to buy all our services through his private, for-profit business?"

Martin seemed offended at the suggestion that Gary was only interested in the money and launched into a spirited defence of the free market as the perfect system for education. Dave gradually tuned out.

He had spent the previous evening in the pub with Heather, reminiscing about his days of being a classroom teacher. She had chastised him for looking back with rose-tinted spectacles. "Don't go doing that senior management thing," she had said, her eyebrow raised in disapproval. "Don't go forgetting how hard the onslaught of back-to-back, five-period days is." Dave had laughed and had assured her that whilst being an assistant head probably involved more hours in school, the hours were far less intense. His current problem was that he could no longer hide. When he had been a classroom teacher, he had always had the option of responding to management's poorly researched ideas by ignoring them and going and doing something useful, like getting on with his job and teaching the students. Now that he was in management, he no longer had that option, indeed, now it was arguably his job to engage with those baseless speculations and to criticise their ill-defined systems.

"But I don't really feel comfortable doing that," Dave had said.

Heather had laughed loudly and had then called across to the regulars stationed in their usual seats at the bar, "Guys, guys, I want to get your opinion on something. See if you agree: Dave says that he is uncomfortable criticising management." When the raucous laughter had died down and Heather had dried her eyes, Dave had clarified further.

"It's more that I don't have any alternative suggestions of my own," he had said. "So I just end up sitting there pointing out how flawed everyone else's views are. But I'm not really putting forward anything of my own. It doesn't really feel like I'm doing anything useful. Not like teaching, that always felt useful."

"But the things management are saying are still wrong, Dave. Just because you don't have an alternative, that doesn't invalidate your criticism. You're still performing a useful role by pointing out their flaws."

"But I'm not creating anything. Like, if the whole of management was filled with people like me, nothing would get done."

"As opposed to what's happening now?" Heather had said sardonically. "Look, Dave, you and I both know that the signal-to-noise ratio on educational research is ridiculously low. It's really hard to get meaningful data and so it's really hard to make an informed strategy. Education is such a wildly complex system with so many competing and interlocking factors that the only way someone could wind up being confident about some educational strategy, is if they had no clue what they were talking about. I call it Marshall's Law of Education: the greater the confidence in a strategy, the less they understand it."

"Marshall? Why Marshall?"

"He was the head at my first placement school. He was a complete idiot. He did that usual thing of assuming that just because something had worked for him when he was growing up, that it would obviously work for all students. Long story short, he mismanaged the school into closure. So I think the fact that you struggle to offer alternative solutions says more about your understanding of education's complexity than anything else."

Dave had taken Heather's analysis to be encouraging, but still thought he would be better off in the classroom. He tuned back into Martin's monologue. Martin had moved onto parroting Gary's logical fallacy that schools would be successful as businesses because successful businesses existed. Dave contemplated challenging his reasoning, but challenging Martin felt as productive as giving a condemned building a new coat of paint.

"So you want me to call Malcolm Willis?" Dave said flatly.

The phone rang several times before being picked up.

"Hello?"

"Hi, is that Malcolm Willis?"

"Speaking."

"Hi Malcolm, this is Dave Winger from Woodford School."

"Ah yes, hello."

"Yes, the management team here are keen to get your input on strategies to help improve the English results."

There was a pause and the sound of papers being shuffled. "Yes, yes, well I think from the book sample I took, it was clear that the marking was quite inconsistent in the English department. The feedback was often unclear and needed to keep in mind the assessment criteria: remember feedback needs to be not just positive, but also constructive. I also found several books that just had whole sections that hadn't been marked for months, and as I always say, a lack of marks leads to a lack of smarts. It always impacts on the results. The students just feel that they're not being cared for and it sends the wrong message."

167

"Uh-uh. Right, well that's very insightful and certainly the conclusion that I think many of the leadership team have also reached independently of the evidence."

"Yes, it's quite clear that the problems are really stemming from your department's marking policy being inconsistently applied. Some people are doing it well, but others are just cutting corners and I'll be honest, it's the students that suffer as a result.

"Yes, I'm sure that's exactly what the leadership team will want to hear, but I still think it would be a good idea if you actually came in to look at the department first though."

There was a pause. "To come in?"

"Yes, you haven't actually visited the department yet."

"Oh, right. I thought I already had a book sample from you."

"No. Not yet."

There was a rustling of papers as though Malcolm was searching for the correct piece of paper. "Oh right, well I think I must have confused your school with another. Woodford school?" He said it wistfully as though recalling a childhood memory. "Oh, I think I must be confusing you with Woodhead Academy."

"Oh right, where's that then?"

He paused for a moment. "I... um... was it Woodhead? Maybe it wasn't. Sometimes I can't see the wood for the trees." He laughed a little bit too loudly and then stopped as though waiting for Dave to say something. Dave remained silent. "Uh, yeah, it's quite easy to get one school confused with another."

"Yes, I'm sure that's extremely easy to do."

"But of course, I'd be happy to come in and look around the department and give you the benefit of my experience. My fee is eight hundred, plus expenses."

MEETING OF
THE MAP

Most afternoons would contain some sort of meeting either with a parent of a student or one of a seemingly endless cavalcade of committees that the school seemed so adept at generating. Dave had found that the meetings often seemed less focussed on finding solutions than they did on people asserting their existence and airing some grievance. Dave's strategy for chairing these meetings had thus far been to smile and nod, and then suggest that the concern be added to the agenda for the next meeting. It meant that each subsequent meeting grew in length, but it achieved the primary goal of making people feel like their voice was being heard. Since Dave hoped he was going to be demoted soon anyway, he would end up leaving all of the slowly accumulating minor concerns for someone else to deal with. His strategy for demotion, however, was still very much a work in progress. He had tried on several occasions to explain to Katarina that his scientific research paper was complete rubbish, but she had dismissed his analysis as being "modesty" and added, "How do you explain all the other research papers that agree with you?" When Dave had tried to explain that these were all terribly structured experiments whose poor design invalidated their own results, she had dismissed him with: "You're just being a scientist," presumably using scientist as some sort of pejorative. Dave had to come up with a clear way of debunking his own research paper, but he recognised that this might take some time and he really needed a demotion as soon as possible so he could get back to some proper teaching. There were plenty of management books giving advice on how to climb the management ladder, but very few describing how to carefully descend a rung or two. Aggressive self-promotion seemed to be a common recommendation for success and so Dave had decided to do the opposite: never telling anyone what he was doing or whether anything he had done had actually worked.

Today was the monthly multi-area partnership meeting and senior management had gathered along with three of the governors and a man from the business committee to discuss the school's progress and ultimately to report to the head of the MAP, Gary Henderson. Dave considered this to be an excellent opportunity to make an impact and a bad impression on his superiors. However, since Gary had failed to turn up to his own meeting, Katarina had begun without him, reviewing the first item on the agenda: the school's new status as a Beacon School. She explained how this was a rare honour and talked for several minutes about the responsibilities the school had taken on. The door opened behind her and ten minutes late, Gary strode into the conference room and sat down at the head of the table. He was wearing a pink-chequered tie with a pink-striped shirt and the combination did not work.

"I'll have a latte," he said loudly to no one in particular. There was a moment of confusion as those around the table looked at each other wondering to whom he was directing this instruction. After a few moments of collective silence, it became apparent that this was a power play, a test of loyalty. Martin leapt to his feet and lunged at the coffee machine in the corner before anyone else could get there. He asked little questions as he undertook the preparation: how strong did

Gary want his coffee? Did he want sugar? And the apotheosis of redundancy, did he want milk? He tentatively slid the completed latte in front of Gary, as though tabling a questionable tribute before a sadistic general. Gary did not acknowledge the drink but instead stabbed his finger at the meeting agenda and announced, "This Beacon School thing is good. Collaboration is what this partnership is all about." Katarina hesitantly agreed with this sentiment, unsure whether Gary was going to make any more sudden pronouncements but, like a volcano, Gary seemed to slip into dormancy. He nodded and rumbled approvingly, as Martin described the collaborative committee he had instigated with both Parkside and Saint Joseph's, the two local schools. Their science results had declined and so Martin had generously offered them help.

"They kept saying that they didn't have a physicist or a chemist, but I explained to them, it's not about the expertise or the knowledge of your staff: it's about your vision and your purpose. If you have a strong vision you can work more effectively with the resources that you have."

"You're so right," Gary said. "It's this whole just-buy-a-new-one mindset. Doesn't help." He then went on to describe how this was a problem in start-ups who would make the mistake of trying to solve their problems by hiring better staff whereas, in Gary's mind, the trick was to succeed with the staff you had.

"Just-buy-a-new-one mindset," Martin repeated with a sycophantic chuckle. "I love it. I'm going to use that in future." Martin proceeded to describe the innovations that had revolutionised Woodford's Science department and how the partner schools had been hungry for his insights. Dave had worked in the Science department for fourteen years and to his mind, the most notable and stabilising innovation had been the paucity of arbitrary management targets. Martin, however, began to describe his three key management interventions, the first being regular homework. "Absolutely vital," he said. "I require that all of the science teachers set regular homework but..." he paused and gave a knowing smile as if to suggest that this was the innovation that made him a genius, "I also require that I'm sent the marks from those homeworks. You see, I told their team, there's no point in just requiring that teachers set homework because without that feedback mechanism it's too easy for teachers to fall behind and stop setting them. If you want to maintain control of your departments, you have to do it through your avenues of feedback."

Dave frowned as he tried to remember the last homework that he had given. He always set revision homework in preparation for tests, but those were only two or three times a term and probably didn't count. He might occasionally set a research assignment for his top set because they tended to enjoy those sort of tasks, but setting a research homework for his bottom set was more likely to deteriorate into an exercise in him setting detentions than in them discovering information. Martin continued to sing the praises of the regular homeworks, claiming that they were crucial in raising standards. There were certainly teachers, like Mary, who would regularly set homework and were brilliant at using them effectively, but likewise, there were some highly effective teachers, like Growler, who rarely bothered. Homework was ultimately just another tool in the teaching shed, making it mandatory was like requiring that a carpenter always use a tenon saw. However, homework was not mandatory in Science, at least not to Dave's knowledge. So the question was why did Martin believe that homework was being regularly set and that he was receiving the marks? It was always possible that Martin was making it up, but confabulation didn't explain the irritating air of smugness that accompanied his claims.

Then Dave remembered the automated, online-homework tasks that periodically sent him emails on how his students were performing. John, the head of department, had subscribed to the system three years earlier and had asked Dave for help in setting it up. The students had all been given accounts so that that they could access fortnightly tasks with drop-down menus and receive immediate feedback on their right and wrong answers. When Dave had asked why they were implementing this system, John had just shaken his head and mumbled something about management being a pain in the ass. It was presumably to this system that Martin was referring, although he seemed to imagine it was functioning more as an obedience barometer.

"If I start seeing those homework tasks dropping away," Martin said. "Then I know it's time for me to step in and start shaking things up. This way I always have control."

For Dave, this explained why Martin had never seemed to bother the science staff about chasing up homework: he had spent three years assuming that real teachers were obediently sending him regular fortnightly updates.

"That's smart management," Gary interjected. "In the business, we call that a canary because it makes a noise when something goes wrong."

Martin paused at Gary's dubious explanation and then obsequiously said, "I did not know that." Dave assumed that his tone of sounding interested was feigned although, he could never quite tell with Martin.

The second way in which Martin believed he had improved the science results was through a system of data analysis and tracking the "flightpath" of the students. Dave had always enjoyed the flightpath analogy with its implication that overachievement was as tragic as underachievement through them both missing the runway. However, whilst Dave agreed with Martin's claim that the data was useful, the department-wide progress tests had been in place for as long Dave had been teaching. It was thus difficult to see how Martin could claim praise for a mechanism that predated his management by several years, although this did not stop Martin from doing so.

His third innovation was mandatory self-reflection, a system where teachers were required to reflect on the progress of their students and submit a written report to Martin on how they would support and encourage each of their students. Such a system would have been onerous and impractical, if not impossible for those teaching three hundred students, but fortunately for the Science department, no such self-reflection regime existed, which again begged the question of why Martin seemed to think that it did.

"At the end of each term, the department e-mails me their reflection reports along with the individualised progress-reports. This way I can see which students are on target and which are under-achieving," Martin said.

Again, it was possible that Martin was fabricating this imaginary department with its detailed reports and kowtowed staff, but the tone of smug self-satisfaction suggested otherwise. Dave tried to remember when he had last written the sort of student-analysis that Martin was describing. The only time he could recall was five years earlier, when John had asked the department to all submit generic reports for nine progress scenarios: over-, average- and underachievement reports for students that were high, medium and low ability. John had then approached Dave and asked him if it was possible to write a mail merge that could take a class of students and assign a comment based on their progress score and yet somehow make those comments seem personal and self-reflective of the teaching. Dave had told him that this was relatively easy and after optimising the bank of written comments and writing a few lines of code to collate the data, he had given John the completed tool. When Dave had asked why he needed this, John had just mumbled something about management being a pain in the ass.

"But most importantly, this management tool gives me access to that self-reflection process. I can see how my staff think about their students and how they reflect on their own teaching and that's like a window into their minds. For me, it's an indicator of how much effort they're putting into their classes. If I start to see that detail dropping away, then that's an early warning sign that they're not as committed."

For Dave the revelation was not that Martin seemed to believe that a mail merge of generic comments was providing him with deep, psychological insights, this didn't surprise him one bit. It seemed far more likely that Martin had never read enough of the reports to pick up on the repetition. No, the real revelation was that over the years, John had been quietly shielding the department from the more exuberant aspects of Martin's management. In effect, John was managing Martin, giving him enough feedback to make him feel like his interventions were doing something whilst saving the Science staff from wasting their time. The real tragedy was that Martin was now foisting these management tools upon another school's Science department. Unless they were lucky enough to have a departmental leader like John, their science teachers would be subjected to Martin's panoply of unrealistic burdens. It was always possible that the automated homework system was improving standards, just as much as the half-termly tests were, but since there was no convincing causal data for either, Martin was not offering evidence-based solutions so much as he was offering guesswork and self-promotion.

"That's a great job," Gary said. "That's top-shelf management right there. We need to make sure that all of our schools are buying into these tools. Great work."   Gary hooked his thumbs onto his red braces, leaned back in his chair and launched into a lengthy monologue about the constant struggle between staff wanting to do less and management driving them to do more. Dave was uncertain of his next step. He had originally planned to appear managerially inept by enthusiastically describing some highly ineffective strategy as though it was brilliant and then waiting to be shot down by his colleagues, but now he was unsure that anyone would notice. They might even celebrate him. Besides, it was going to be tough to appear incompetent when Martin was so clearly dominating the field.

"And that's why it's so important to share these ideas with our partner schools," Gary concluded. "Collaboration in business is vital. It always has been." He looked down at the agenda. "Right, what's next? Results." Gary's tone shifted and he slammed the palm of his hand onto the agenda as though it was about to blow away. The three governors jumped. "This needs sorting," he said loudly. "Schools are judged on their results. This is what matters. If your results drop, you lose your students. And if you lose your students, you lose your revenue. You understand? You're a business. And business is all about results." He glared at everyone around the table, sweeping his gaze from left to right. "This is a race and if you want to win, you've got to look at who's trying to beat you and you've got to work out how to crush them." He held his hand up and slowly scrunched his fingers into a balled fist, presumably in case anyone was unsure what crushing was. "Because trust me, they're trying to crush you. So you've got to crush them harder, you see? You've got to scope out the competition. You've got to know who your rivals are and work out your attack strategy." He placed both hands on the table and leaned forward. "So, ask yourselves: who are your rivals?"

"Well, locally, I suppose Parkside and Saint Josephs are," Katarina said.

"Right, you've got to crush them," Gary shouted. "Crush them in the exams. Crush them in the league tables. Crush, crush, crush!"

Those in the room nodded earnestly at Gary's insistence that they crush their partner schools in the pursuit of excellence, whilst presumably continuing to agree with his earlier invocation that they support those same partner schools in achieving excellence. It was the same criticism that Dave had pointed out during his interview and to which Gary had responded with non-sequiturs.

"But we're still supporting those schools, right?" Dave asked.

"Of course you're still supporting them," Gary said with a fist shake that vibrated the table. "You're a Beacon school. You can help them raise their game, but..." he paused and glowered at everyone in turn. "You're not in the business of cutting your own throat either. That's not good for business. You don't go telling them all your tricks and strategies, that's just dumb. No, you still give them support so that everyone can see that you're helping them, but you make sure you stay competitive. You're in the business of raising your own game. You see? By helping, you look powerful. And if people think you've got the money and resources to help others, that gives you a better negotiating position."

It was not clear what Gary imagined the school would do with this improved negotiating position or indeed what they would be negotiating over, but as with many of Gary's monologues, it seemed like the goal was less about the expression of actual ideas than the theatrical impact.

Katarina tried to explain that in absolute terms last year's English results had not actually dropped, which prompted Gary to bellow the word "No!" as though her attempts to try and alter his opinion were a crime.

"I don't care what the numbers say," he said forcefully. "I know that the results dropped: the numbers prove it."

Katarina paused at the self-contradictory statement but decided against mentioning it. "We've begun to put together..." she began.

"I'm not interested in words," Gary snapped. "I want solutions." Given the strong possibility that any subsequent solutions would be couched using words, Dave suspected that Gary might wind up disappointed. Katarina tried again to explain her solution as Gary sighed impatiently and shifted in his chair.

Martin nodded with the disinterested agreement of someone waiting to pounce on a pause and sure enough, the moment Katarina hesitated, he leapt in with, "I think the biggest problem in English is the permissive culture that has taken hold. We need to nip that in the bud."

"Now that's something we can work with," Gary said, nodding in approval at Martin's baseless speculation. "Suggestions?"

Sandra slapped her palm on the desk. "We need to come down on them like a ton of bricks," she said. Gary visibly brightened at the posturing. "They need to know we're not playing around anymore. They need to realise that their performance is going to directly affect their pay."

"Now that's how you motivate people," Gary said. Dave was fairly sure that this was a terrible way of motivating people, but Gary was not there to learn, he was there to preach. "I've turned around failing businesses before," he declared. "You've got to go in there hard. You've got to fire the bad apples, kick over the barrel and see who salutes." He continued with a few more confusingly mixed metaphors until Martin who, not wishing to be outdone by Sandra, offered his own input.

"I called up Malcolm Willis. I invited him to come back so he can give us the benefit of his experience. You know, because he was so helpful last time."

This also pleased Gary because Malcolm turned out to be a "personal friend" whom he often beat at golf. Inviting Malcolm was, in Gary's opinion, a stroke of genius and for a brief moment, Martin was able to bask in the sunshine of Gary's approval.

"When's he coming in?" Gary asked. Martin's smile faded and his gaze darted between Dave and Katarina: hiring Malcolm had been Katarina's idea and since Dave had been given the job of arranging the meeting, Martin knew very little.

"I...um...I can't remember the exact date at the moment," he said, fumbling over his words. "I delegate a lot of the day-to-day diary stuff to Dave. He's a physicist, he's good with time."

Dave raised an eyebrow at this nonsensical accolade and glanced down at the calendar on his phone. "The twenty-third," he said.

"I had to convince Dave that it was a good idea. He thought it was a bad idea, kept telling me it was a bad idea. He didn't want to get Malcolm in. He wasn't keen on the idea at all," Martin said, trying to deflect attention away from his earlier uncertainty.

Sandra frowned at Dave. "Why would you have a problem with us getting advice?" she said. "Malcolm is a leading expert."

There was something both tragic and meaningless about Sandra's political posturing, like a child pretending to be a doctor at an actual car crash. What the school really needed was effective, evidence-led management and what it was getting was political theatre. Dave sighed. This was not his world. He was more useful teaching physics in the classroom than spectating at an ego parade, but he was trapped. His original hope that an admission of academic fraud would result in his demotion had been nullified by Katarina's refusal to believe his confession. His plan B had simply been to undertake his assistant headship badly, but he had not anticipated such strong competition in the marketplace of ineptitude and so Dave was finding it difficult to stand out. However, if this meeting had shown him one thing it was how conspicuously absent dissenting voices were. Katarina had occasionally tried to use facts, which Gary had countered by shouting at her, but no one had actually challenged Gary or criticised his method – although 'method' was probably a strong word for what Gary was doing. Dave had wondered whether being belligerently honest might be a more successful strategy in achieving demotion. A squeaky wheel might get the oil, but a really squeaky wheel would hopefully just get replaced.

"If he's a real expert, then it's not a problem," Dave said. "I just don't want him to be one of those charlatans who go around charging schools eight hundred quid for the privilege of telling them that they need to overhaul their marking policy and then justifying it with some nonsensical rhyming aphorism like, a lack of marks leads to a lack of smarts." Dave was reasonably confident that in a week's time he would be cashing in on this prediction.

"Oh no, Malcolm knows what he's talking about," Gary said with total conviction. "He's a professional."

THE TRIUMPH OF TREVITT

Dave drained the remains of his coffee and peered at the brown residue that clung to the bottom of the mug. He was poised to unleash his new belligerently honest persona, but the meeting was turning out to contain very few opportunities for brutal, paradigm-shifting truths.

"How's my Ex-army guy doing? What was his name? Privit?" Gary said.

"Trevitt," Katarina corrected.

The previous year the school had made a big show over cracking down on discipline. Nothing had really changed to necessitate this except that management had suddenly decided that discipline was a problem that needed solving. Gary was confident that he knew how to solve discipline because he subscribed to the idea that what ill-disciplined children lacked was a rigid set of rules and being shouted at really loudly for any transgression. Thus, the school's discipline problems could be solved by getting in shouting experts and the best people in the world at shouting were naturally, the army. As part of a government-sponsored programme to encourage ex-army officers to enter teaching, Katarina had hired Lance Corporal Gordon Trevitt as a maths teacher. He wasn't a mathematician and nor did he particularly enjoy maths, but he knew how to direct students to the correct pages in the maths book and he was really good at shouting.

Trevitt had a truly stentorian voice. Its amplitude seemed completely disproportionate to his short, stocky frame. When he got angry, and he often got angry, his booming voice sliced through the breeze-block walls and double-skinned fire doors like a knife through summer butter. Students in unrelated lessons would flinch at his explosive rage. And when Trevitt ramped up into apoplectic, and he often ramped up into apoplectic, his voice could be heard in the adjacent buildings. Confident in the volume of his voice, Trevitt had been convinced that he was going to turn the school's discipline problem around.

"Just send them to me," he had confidently announced at a Monday morning staff briefing. "I'll whip them into shape." His entire philosophy of discipline was predicated on the notion that people disliked being shouted at, which was mostly true. However, teaching arguably had slightly more to it than just shouting at students. The problem was that when students in his lessons came across tasks they found hard, they would disengage, get bored and then try and entertain themselves by throwing bits of paper around or by stealing someone's ruler. When Trevitt bellowed at them to stop, they would temporarily desist, but the volume of his voice hadn't dispelled their underlying ignorance nor stopped the textbook from being boring. And so the situation would repeat. And each time the students misbehaved, Trevitt, believing that the problem had been a lack of amplitude, would shout a bit louder. But again the book remained boring and the students mathematically ignorant and so Trevitt would start having to make threats of detentions, telling them that far off in the future they would be punished by losing their free time. But this abstract idea still didn't stop the book from being boring nor address the underlying problem of them not understanding the maths. However, Trevitt's shouting was now far more interesting than the maths book could ever be and so Trevitt found that students seemed to be actively trying to wind him up. Trevitt would demand that the students respect him, backing up his assertion with the information that he was a teacher and thus they should respect him. When this teleological line of reasoning failed to win the students over, he began threatening them with ever-increasing lengths of detention: a week, two weeks, a month! Unsurprisingly, these demands for respect had the opposite effect. There was widespread speculation amongst the students as to how mad Trevitt could get, how loud his voice could go and how red his face could turn. Some began taking bets on the maximum ceiling for the length of his detentions. Would he ever get so mad that he would give out a year's worth of detentions? Maybe two years? And who was going to be the recipient of this legendary punishment?

Unfortunately, for Trevitt's strategy, many of the school's most troubled students came from homes where shouting was not so much a signifier of bad behaviour than simply the way in which people communicated with each other. For some of them an increase in volume wasn't a call to compliance, but a likely precursor to violence. And whilst Trevitt's threats of detentions might have worked for the majority of students, a detention always assumes that the students want to go home. As the Christmas holidays approached, Trevitt found himself getting embroiled in ever more arguments over increasingly trivial issues. Entire classes seemed to have made a sport out of pushing his buttons because what Trevitt had failed to appreciate was that by making his confrontations so public, he had given the students an arena within which to challenge his authority. His shouting began to be reciprocated by students who had realised that in terms of social kudos, they had more to gain from challenging him than by deferring. Inevitably, Trevitt's shouting matches escalated to the point where one afternoon he finally threatened a student with a year's worth of detentions. The student, feeling that they now had absolutely nothing to lose, decided to set the controls for the heart of the sun and began ploughing through the desks, upending them one by one and scattering books and pencil cases as they went. Trevitt had not left himself much headroom with his year of detentions and so he finally reached the logical limit of his threat elevation and above the screaming mayhem of an entire class shrieked, "You're in detention for life!" Everything stopped. For three or four seconds there was complete silence as an entire class tried to comprehend the absurdity of this sanction. It was so extreme, so completely unlike anything that had ever happened in a lesson before, that no one knew how to respond.

The student who had been halfway through toppling another desk let it rock back onto its four feet, stood up straight and scornfully said, "That doesn't even make any sense."

Thus, Gordon Trevitt became a joke. Students would gleefully mimic his common invocation to, "Stand down!" and loudly tell each other, "No, *you're* in detention for life!" Trevitt did not return after the Christmas holiday, deciding instead to pursue what he described in his resignation letter as, 'a lucrative consultancy offer'.

"Uh, no he left last year," Katarina said.

Gary shook his head in disappointment. "Shame," he said. "We need more good men like him. Men who understand discipline."

CUTTING COSTS AND CORNERS

The meeting ambled on through the agenda items with all the banality and consequence of a tourist shuffling through a museum. With each uninspiring item, Dave slumped a little lower in his chair. The man from the business committee described the cost-cutting services that were now available to the school through the MAP and Sandra enthused over how being more like a business had given them the financial autonomy to spend money on new educational opportunities.

Gary reminded everybody that the school was a charity and so this precluded them from making a profit, however, the school was currently running a deficit and this was a bad thing. It was essential that they cut costs and get back to being profitable because then they could use the profits to invest in infrastructure. Gary then embarked on a rambling monologue about how harnessing the engine of the free market could help drive the MAP along the educational road to an academic utopia. Martin jumped onto the tail end of Gary's manifesto and pledged his commitment to this financial model, suggesting that he and the rest of senior management would work tirelessly towards cutting costs and making the school more profitable because any profit they made would be fed straight back into improving the school and the education of the students.

"We can start straight away with some really simple measures like cutting down on photocopying," he said. Around the table came the nods and murmurs of affirmation. Dave had now slumped to the point where he was approaching horizontal, his chin resting on his chest, but Martin's comment sounded like an opportunity for some minor dissent, so he shuffled his way back into an upright position.

"Is photocopying a particularly large expense?" he asked.

"Of course. It runs into the tens, maybe hundreds of thousands," Martin said.

"Hundreds of thousands?" Dave said, not bothering to hide his scepticism. "Okay, so how do you suggest we practically go about reducing those huge photocopying-costs?"

"There's a whole host of things we can do, Dave. The point is that we need to commit to a vision of cost cutting. These are difficult times and I think teachers have been, well, quite frankly, insulated from the financial realities of the real world. They need to start being realistic and finding alternatives. And there are alternatives out there. They could start by asking themselves simple questions like: can I cut down on the number of worksheets and past papers I print out? Can I use technology more effectively?"

"And those savings, you're suggesting that we would spend those on, what? Educational resources?"

"Exactly. That's the whole point of becoming more profitable, Dave. We can really start ploughing that money back into the resources that have a direct educational impact."

"So things like past papers and worksheets and things like that?"

"Yes, exactly," Martin said, deaf to the circularity of his own argument.

Dave shifted in his seat. Maybe he was being too subtle? "So, are we also going to stop printing out thousands of those glossy school-prospectuses?"

Martin shook his head. "No, no, that's a different account entirely, Dave. No, that's advertising. Those prospectuses are crucial in maintaining our intake; it would be foolish for us to cut those."

"Has anyone ever been swayed by them? I mean, do we know how many parents changed their mind on the strength of the prospectus?"

Martin made a dismissive snort. "How could we possibly know that, Dave?" he said. "Think about it: how can we know what parents were thinking?"

"Well, we could ask them. That way we'd at least know if we were wasting our money."

Gary slapped the desk with his hand as if he were slapping an old friend on the back. "I like it!" he bellowed and pointed at Martin. "Write a survey. Send it out to parents. Find out." He turned and pointed at Dave. "I like your blue-sky thinking." He said and added, "It's outside the box."

Dave was reasonably confident that the notion of getting data to see whether something had worked was not a revolutionary idea. However, it was clearly enough to impress Gary. Predictably, Gary's praise had ignited excited posturing from both Sandra and Martin who talked over each other like children competing for paternal validation. Martin was trying to pretend that he had already written a survey – he just hadn't sent it out yet – and Sandra was trying to remind everyone that performance-related pay was going to both raise standards and save money.

"Great point," Gary interrupted, shaking his fist enthusiastically and then rearranging his fingers to point at Sandra in a gesture that came across as oddly threatening. "I've always said performance-related pay is the key. Look at any successful business. Number one priority: get the right people. Number two: keep the right people. Now clearly the best way to do that is to recruit good people and reward good performance. That's just obvious." Sandra nodded with the smug, self-satisfaction of a lifetime-achievement award recipient. Gary continued, "We set the high standards and teachers will up their game. It's simple. It's effective. The higher we set those standards the fewer the teachers who can meet them and the less we have to pay out. Genius. Improves output, saves money."

Katarina cut in, quickly adding, "Which is obviously not why we're doing it. We're doing it to drive up standards. We're encouraging teachers by rewarding them when they reach those high standards."

"Sure, sure," Gary said with a hand wave that seemed more dismissive than acknowledging. "It's about kids and higher standards and all that. But this is a business. And setting higher standards will make us more profitable."

Dave was unsure for whom Katarina had made her anxious clarification, whether it was an attempt to convince herself of its virtues, or others. Gary clearly viewed performance-related pay as a mechanism through which to reduce teachers' wages and for Sandra, it was more of a personal vendetta against what she called "coasting teachers", an imaginary group upon whom she was now heaping the manifold failures of education.

"What are coasting teachers?" Dave asked after she had finished.

Sandra frowned. "I'm sure you know what coasting-teachers are, Dave. They get to the top rate of pay and then they just sit back and get complacent."

"What? You mean as in, they go into senior management?"

"No, that's not what I mean," she said coldly. "We all know classroom teachers who've been in the job for years and just phone it in."

"And you have evidence of this complacency?"

"Yes," Sandra said curtly. "Their results stop improving."

"I'm not sure that that constitutes evidence. The students' results might plateau for any number of reasons. It might be teacher complacency, but equally, they might have just reached equilibrium. Expecting grades to continually improve is like expecting kids to continually grow taller."

Sandra narrowed her eyes. "I know when teachers are coasting, Dave. I can just tell. You get a feel for it."

"You just feel it?"

"Yeah."

"I'm not sure that pay decisions should be based on your feelings."

Sandra made a 'pffftt' sound like the releasing air brakes of a lorry. "So tell us your solution, Dave?"

"We could shift the school day to start two hours later. Sleep research shows that teenagers struggle to wake up early, not because they're lazy or going to bed too late, but because they're in a developmental phase where their brain releases serotonin two hours later than in adults or young children. The studies I read showed some impressive improvements for those teenagers who get to start their school day later."

Katarina shook her head. "No, that would be far too disruptive. Rescheduling all of the school buses alone would make it too expensive."

Sandra raised an eyebrow. "I'm sure if we wanted, Dave, we could all come up with expensive ways to improve students' lives, but unfortunately none of them would help return the school to profitability," she said pointedly.

"I'm not even convinced that profitability should be our goal," Dave said. "Obviously I don't think we should be running a deficit, but I think there's a danger that we end up focussing on becoming profitable at the expense of what we're actually here for, which is the education of the students."

"That's fine, Dave, if you can't think of a practical way to help the school cut costs, you don't have to."

Dave rolled his eyes at the pettiness and decided that it was time to double down on his demotion attempt. "I suppose we could stop paying senior members of the MAP £800 for just showing up to meetings."

The room fell silent and the collective gaze fell upon Gary for his response. Dave had hoped that this barbed suggestion would elicit spluttering outrage and his angry dismissal from the room, but disappointingly, Gary responded as though this was a frequently asked question.

"Well, they're a courtesy fee, Dave. The MAP employs some very important businessmen and women and their time is extremely valuable. These payments acknowledge that and give us access to their expertise."

"Well given our contractual requirement to have at least one senior member of the MAP at all of our budgetary and managerial meetings, it's less of a courtesy and more of a mandated fee."

"I can see why you'd think that, but no," Gary said with a shake of his head. "You can't lose the courtesy fee. Successful businessmen and women need to be compensated for their superior wisdom and experience otherwise they won't come to the meetings. In a way, having them at the meetings is like hiring an expert consultant. They're adding value to the school. They're an investment in your future. I'm sure there are other larger costs that can be cut ahead of them."

Dave could not recall a single instance where a member of the MAP had provided useful advice, let alone advice that would have compensated for their attendance fee, but whilst Gary being wrong was infuriating, it was more infuriating that he seemed oblivious to the possibility of his own fallibility. Dave thought back to earlier in the week and Bob's insistence that the MAP was little more than a value-extraction tool for a select few, notably Gary. It now seemed incisive and Dave wished that he had paid more attention to the arguments that Bob had made. He dredged his memory and threw out the few facts he could recall.

"We could focus on a much larger saving: the twelve administrative and estates staff we employ through Henderson Support Services. Their wages vary between £12,000 and £16,000..."

Gary Henderson surged into the momentary pause as Dave took a breath. "Yes, that's a real benefit of Woodside being in the MAP. You get to benefit from the economy of scale that these world-class support services can offer."

"Sure. Well looking at the maths, if we employed them ourselves, it would cost just under a £120,000 a year. But we currently pay Henderson Support £200,000. So we can make an annual saving of £80,000 just by cancelling that contract."

Gary furrowed his brow. "No. No, you can't do that. It's far more complex than that. There's lots of legal and financial stuff they do. Lots of extra costs that come along with hiring people and you're just not factoring those in."

"Like what?"

"You'd have to ask the people. I'm a big picture kind of guy. But I can assure you, Henderson provides a world-class service. Ask anyone. If someone's sick you don't have to recruit a temporary replacement. Henderson gives you a replacement at no extra cost. That's a guarantee," he said with an accompanying finger point.

"Well, it's doesn't really come at no extra cost," Dave said. "It comes for an additional £80,000 a year."

Martin jumped to the defence of Gary's business. "But Dave, we haven't had any complaints about the support services. They do an excellent job."

"I'm not saying we've had complaints. I'm saying that they're over-charging us. If the objective is to cut costs, well, we can get those services cheaper elsewhere."

"But you haven't understood, Dave. Henderson services are a part of this MAP. We have a contract with them. The reality is, we're tied into Henderson services, we couldn't change provider even if we wanted to."

Dave thought back to Bob's rambling monologue. "No, I believe that the contract just has a penalty fee for early termination," he said. "If we cancel now we'd pay £50,000 for the two or three months we've used them, pay the £100,000 penalty and rehire the staff for the remainder of the year at £90,000. In two years, we would still have saved

£40,000. I mean, obviously, that's not as much as we could save on photocopying, but still."

Gary gave a knowing smile and cut across Martin before he could respond. "I see what you're doing, Dave." he said. Dave was not entirely sure what Gary thought he was doing but rather than dispelling Gary's assumption, Dave just waited to see where this was going. Gary shook his head in silence for a few seconds as though internally debating something and then with a sigh and slap of his hand on the desk he said, "Fine, I'll have a word with them about renegotiating the service fee." He turned to one of the governors and added, "Make a note of that." The woman looked at Gary with an expression of confusion, presumably because she wasn't his secretary nor was she expecting to take any kind of notes. Gary continued, "I think you've got the right idea to look at recruitment, but I think you're focussing on the wrong area. The school's biggest expenditure is teaching staff, not support. It's ridiculous. The school needs to cut down on their old, expensive staff and replace them with highly motivated, new teachers."

"Or we could cut the wages of senior management?" Dave suggested. The room looked at Dave as though he had dropped his pants and started dancing: their initial expressions of shock transitioning into a mixture of disgust and anger. Dave continued despite the glares, "I don't feel I'm working any harder than when I was a classroom teacher, but for some reason you're paying me more than twice my old salary."

"Speak for yourself, Dave." Martin said Dave's name with more than a little animosity. "I certainly earn *my* wage."

Sandra folded her arms. "Well, maybe you don't do any work, Dave. But *I* certainly do."

Dave looked sceptical. "Do you really think you do twice as much work as a full-time teacher?"

Katarina cut across him. "It's not about how many hours you work, Dave: it's about the value of that work. Our salaries reflect the value that we bring to this school."

"In that case, I would have thought we'd be paying teaching assistants far more than we are."

Katarina cheeks flushed red and she narrowed her eyes.

"If you don't like the way we do things, you don't have to work here, Dave."

"I'm only suggesting ideas that might save the school money."

"No, you're being deliberately antagonistic."

"I'm not opposed to people getting pay rises, but maybe we should think about capping our pay to a multiplier of the lowest wage in the school. That way, if we wanted a pay rise we'd have to start by increasing the wages of the lowest paid people first."

As usual, Gary seemed to have been party to a completely different conversation. "I love it!" he said. "You're a radical thinker, Dave. It's refreshing; we need more radical thinkers like you." Katarina, Sandra and Martin looked at Gary in confusion; he seemed to be agreeing to a cap on his own pay. "Sometimes, these out of the box suggestions can have something in them that we can take and use," he said. "The school needs to cut down on their old, expensive staff and one way the school can do that is through Dave's suggestion of capping their pay."

"That wasn't my suggestion," Dave said.

"And he's so modest," Gary said approvingly. "This guy just keeps hitting it out the park."

Dave sighed.

"Absolutely," Sandra said, seizing the opportunity to recapture the narrative. "I completely agree: expensive teachers are draining the resources from this school."

"So you want us to replace our experienced staff with inexperienced staff?" Dave said.

"No, no, no," Gary said. "We want to replace the expensive teachers with cost-effective teachers. Some of these older teachers are on ridiculous five-figure salaries."

"Five-figures? You mean, like £35,000?"

"Exactly. Silly money. The school can't afford large numbers of staff on those kinds of inflated figures."

"I thought investing in good people was the first rule of business?" Dave said, using Gary's own argument against him.

Gary laughed loudly and pointed at Dave. "This guy's great; he learns fast. You're absolutely right, Dave. Investing in good people is vital. Spot on. But your results are improving, so I think the school can afford to be a little more cost effective in its approach. Currently, you're top heavy with expensive teachers but I think by slimming them down, you'll become more agile. It's all in this great book I've been reading called the Carson Method."

The name sounded familiar and it took Dave a few moments to recall the incoherent mess of methodology that failed SLT candidate, Mel Carson had plied at his presentation. Dave had not read the Carson Method, but given Mel's bizarre attempt to base his financial strategy on a motivational business slogan, he suspected that the rest of the book was probably as ill-informed and confusing. The problem wasn't that Gary was reading Mel's book, but rather that without the skills to critique it, he was unable to distinguish between damaging nonsense and harmless nonsense. Firstly, agility had no meaning in this context. Secondly, ditching your experienced teachers because your results were improving was like throwing away your umbrella in a storm because you weren't getting wet. Dave didn't know where to begin.

RIVERSIDE WALK

"So what did you say?" Heather asked tucking back her hair back beneath her woollen bobble hat as the wind whipped around and tried to pluck it free. Dark-grey, fractured clouds hurried beneath a silvery duvet of altostratus.

"I can't remember exactly what I said, but I sort of made the point that you couldn't really call them expensive teachers when for the equivalent of his pay, we could hire fourteen of them."

The leaves roared as the wind lifted them from their branches. Heather stopped walking and faced Dave. "You actually said that?" Dave nodded. "Oh my god. What did he say?"

"Well I was kinda hoping it would be a real mic-drop sort of moment."

"And it wasn't?"

"No. He just sort of shrugged and said, 'yeah I've heard that argument before. It's like when people complain about footballers.'"

Heather pulled a confused expression and resumed walking. "How is he like a footballer?"

"He had some argument about individual footballers being popular and so their success gives clubs access to a larger market. I think his point was that their pay makes sense when you consider it from a global market point of view. The scale of the market is disproportionately larger."

"Right but that's for football. How does that in any way apply to him? There isn't some global education market that he's giving you access to."

"No and I pointed that out, but you know: it's Gary. He just kept repeating that it *was* like football." The wind rose again hoisting a cascade of leaves skyward and sending them swirling and whirling like a murmuration of starlings. Heather jumped over a large puddle on the muddy riverside path.

"That sounds like a productive meeting." She said, waiting for Dave to join her.

Dave jumped the puddle. "It gets better."

"Oh?"

"Yeah, so Gary basically began justifying his pay by saying he works really hard. So I asked him whether he thought he worked fourteen times harder than a classroom teacher. He said, yes."

"What were you expecting him to say?"

"I don't know."

"Do you think he believes that?"

"Quite possibly. He went on and did the whole 'those who can, do; those who can't, teach', spiel. In retrospect, this was quite ironic."

Heather narrowed her eyes. "Well, if he thinks it's that easy, maybe he should try it sometime."

"Yeah, that's normally what I'd have said, too. But I was just trying to do some damage control and mitigate the situation; the whole meeting felt like it was getting really personal. But it was weird. Gary was really insistent that he had to show me how easy he would find teaching."

Heather furrowed her brow. "What? As in, he wanted to show you he could teach a lesson?"

"Yeah. He was really insistent. He was all," Dave began mimicking Gary's tone and syntax. "You don't believe me, Dave. I could teach. If you're confident, you're smart and you know how to talk to people, you don't need to be trained in teaching. You can just walk in there and do it. I could teach a business studies lesson right now if I wanted. I'd walk in there: Boom. I'd teach them."

Heather shook her head in disbelief. "And this guy runs what, twelve schools? It sounds like he doesn't have the first clue what teaching actually entails." The two of them paused to clamber over the trunk of a fallen tree, its top half partially submerged in the river, its branches decorated with weeds and detritus like a depressing Christmas tree. "So what did you say to him?" Heather asked.

"I told him, there's no need for you to do that. You don't need to prove anything. It's fine. Don't worry about it. But he was having none of it. He just started shouting at Martin to go and sort out a lesson for him to teach."

"Oh my god, that's ridiculous. A single lesson? That's nothing. Even if he did that, that wouldn't prove anything. It wouldn't give him any sense of what being a teacher was actually like."

Dave agreed with her. "It's always amazed me how little of teaching is actually teaching the students."

Heather waved a hand in frustration. "The problem is he'll stand in front of those kids, talk at them for an hour and then imagine that he's a teacher. It's like putting the key in the ignition and imagining that, now you know how to drive."

Dave nodded. "I totally agree. So what I said to him was, if he's going to do it, he needed to do it properly: you can't just teach a single lesson. You know what it's like, you put an unknown adult in front of a group of kids and unless they're a complete disaster, kids'll be pretty well-behaved."

"Yeah, for all they know, you're an axe murderer. I'd say you've got to give it at least three or four lessons."

"Right, which is pretty much what I said to him. So after the meeting, we found him a class, found out where the students were up to, gave him two or three learning objectives off the business-studies specification and told him he should take at least three lessons to teach the material to the students. We'd give the students a test at the start to establish a baseline and then we'd assess their progress with the same test at the end."

Heather smiled at the idea. "That's funny. I like the rigour, but there's no way he'd go through with that."

"Well, to Gary's credit, he was a man of his word. We did the whole thing last week."

Heather stopped walking, her eyes widened in anticipation. "What? He's already taught them?"

Dave paused and turned to face her. "Oh, I don't know if I'd go as far as using the verb 'taught'. He was definitely in the room at the same time as the kids, though."

Heather grabbed Dave by the elbow and pulled him closer. "Oh my god, what was it like?" She said, her movements light with enthusiasm.

Dave chuckled. "Well in the same way as if someone had a go at brain surgery without any training, it went pretty much as you'd expect."

Heather stifled a laugh with her hand. "Okay, let me guess: he treated the whole thing like a presentation and the kids like an audience?"

Dave smiled. "Yup. He was basically your worst career-change trainee ever."

Both of them had trained several student teachers over the years and so had come to recognise some common student pitfalls. Trainees were often a real mix, but those that did well often did so through a willingness to learn their new trade. In Dave's experience, some of the more problematic trainees were those in the process of a career change who imagined that their existing skills and experience would carry them through the majority of the training.

The trees hissed at another gust of wind and Heather readjusted her bobble hat. "Let me guess: did he read off a PowerPoint slide?" Dave nodded. "...that had way too much information on it?"

"Of course," Dave confirmed. "That's what we're trained to do, right? Put the whole thing into eight-point font and assume complete illiteracy? Kids love that."

Heather resumed walking. "This is fun," she said. "I'm guessing there was no development of ideas?" Dave shook his head. "Little to no assessment?" Another headshake. "Lots of vague, open questions and very little in the way of structure?"

"Yup, all of those," he said, following closely behind her as the path narrowed. "I mean, it did have some structure. It was structured in so much as there was a period where he told them what they needed to know by literally reading off the exam board's specification and then there was a much longer period of autobiographical rambling, where he told them how successful he was."

"He just read out the spec?" Heather laughed, picking her way over an outcrop of rock. "I don't think I've ever had a trainee even try and do something that stupid. That sounds like a joke." She slid down the other side of the rock. "Did he have any activities or anything with which to engage the students?"

"Well if you consider being sent out of the room an activity, then yeah. Twelve kids got to take part in an activity."

"Are you joking?" Heather said, looking back over her shoulder to scrutinise Dave for sarcasm.

"No."

"He sent out twelve students? Oh my god. That sounds awful." She paused as she tried to imagine sending out a third of her students. "How does that even work? Where do you send twelve students? I mean, firstly, how can you have so little control that you need to eject a third of your class?"

"Yeah, I know."

"But where did he send them? I mean, you can't just send out twelve students unsupervised into the corridor. That's not just incompetent, that's irresponsible."

"Oh yeah, it was a complete car crash of a lesson. I don't think I've ever seen someone so completely incompetent and yet so comfortable with it. It was obvious that he had no idea what he was doing but it was weird how little this seemed to bother him."

"What? Like he didn't realise it was going badly?"

"Yeah, I think that's probably exactly what it was. Normally when trainees mess up they're acutely aware that it's all going wrong and they just get more and more frantic as the whole thing just unravels and slips away from them, but this guy was like a derailed freight train. He just ploughed on with this rambling monologue. He was completely oblivious to what was happening. It was amazing. Occasionally he would just shout at them and demand that they respect his authority."

"What? Like Cartman from South Park?"

"Almost exactly like that, yeah," Dave said, chuckling. "And the students quickly picked up that they could just leave the lesson with no apparent consequence. He was so completely out of his depth it was embarrassing. If he had been a trainee, I'd have intervened after something like the first five or ten minutes. It was obviously only going to get worse. But you know, this is Gary we're talking about. He's not just some trainee, he's the boss. It's got this whole unique tension. You know what Gary's like. I don't think he'd have let me intervene even if I'd tried."

"He might have been grateful for the help?" Heather said speculatively and then changed her mind. "No, you're right. It's probably more likely that he'd have just ignored you."

"Yeah, that or he'd have sent me out of the room as well."

They stopped midway across an old, stone bridge and peered over the edge into the brown, churning water beneath them. "That's a difficult situation." She said. "You're the responsible adult in the room; you've got a duty of care."

"Exactly, and there were a growing number of them who were being sent out into the corridor of oblivion." Heather smiled at the description as Dave continued. "I mean it's funny looking back on it, but it definitely wasn't funny at the time. The stupid thing is, it panned out almost exactly as I would have expected, but I hadn't really thought the consequences through. I just thought it would be funny to watch him fail, but I hadn't actually considered what action I would have to take if he went completely off the rails and became a liability."

"So what did you do? Get help from another member of staff or something? I dunno?"

"Well, in the end that's sort of what I did. Linda's their normal teacher and she was sitting in the class with me, so after the third student was sent out I sent her to take them all to an empty classroom. She basically did a proper lesson with them."

They finished crossing the bridge and re-joined the riverside path. "Oh, so they weren't just going out into the corridor to wreak havoc?"

"No, they were going to B5 to wreak havoc," Dave said chuckling. "Actually, by the sounds of it, Linda had a pretty good lesson with them. I mean, there were only twelve of them and she *can* teach."

"So did Gary know you were doing that?"

"What? Constructing a parallel lesson to cover for his monolithic ineptitude? No. He had no clue where they were going. I think once they'd left the room, he stopped caring. He was just ejecting whoever wanted to be ejected so that he could go back to waxing lyrical about how amazing he was at negotiating."

"Sounds like a really annoying lesson to be in," Heather said. "I'm guessing you didn't let him teach a second lesson."

Dave grinned. "Well this is where it gets really funny."

Heather laughed. "You mean there's more?"

"Well Gary was convinced that he'd just taught an epic lesson. So as far as he was concerned, he'd completely proved his point that teaching was easy."

Heather stopped and let her mouth hang open. "Are you kidding? How could he possibly think that?"

"Dunning-Krueger."

She resumed her step. "But even then, you said it was a complete car crash. He sent out a third of the group! There's no way that someone could interpret that as a success. No one's that ignorant."

"That's the whole thing with Dunning-Krueger. He doesn't even have enough knowledge to assess the level of his own ignorance. Think about it: Gary thinks teaching is standing in a room and talking about yourself. So by that measure, he was a massive success."

The muddy path gave way to paving slabs as they approached the next village. "He probably does realise it was a disaster, Dave. It's probably more likely that he was embarrassed by the whole thing and wanted to try and paint it as positively as possible."

Dave laughed. "That's a very generous interpretation, Heather. I love how you do that: always giving people the benefit of the doubt." Heather smiled but seemed unsure how to take the compliment. Dave continued, hurriedly trying to distract her by filling the uncertainty with words, "I'm not sure that in this case it's warranted, though. I don't think he was being optimistic. He came out of that lesson positively bragging that he'd just managed to teach them half a year's worth of work."

Dave explained that before Gary's lesson, the students had achieved an average of twenty percent on the test and Gary was convinced that on their retest they would achieve somewhere between ninety and a hundred percent. Such was his confidence, Dave had suggested that they tie Gary's wage to the final average and Heather had laughed at this caveat.

Heather took off her hat and shook her hair loose as they entered the village pub. "So have they done the re-test?" she said, picking up a menu from the table.

"Yeah," Dave said.

"What was it? Twenty percent again?"

"Oh come on, Heather, they got twenty percent when they hadn't been taught anything." Dave said putting his coat onto the back of the chair.

"Well, exactly."

"No, they got fourteen percent."

Heather laughed. "So they did worse after his lesson?"

"Maybe," Dave said. "To be fair to Gary, that drop was probably more an artefact of the group being split and the sample size being small, but they certainly didn't improve." Heather was distracted as she looked at the specials menu. She had bought dinner last time, so this time it was Dave's turn. He ordered at the bar and returned with two pints of ale.

"So what did Gary say? Have you given him the results?" Heather asked, taking her pint from him.

Dave sat down opposite her. "Aw, he just blamed the students and said that they were stupid and badly behaved."

Heather looked irritated. "Did you explain that, as a teacher that would be his job to rectify that?"

"No, there was no need. That average of fourteen percent was just from the students that had remained in his lesson. The twelve kids that he'd sent out and who'd ended up getting a lesson from Linda, they got an average of sixty-three percent."

Heather put her hand to her mouth and stifled a laugh. "Oh that's beautiful. So how did he explain that?"

"Well, he couldn't really. He just looked confused, so I took the opportunity to suggest that we could either scale his salary down to fourteen percent of its current value, or we could pay Linda five times his salary, since she was demonstrably five times better than he was."

Heather stifled another laugh. "And what did he say to that?"

"He didn't seem all that keen to pay Linda two and a half million. He just laughed and said that they're two totally different jobs. Which is true: they are. But he just couldn't let the whole test thing go. He spent something like five minutes justifying that it wasn't a fair comparison because of this and that and saying that it wasn't fair because Linda knew what the test questions were beforehand."

"I thought you said he had a copy of the test beforehand?"

"Oh yeah, absolutely. And the kids had all sat the test. So he diverted and went for the philosophical high-ground and said that teaching is about so much more than just test results."

"Oh, you're kidding!" Heather gasped with outrage. "Isn't this the guy who was all for performance-related pay based on exam results?"

"Yeah, you know, but that's for other people. I don't think his own words apply to him."

"What a complete jerk." Heather said and spent a few seconds looking carefully at Dave. Finally, she said, "I'm glad you're not like that."

"What? Blithely unaware of my own ignorance?"

Heather laughed. "Oh no, you're definitely that."

"That's what I thought." Dave said.

IDEALISM VS PRAGMATISM

At the end of every lesson or meeting, Dave would check his emails. Checking emails was different to dealing with emails: Dave had discovered that a swift email response might appear efficient and convince people that he was on top of things, but ultimately it just encouraged people to hand him more of their minor concerns and grievances, thus reducing his overall efficiency. Now, he would strategically wait a few hours or even days, before replying. As assistant head, most of the problems in his inbox were usually resolved without his intervention. That morning he had received an email urgently requesting the key to a maintenance cupboard and then half an hour later a follow-up email telling him that he should no longer worry: they had ended up getting the key from the caretaker. As in many organisations, the proportion of useful emails was small when compared to the total number of emails received and the signal-to-noise ratio was not helped by staff having access to the all-staff mailing list. On any given day, a slew of emails would fill inboxes across the school to keep staff fully informed on the day's major issues.

Lost items:

Sorry for the blanket email. Has anyone seen Johnny Bobbleknocker's pen? It's a black biro with a black lid. He's very upset because it has sentimental value. Thanks.

Found items:

Sorry for the blanket email. A key has been found on the ground outside B12. It is made from shiny metal and has no distinguishing features. Please ask around to see if anyone has lost a key. Thanks.

Wanted items:

Sorry for the blanket email. Martha Simkins in 10D is doing an art project and needs 600 plastic milk bottle caps and five kilos of weapons-grade plutonium. If you can help, please drop the items into the Art department. Thanks.

The first thing these emails told Dave was that no one felt any sense of remorse for sending blanket emails and the second was that anything with the adjunct, "Sorry for the blanket email," was almost certainly not worth his reading. To this end, he had placed a filter that redirected these offending emails into the junk folder. Of the remaining emails, Dave had applied a filter that highlighted any messages that were only directed to him because, if someone had written an email just to him, the likelihood of them wanting a response was quite high. This way he could deal with personally-directed correspondence ahead of the choking smoke of information that swirled around the school like that of a damp bonfire.

Today's selection of all-staff emails contained an entertaining contribution from Sandra, who had spent two whole pages spewing vitriol and condescension as she lambasted the "deplorable quality of staff's written reports" and then went through all of the common mistakes of spellings and incorrect capitalisations. The email did not read as a helpful guide so much as an assertion of Sandra's powerful command of the English language and her superiority when it came to undertaking teachers' paperwork. Of course, if one is going to criticise others over their failure to proofread, then the universal law of irony dictates that they should very carefully proofread their own text. Sandra however, had made at least two minor punctuation-mistakes and a spelling mistake but her main error was arguably in sending out the email in the first place. Since the school no longer operated a system of written reports, Sandra's rant over inadequate writing had been completely obviated by Debbie's introduction of the school's new system of drop-down menus and prefabricated comments. The written reports that Sandra was presumably referencing had been the last set in the phased withdrawal of written reports from the previous year, just before Debbie had resigned. Thus, Sandra's two pages of splenetic condemnation was not just irrelevant but an entertaining indictment of how little she was engaged in the workload of classroom teachers.

A highlighted email appeared on the screen from the organiser of a TED-X event in Cambridge. Dave assumed that the email was probably attempting to sell him tickets or something, but it seemed odd that the message was addressed to him personally. TED, an acronym for Technology, Entertainment and Design, held a big conference once a year where innovative and leading thinkers from around the world would talk for between ten and fifteen minutes on a topic of their choice. Millions accessed the resulting online videos and the main conference had spawned a series of franchised spin-offs: the TED-X events. These local events tended to have individual themes and this year's Cambridge event was to be focussed on Education. Dave skimmed the email for the usual signs of advertising like big colour pictures, bullet-point lists and repeated phrases like "exciting opportunity". This email contained none of those. Indeed, the email was remarkably personal, asking Dave how his preparation was coming along, whether he had decided on a more concrete theme for his talk and whether the organisers could assist him in any way. Dave scrolled back up to the email header to check whether the email had been sent to the wrong address, which was completely pointless. Unlike postal mail, email did not arrive at the wrong address by mistake: it arrived at the address to which it had been sent, which in this case was Dave's email address. Confused, he read through the email again. The sender, a woman named Sally Tate, clearly thought that someone called Dave at Dave's email address was due to give a TED talk in February. He scrolled down to below Sally's message where he came across a reply chain that gave a reverse chronological account of the preceding exchange.

The most recent reply was from Katarina and simply contained Dave's email address. This alone was enough for Dave to let out a heavy sigh of resignation.

The reply below that was Sally asking whether Katarina could send them Dave's email address.

Below that, Katarina was describing Dave as a leading educational theorist and assistant head at Woodford school and suggesting that he would certainly give a talk. Katarina imagined he would probably want to describe his groundbreaking research into dynamic enacting ratios and the strong, visionary support he had received from the school's senior leadership team.

Before that, Sally was asking for more details about this visionary academic, Dave Winger and asking whether he would be interested in delivering a talk?

Before that, Katarina was explaining that she understood there were limited places, but that her forward thinking leadership of Woodford School had encouraged and nurtured the visionary academic, Dave Winger, the father of dynamic enacting ratios.

Before that, Sally was thanking Katarina for showing an interest in the TED-X event but regretfully explained that they get a lot of visionary headteachers and that there weren't currently any spaces for another talk of that nature.

The original email at the bottom, the one that had kicked off the whole chain, was Katarina introducing herself to Sally as a, "Progressive, data-driven headteacher whose visionary ideas would provide a strong contribution at the February TED-X event."

What remained unclear was whether Katarina thought she had already discussed this with Dave, or whether she just figured a random email from the organisers of the event was by far the most professional way for him to find out. Dave walked over to Katarina's office where he found her door open and Katarina sitting behind her desk. Wearing a purple suit jacket and a white-silk blouse, she was peering at her computer screen. The plant in the corner was now fully and unequivocally dead, its brown, desiccated remains draped over the plastic rim of the pot. The soil however, looked thoroughly and freshly watered, presumably in the belief that doubling the amount of water now would somehow compensate for the earlier neglect.

"Hi," Dave said, knocking on the door as he walked in. "I just got an email from the organisers of a TED-X event?"

Katarina looked up from her monitor. "Oh great, have you come up with a theme yet?"

"A theme? A theme for what?"

"For your talk."

Dave gave an exaggerated shoulder shrug. "Why would I be doing a talk? I don't know anything about a talk."

Katarina answered with a raised inflection at the end of her sentences, as though reminding a forgetful relative about visiting their niece. "It's for your TED-X talk. At the start of February."

"Why would I know anything about that?"

"TED talks are a global phenomenon, Dave. They're very prestigious."

"I realise that. But why are they contacting me as though I'd agreed to do one?"

Katarina lifted her hands from the desk as though the answer was self-evident. "You're a leading academic, Dave. I think you just have to accept that people will want to hear about your work. You're the father of dynamic enacting ratios. I'm sure there are a lot of people out there that'll want to hear about your research and the forward-thinking approach of the school that supported you."

"But why do you seem to know about it, when I don't?"

Katarina seemed not to hear Dave's question and continued to talk about the fantastic opportunity he had to promote the amazing work of the school.

Growler was standing in front of Martin's desk. He was wearing his trademark tweed jacket and standing with his feet shoulder-width apart, his hands clasped behind his back like a soldier standing at ease. Dave shuffled past and over to his desk where he politely began looking like he was doing some work.

Growler often complained in the staff base and his complaints could tackle a wide variety of topics: the inability of politicians to enact beneficial change, the poor wording of exam questions, why stupid people were allowed on TV and a whole pantheon of other minor irritations he had encountered in the previous twenty-four hours. However, these complaints were always good humoured and limited to the conversations within the staff base. Dave could not recall a time when Growler had ever elevated a complaint to a formal level and approached senior management.

Growler spoke softly and simply in his deep rumbling baritone, his words having an economy of meaning that Dave had always admired. He told Martin that performance-related pay was not having the effect that they had intended. Rather than the competition motivating teachers to perform better, it was fragmenting the department, producing an unwillingness to share resources and a reduction in support for their more vulnerable staff. Growler didn't belabour the point or provide unnecessary anecdotes, he just stopped talking when he had finished. Martin leapt in, thanking Growler for his opinion and then speaking for several minutes about why he was wrong, dropping some of his favourite management phrases into the mix like 'turnkey solution', 'leveraged position' and 'global insight.'

Growler remained silent throughout, his face immobile and when Martin had finally finished Growler responded by ignoring the majority of what had been said and simply refuted Martin's first sentence, explaining that he wasn't expressing an opinion he was giving him a synopsis of his observations. Martin tried asserting that of course it was his opinion, all Growler could do was express opinions because of the nature of subjectivity. To back up his point he name-dropped a few enlightenment philosophers and then concluded that performance-related pay was working just fine.

Growler raised one of his huge furry eyebrows. "No, that wasn't my opinion: I was telling you what I had observed," he said. "But I'm happy to give you my opinion." Martin reiterated that his observations were still opinions but

Growler ignored the distraction and instead laid out his complaint.

Teaching was a complicated profession with many interlocking roles and skills and like any complicated profession, it took most practitioners at least three or four years to become comfortable with the basics. Growler believed that it would take a similar amount of time again for a teacher to become truly good at the job. The old pay system of incremental progression rewarded teachers for staying in the profession long enough to reach a certain level of proficiency, it understood that excellence took time. One set of bad results didn't make you a bad teacher, any more than one set of good results made you a good one. But by basing pay on results, Growler believed that newly qualified teachers would be unfairly disadvantaged because, in those first few years, they would still be learning the job. He argued that keeping them on low pay for three or four years was likely to contribute to them quitting the profession.

Martin was not impressed with the argument. He suggested that those unable to hack the job were better off leaving so that the profession as a whole would be stronger. He accused Growler of being melodramatic and asked: what could be more egalitarian than a system that pays people what they're worth? Growler nodded slowly as he considered this.

"You're assuming that your system measures worth," Growler said. "But it doesn't: it just measures grades. And as I previously stated, it appears to be reducing both productivity and morale."

Martin gave a disapproving snort. "I think morale will be pretty high when people start getting bonuses for their great exam results."

"I'm not saying that the previous system was perfect. I'm sure you could find examples of some terrible teachers who were essentially being overpaid..."

"There were plenty of those," Martin scoffed, talking over Growler.

"...but then likewise there were also plenty of excellent teachers who were being very much underpaid. Paying teachers their market value cuts both ways."

"Oh does it? I didn't realise you were such an expert in economics?"

Growler ignored the sarcasm and continued talking in the same measured tone. "Some of your science and maths teachers are highly employable individuals."

"Oh are they?" Martin sneered.

"And employable not just within teaching. My concern is that once you commodify teachers' pay, your problem is going to be that of a low-league football team. You're going to have problems raising enough money to attract the good teachers."

Martin let out a frustrated sigh, bored by Growler's argument and irritated with his impassive delivery. "Right, well you're making a lot of assumptions there. Firstly, we're just paying people for the job they do, that's all. Secondly, we're not starting some global market. If they do a good job, they get paid more. It's quite simple. I honestly can't see what your problem is."

Growler patiently explained that by moving to performance-related pay they were decoupling from the National Pay Scale. Growler believed that the National Pay Scale was the key to social mobility. It was the great leveller. It meant that the education available to those in the poorest parts of the country was essentially the same as that which was available to those in the wealthiest because there was very little difference in pay.

"So what I'm hearing is: you're hugely employable and that we should be paying you more?" Martin said.

Growler frowned. "No. That's almost the opposite of what I was saying."

Martin sighed. "Okay, you don't like the pay system. You think it's destroying morale, the Science department and the whole country?"

"That's possibly overstating it, but somewhat closer."

"Okay, well we're not going to change the pay system," Martin said delivering a dismissive wave as he said this. "It works just fine."

"Do you have any evidence that it's working fine?"

"Yeah, I'm telling you that it's working, okay? That's your evidence."

"That's not evidence."

"It is if I say it is," Martin snapped. "Where's your evidence that it's not working?"

Growler took a step forward and placed two sheets of paper in front of Martin. "The data is really noisy and I would caution against over-interpretation." He said. "However, my concern is that the science progress trend lines appear to be declining across all the year groups, and the drops are all pushing significance levels."

"These are just numbers," Martin said without even looking at the paper. "They've got nothing to do with pay."

"I agree that there's no evidence for a causal link."

"So why are you bothering me with it? The new pay system will solve it: people will work harder and earn their bonuses."

"I'm just giving you the data."

"No, you're not. You're being negative and that's not helpful. Why can't you be positive about the new system? Plenty of staff have told me that they're delighted with the new system."

"Like who?"

Martin scowled at the question. "It doesn't matter who," and then becoming even more irritated added: "In fact, it's none of your business, who. All you need to know is that plenty of people have told me how great they think this new system is. You don't speak for them. In fact, I'm shocked that you would have the audacity to come up here and talk to me like you know what's best for the school when..."

"I'm just giving you the data."

"No. No, you're not. You're not giving me data. You're telling me that you want the pay policy changed because you don't like it..."

"That's not what I said."

"...which... no, let me finish. I find that incredibly arrogant of you. And if I'm honest, this attitude is all part of a much bigger problem. I don't know where it's come from, but it seems like the whole Science department thinks it's better than the rest of the school. And I'm getting sick of it. People like you and John," he gestured accusingly with an outstretched finger. "You treat Science like it's your own personal fiefdom, as though the rules don't apply to you. The whole department is infected with this permissive culture, this whole negative, anti-management ethos. You seem to think that you know better than everyone else. But I remind you. That's not your job. Your job is to teach the students. Mine is to run the school. You're just a classroom teacher. Now if you don't like the way we run things or you don't like the idea of teachers being paid for their results, then that's fine. Feel free to go out there and find a job where everyone agrees with you. No one's forcing you to work here."

There was a moment of silence. "I'm sorry? Are you suggesting I should leave?" Growler said.

"You can do whatever the hell you want. But I'll be honest with you. If there's one thing that's undermining morale in this school, it's not the pay system: it's the corrosive attitude in Science. What we need are teachers that have got the right attitude and are willing to work with us rather than against us."

"You make it sound like you think you'd be better off without me."

"Hey, like I said, it's your decision. I'm not going to beg for you to stay," Martin said scornfully. There was silence for several seconds in which Martin seemed to be awaiting Growler's apology.

Growler gave a little sigh. "Well, my contract stipulates a term's notice, so that should take you nicely up to February."

"Okay. If that's your decision, fine. I'm not going to stand in your way. A term gives us plenty of time to find your replacement. There's a whole load of NQTs out there who will jump at the chance to work in a school as successful as this. Teachers with the right attitude who can work as part of a team."

"Okay," Growler said with a resigned shrug. "I'll put my resignation onto Katarina's desk this afternoon. Have a good day." He walked out of the office and closed the door carefully behind him.

Martin turned to Dave. "Can you believe that guy? Coming in here with an attitude like that? Where does he get off telling me how to run the pay system? Seriously, what was he expecting me to do? Go back to the old system just because he doesn't like it? He marches in here... who the hell does he think he is?" Martin swivelled in his chair, expelling some of his frustration. "That guy needed to be taken down a peg or two, coming in here with all that." He made a flappy mouth gesture with his right hand. "Someone needed to kick that guy back into line." He said and rocked back in his chair. "I don't think he was expecting me to call his bluff though," he said with a self-satisfied chuckle.

Dave looked at him quizzically. "His bluff?"

"Absolutely. Didn't you see what he was trying to do? He was trying to strong arm me. He thought I'd back down and beg him to stay, but you can't play that game with me. I'm an expert negotiator. He messed with the wrong guy."

"So you don't think he's actually going to resign?"

"Hell no. That was just all posturing and ego. Trust me. I've seen it a million times. He'll be angry for a few hours but he'll cool off and realise his mistake."

"He didn't seem all that angry."

"No, he was. I can tell. He was holding it in, but he was angry."

"And if you're wrong, you've just told the school's only chemist to get lost."

"No. A good manager's always one step ahead, Dave. Before he even started talking, I'd already got him all figured out. See I went through all his options in my head. He's what? In his sixties? He'll be looking to retire in fifteen, maybe twenty years. This is a good school and he's on a good wage. Now, if he tried to go somewhere else he's more than likely looking at a pay cut. Chances are they probably wouldn't even take him: he's old, he's expensive. There are not many schools that'll take him and he's not going to up sticks and move just to prove some stupid point." Martin shook his head as though agreeing with his own argument. "No, he's not going anywhere."

"You're assuming he's a pragmatist," Dave said. "But I don't think Growler's a pragmatist. I think you may have just lost the school's only chemist."

Martin gave a derisive snort. "No I haven't. I've just told you, I've run through all the scenarios: he's not going anywhere. He stands to lose way more from leaving than we do."

"You realise Growler's a millionaire, right?"

Martin furrowed his brow at the information. "What? What do you mean?"

"I mean, he's a millionaire."

"Why would he be working here if he's a millionaire?"

"He's not a pragmatist, Martin. He's an idealist. He's not here for the money. He's here because he feels like it's giving something back to society."

Martin's joviality diminished substantially. "So why was he complaining about his pay then?"

"I don't think he was."

"Yeah he was. He was going on about how the Science department were being underpaid and how the pay system was unfair and damaging morale. Which is nonsense, people love the new pay system."

"It sounded to me more like he was opposed to the new pay system because he believes it undermines the cohesive and collaborative nature of teaching, disproportionately punishes those who are new to the profession and would result in future recruitment problems for the school."

"He's expensive and he's got a bad attitude," Martin said huffily. "We don't need teachers like that. We're better off without him. We need team players: teachers who are on board with the school's vision."

Dave shrugged and returned to his monitor. Half an hour later Katarina walked into the office and over to Martin's desk.

"Martin, why have I got Grantham's notice on my desk?" she said and before he could respond added, "He's saying that you want to replace him because he's arrogant and his bad attitude is damaging morale."

"That's not exactly what I said," Martin began and then launched into a largely fictitious account in which he was an implacable figure of wisdom who had unsuccessfully tried to council the childish petulance of Growler. "I tried to stop him, but he was having none of it," Martin concluded with a regretful shake of his head.

"He's the school's only chemist, Martin. Why would you say we can replace him with an NQT?"

"Well we can. There's plenty of NQTs..." Martin began.

"Not ones that consistently get excellent results. And John tells me Grantham's the one who runs all the science trips because he has all the industry links. You think we'll find a replacement with those skills?"

"I get that he's an experienced teacher and he does lots of extra stuff," Martin said and then added: "But I wouldn't necessarily take John's word for it. They're thick as thieves down there. We have to look at the bigger picture. In the long run, we have to think about how we can build a more cohesive department and someone like Grantham is a major disruptive influence. I think he is bad for morale. There are loads of NQTs out there, Kat. We can replace him at a fraction of his cost"

"Martin, there's a national shortage of chemistry teachers. We're in the middle of rural nowhere. Grantham is probably the only chemistry teacher with a chemistry degree in this whole county. Go and talk to him. Apologise, do whatever it takes."

"But I haven't done anything wrong. He was the one who came in here trying to tell me how to do my job."

"Martin, I want the school to have a chemistry teacher. Go and talk to him."

Martin gave a plosive sigh like a reprimanded teenager and stalked out of the office. Katarina waited for the door to close and then she slumped back against Martin's desk, her shoulders hunched up, her head hung forward. She seemed unaware of Dave's presence and for a moment, Dave saw Katarina, not as an ambitious mountaineer scaling the career mountain but as a woman concerned for her school and compressed by circumstance.

"I doubt Martin will convince him," Dave said cutting into her reverie.

Katarina took a deep breath and looked across at Dave, the tension returning to her shoulders. "Why not?"

Dave explained that Grantham was probably looking to make a larger point about the commodification of teachers' pay and that he was hoping to highlight the hypocrisy of management. "He believes that the goal of the pay system is not to reward performance, but to suppress wages."

"I don't understand how him leaving, makes that point?"

Dave explained that if Grantham left, the school would no longer be able to offer A-level chemistry, the GCSE chemistry results would nosedive and the science results would go along with them. The school was unlikely to find a replacement chemist and so after a year or two of the results

217

being on the floor Dave predicted that Grantham would return and offer his services.

"Only he'll have established the market rate for a chemistry teacher with his experience and performance record," Dave said. "Which, given the scarcity of chemistry teachers, might be as much as twice what you're currently paying him, maybe even as high as Martin's wage."

"Well that's ridiculous, there's no way we could afford that."

"Right, and thus he will have highlighted your hypocrisy."

Katarina scowled. "How does that make us hypocrites?"

"Martin claimed that the goal was to pay teachers what they're worth, so if you refuse to hire him back because he's too expensive, he'll just say: look I told you it was really about wanting cheap teachers."

"That's not how markets work, Dave. You don't get to turn up and say I want three times what you used to pay me."

"You don't think there are schools out there with the resources to pay for him?"

"He might if he looks hard enough, but that's a ridiculous argument. If he costs that much, they can have him."

"Right, but that's his point. Under your new system, you can no longer afford a chemistry teacher of his calibre. And you used to have him working for you at a bargain-basement rate."

"He clearly doesn't understand economics, then." Katarina said pointedly raising an eyebrow at Dave. "Because if being a chemistry teacher becomes that lucrative, there'll be a surplus of them."

"Except that the supply problem was never from a lack of incentive. It's because there aren't enough chemistry specialists training the kids to become chemists in the first place. And I realise that that's not your fault, that's a larger government issue and it has been for a while. But Growler's argument is that by making chemistry teachers expensive, you're not incentivising their creation or increasing the supply, you're just turning them into a luxury that only wealthy schools can afford."

"You say that like it's my fault, Dave. I didn't choose for it to be like this." Katarina spoke with a pained expression. "Performance-related pay is just the way that things are going. The government inspectors want us to show that we're denying some of our staff pay progression and this system allows us to show that. Even if we had a perfect staff of excellent teachers, we'd still be required to penalise some of them. It's just an economic reality. I'm just trying to do the best for the school."

Dave saw for the first time that the changes in the school were not necessarily being driven by malice. Katarina was not masterminding the demise of his profession or persecuting his colleagues. She was just responding to the immediate needs of the school at that moment. Maybe the problem was government incompetence, but Dave was always reluctant to assign such a simple explanation to something as complex as education policy and finance. Changes in policy took years or even decades to play out and so assigning responsibility for a failure was often as difficult as it was ineffective.

Martin returned half an hour later. He did not look happy, but Dave asked him how it had gone anyway.

"He's not interested," Martin mumbled as he sat back at his desk. "We don't need him. It's not hard to find teachers."

"So he's just quit teaching entirely?"

"I guess so. I didn't ask," he said, stabbing the keyboard aggressively with his fingers. He hammered out a few more words, mumbling. "So arrogant. So, so arrogant." He paused and faced Dave. "He said if we still needed him in a few years' time he might reconsider. Can you believe that guy?" He turned back to his monitor. "So arrogant."

CYBORG JUSTICE-RANGER

The students from Dave's only lower school group tumbled into the laboratory and seated themselves at their benches.

"It's Christmas, sir." A boy on the front row chirped, presumably thinking Dave might be unaware of the season. "Are we going to watch a film?"

Dave looked up slowly from his laptop and met the boy's eager face. "You've got two weeks until Christmas. We're not going to sit and watch films."

"Are we going to have a fun lesson?" The girl sitting next to him said.

"What do you mean?" Dave said in mock confusion. "Aren't all my lessons fun?"

"No." They both said in unison.

"Then I'd say that the outlook probably doesn't look that good for this one either."

The boy rolled his eyes. "Oh man, physics is so boring."

"How'd you figure that?" Dave asked.

"Physics is just boring. It's just always numbers and writing."

"What about that lesson when we fired rockets out the window?"

"Oh, yeah that was fun," the boy said, as though that went without saying.

"Well, that was physics."

"Right, but all the other lessons were boring," the girl said.

"What, even the lesson where we ran the zip line off the roof?"

The girl took a moment to think back and then said, "Oh yeah that was fun."

"That was awesome," the boy added.

"Well, that was physics."

"Right, but you know what we mean?" the girl said.

"No, I don't know what you mean. You tell me what you mean."

"Physics is just all equations and it's boring," the boy said.

"When am I ever going to use physics?" the girl said.

"You tell me a topic that's been boring."

"Momentum," the boy said.

His friend sitting next to him chipped in. "Oh yeah, momentum was so boring."

"What, even the lesson where two of you wore sumo suits and ran into each other."

They took a few seconds to recall the lesson and then both concluded. "Oh yeah, that was great."

"And the lesson where we did the calculation to work out how fast you'd fly back if you'd been shot with a sniper rifle?"

"Oh yeah, that was pretty cool," the first boy said.

"And then we tried it out by firing the air cannon into Terrence the Teddy bear?"

"Oh yeah that was awesome!" his friend said. "I remember, we made him that bulletproof vest out of playdoh."

"Right well, that was all momentum!" Dave said.

"Electricity was boring," the girl said.

"What, you mean the lesson where we used the Van de Graaff generator to detonate a can of custard powder?"

"Oh right, yeah, that was cool," she conceded. "But the rest of electricity was boring. All the circuits and stuff."

"What? Even the lesson where you heated up the wire with a current and used it to cut through plastic?"

"That was awesome," the boy said.

"Yeah, I cut right through my pen and you said I still had to use it!" The friend gleefully recalled.

"Right, so that was electricity."

"Well obviously that was fun," the girl said.

Dave looked at the three of them sceptically. "You know, I'm beginning to think that you guys don't know what you're talking about."

"Obviously we're not saying your lessons aren't fun, sir," the girl said. "We're just saying that physics is boring."

"Yeah," the boy agreed.

"What the hell are you talking about? All of my lessons are physics. If you're enjoying the lessons, you're enjoying physics."

"Yeah but answering questions is boring," the boy said.

"But that's true of all subjects. All your subjects ask you exam questions. Why single out physics as being the one subject that's boring because it asks you exam questions?"

The three of them looked blank. "I don't know," the girl said.

"Right, well I think I can safely ignore your complaints from now on: we've established there's little evidential basis for them."

"We've not got a test next lesson, have we?" the first boy asked.

"Yes. That's still happening."

"Oh, but it's Christmas," he said.

"No, it's Christmas in two weeks' time. This is just December. We don't suspend work for the whole month just because that month contains a particular day." Dave said and handed out the past-paper questions with which they could start their revision.

Mary peered round the door of the lab and, seeing that the students were all happily working away, asked, "You busy?"

Dave walked over and positioned himself so he could continue to monitor the class whilst holding his conversation.

"It's done," Mary said. "I've handed it in."

Dave nodded and rested a hand on her shoulder. "This place won't be the same without you," he said. "You do so much for the kids and they're always saying how great you are. You're one of the best biology teachers around."

Mary smiled weakly. "Well, someone should tell her that," she said.

At the end of September, Sandra had begun her campaign of weeding out those teachers that she deemed to be coasting and for some reason, Mary had been one of her targets. Dave had come across plenty of unsuitable or incompetent teachers in his time. Sometimes they would be well-meaning individuals whose constant dithering and mumbled apologies made them woefully ineffective at managing teenagers. Other times they would be cynically disengaged individuals who would write up the lesson information on the board because 'that was their job', but then completely ignore the students' behaviour, allowing them to run around the classroom or huddle together in conversations because, 'if they don't know any better, that's their problem'. Eventually, their shortcomings made it to the attention of management who would start their support programme and after several months, the teachers would usually choose to leave the profession or join less discerning schools. Dave had come to believe that the school's steady improvement in the last decade was largely due to this erosion of the weaker staff. The problem, however, was that of an overactive immune system. Once management had weeded out all of the obviously incompetent staff and pegged this to the commensurate rise in results, they began turning on perfectly competent teachers who they thought were possibly a bit old or a bit odd. Sandra had approached Mary with a friendly offer of help, suggesting that she observe one of Mary's lessons to help in supporting one of her students. Mary, who was always looking to learn new techniques and improve her teaching, had agreed. Unfortunately, rather than providing constructive feedback on the lesson, Sandra had informed Mary that her teaching was now a cause for concern and that her books and lessons would be monitored to ensure improvement. John, the head of department, had angrily condemned Sandra's meddling, but it was too late. Sandra's single observation was the hammer with which she then proceeded to beat Mary down.

Throughout November, Mary had faded. Each day she had seemed paler and more withdrawn as the joy and enthusiasm that had previously permeated her character, ebbed away. Her lessons had grown more cautious and less adventurous lest they incur Sandra's ire. Dave's visits to the staff room were less frequent than they used to be, but with each visiting snapshot, he had seen Mary halve. By the end of November, she had resolved to leave, not just the school, but teaching as a whole. Fortunately, Mary had contacts in biomedical research and after a few days of interviews and negotiations, a research firm in Oxford had offered Mary a job heading up their new bioethics committee. Her years of teaching had honed her presentation skills, and her confidence in explaining concepts by breaking them down had made her almost the perfect candidate.

"Are you okay with it all?" Dave asked as they stood in the doorway together. "I mean... you look a lot happier now."

Mary sighed. "I guess so. I think what saddens me is just how unnecessary it's all been. I really enjoy teaching and I've really enjoyed my time here. There's something really great about helping the kids and getting to know them. And I think that's probably been the big problem this last month: I didn't really want to let it go. It felt like I was just letting her win. You know?" Dave nodded sympathetically. "That really frustrates me, that idea of letting her imagine that she's some great manager. But she's not. I thought maybe she was being vindictive as though she really didn't like me for some reason. But, the more I think about it, the more I realise, she's just incompetent."

"Hanlon's razor."

"I don't know what that is."

"Don't ascribe to malice what can be explained by incompetence."

Mary smiled. "Yeah, that sounds about right. I feel like she doesn't really understand the impact that she has. I'm sure she thinks she does and I'm sure she thinks she's brilliant. She'll probably be patting herself on the back now that I'm leaving, but I don't think she's intelligent enough to understand the consequences of what she's doing."

"I don't think she's stupid but I think you're right that she doesn't understand the consequences of her actions."

Mary shrugged. "Maybe. But to me, that's stupidity. After Christmas they won't have anyone to teach A level; my new job starts in January. And now that both Growler and I have gone, John's started looking for another job."

"Really?"

"Yeah, he said he felt like the department was dying. I think he wants to go abroad."

Dave was distracted as a student waved at him. "Hang on," he said to Mary.

"No, no it's okay, Dave. I just wanted to let you know about the Oxford job and that I've handed in my notice. That was all."

"Honestly this won't take a moment," he said, half returning to the classroom.

"No, I'll let you get back to your lesson. I can always catch up with you later."

Dave smiled and walked over to the group of girls. "You okay?" he asked.

"Do we have to do *all* the practice questions?" one of them asked, emphasising the word 'all' as though it were some Herculean task.

"Only if you want to get good at *all* the topics," Dave said with similar emphasis. The three of them looked disappointed with this response but reluctantly returned to their revision.

Dave had hoped to find Mary after the lesson, but before he could find her, a call came down from the front office for him to deal with a parental complaint. After half an hour of listening to an irritated parent, Dave had to sit in on an educational-strategy meeting for two hours and so by the time he had finished, Mary had gone home. He didn't blame her. She was no longer motivated to give the school any more of her time than was contractually necessary. Dave buried his chin into his scarf and headed down the hill towards the town centre. It had rained most of the afternoon and in the yellow streetlight, the wet road appeared as an oily-black streak. Dave took out his phone as he waited at a pedestrian crossing, his thumb hovering over Heather's name. It was unusual for him to call her: they usually arranged to meet up by text and only then every two or three weeks. He slid the phone back into his pocket and crossed the road. Despite the lattice of gaudy Christmas lights that spanned the high street, the evening felt darker than usual. He stopped opposite the bank and took out his phone again. Phoning Heather felt like he was breaking some unspoken communication-rule, as though their friendship was contingent upon keeping a certain distance. He could always walk down to the Drovers, sit in front of the fire and talk with some of the regulars instead. He went to put his phone away for a second time but stopped. He didn't just want to talk to anyone, he wanted to talk with Heather. He wanted the warmth of her company. He sighed heavily, his thumb hovering over her name. It seemed silly not to even try. He dialled her number.

"Hey, Dave?" Heather said managing to sound both curious and pleasantly surprised.

"Hey, how you doing?"

"Yeah, I'm good. You?"

"Yeah. I realise this is short notice and everything and it's okay if you're busy..." Dave winced at his self-erasing introduction: he hated it when people started a sentence with mitigating caveats. "I was just wondered if maybe you were around later? I thought perhaps we could hang out or maybe go and see a film or something?" There was a little pause as though Heather was still processing the situation. "...it's okay if you're not."

"No, that sounds good," she said. "I had planned a wild evening of sitting at home alone and marking, but I could probably put that on hold."

Dave smiled, both at the humour and at the prospect of an evening with Heather. "Oh, that marking sounds like way more fun; I don't want to tear you away from that," he said.

He could hear Heather smiling in the tone of her voice as she suggested that they get something to eat at the chain pub. Dave agreed.

On the outside, the high street's chain pub looked like the old coaching inn it had once been, but the interior was all neat floorboards, smooth plastering and pithy aphorisms painted onto its Farrow and Ball walls.

Heather took off her dark-red coat and draped it over the back of the sofa. As usual, she wore a stylish combination: a thin, burgundy sweater, a velvet jacket and a dark-green skirt that ended below the knee.

"I got you a drink," Dave said, indicating a pint on the table. "It's a guest-ale with some weird name like Crunk-Wallop. Hope that's okay?"

Heather took off her soft, woollen hat and pushed it into the sleeve of her coat. "I'll let it slide just this once," she said with a smile.

How's it going?" he asked.

"I'm really glad you called," she said, sinking into the sofa opposite Dave. "I was just sitting at home being miserable and thinking how rubbish everything was. It's difficult this time of year. I try to be optimistic but it's so dark all the time. I get up in the dark. I go home in the dark." She gave a little shrug. "But I guess the same is true for everyone else."

"Help yourself to the chips," he said, indicating the bowl on the low coffee-table. Heather thanked him and reached forward to take a chip. "I know what you mean," Dave said. "We don't tend to use 'cold' and 'dark' as particularly positive descriptors. November into December always feels like this gradual, creeping sadness. I end up feeling more and more isolated and detached and then I don't really feel like going out, even though I know that's what I need to do."

"Same here. I suppose the payoff is the long summer evenings," Heather said. "You can't really have one without the other. When I was in Ecuador the sun would come up at six and set at six; it didn't really matter what time of year it was. It would set like that." She made a chopping gesture with her hand. "We didn't really get any twilight."

"Yeah, that's the ecliptic plane for you."

"Anyway, how are you doing? You don't usually call during the week," she said and then hastily added. "Not that I mind."

Dave sighed and described his earlier conversation with Mary, about how the department had now lost two experienced teachers and by the sound of it, about to lose John.

"That's huge," Heather said. "A department is the people that work there. You change the people and you change the department. How do you feel?"

Dave poked his thimble of tomato ketchup with the end of a chip as he considered her question. "Yeah, I mean, I'm really glad that Mary's found something and, you know I'm pleased that Growler's doing well..." He paused. "Well, I think he is. It's a bit difficult to tell with Growler. He's certainly the same as he was so that probably means he's fine. And it makes sense that John would want to leave. You know, John'll be good wherever he goes: he's a great manager. But I feel like I should have been able to do more, you know?"

"How do you mean?"

"I don't know. Maybe I could have kept the department together or something. You know? I'm an assistant head. I feel like I should have been able to do something. Intervene in some way."

"I don't think you could have done anything, Dave."

"But that's just it. I don't feel like any of us could have done anything. The whole school's just crumbling away and all we can do is just sit and watch it go." Dave sighed and chewed on his chip as he considered how to articulate his feelings. "I guess... I guess it just feels lonely. I feel like it's just me being selfish, but I feel really sad that they've gone. It's like this whole era has just imploded."

Heather reached across the coffee table and rested her hand on his arm. "I don't think that's being selfish."

"It kind of feels like it. They're all going off and doing things that'll make their lives better and here I am complaining that it's making me feel sad and lonely."

Heather straightened up. "But you're not feeling sad because they're doing things with their lives, Dave. You're sad because they won't be around. That's not the same thing."

"I suppose."

"It's not selfish to miss your friends. If you were being selfish, you'd be forcing them to stay."

"Yeah, I guess," Dave agreed. "I just feel a bit lost. Like... I dunno. What am I doing with my life? What's it all for?"

"Well, what do you want to do with your life?"

Dave thought about it for half a minute. "I dunno. I don't really feel like I'm in control of it."

"Are you happy with how things are going?"

"Well, I'm not unhappy."

Heather laughed. "You should get that on your gravestone. Dave: he wasn't unhappy."

Dave chuckled and as he considered the absurdity of such a weak epitaph, the chuckle grew into a deep, cathartic laugh. Some of the sadness that had weighed on his heart all afternoon began to lift. Nothing had changed. The sane people in his department were still leaving. He was still struggling to achieve demotion from the same tedious, unwanted management role. He still had an impending TED talk to write on a spurious topic that he had fabricated in the pub. The only difference was that when he was with Heather, he had someone with whom he could share all of this absurdity. When she laughed along with him, it all seemed so inconsequential.

"Are you happy?" he asked.

Heather considered the question for several seconds. "Sometimes. I think it depends on what's happening. I'm happy right now," she said and thought about it a little longer. "But I don't think happiness should be a goal in itself. That's never really made much sense to me. Happiness is more like a measurement or a way of knowing whether something is working for you. It can't ever really be the goal."

"Yeah, I think I see what you're saying. You can't make the weighing scales your weight-loss target."

Heather looked a little confused as she considered Dave's analogy. "Uh something like that," she said, generously. "I think I'm probably happiest when I'm working towards something. But the happiness is not the goal. The happiness is telling me that my goal should be to work towards something."

"Like what?"

"Well, it depends. It can be a relationship or something professional. I really enjoyed setting up that project with the students and then getting to present it at the Royal Society."

"I remember that. That was really impressive."

"Yeah, it was a lot of fun. The presentation and the recognition were exciting, but if none of that had happened, we would still have had an amazing time. It was more the journey. It was having a target and working towards it."

"Oh right. So, uh, how would that work with something like a relationship?" Dave said, avoiding eye contact as he became very engaged in picking up another chip. "I mean, once you've achieved a relationship, your journey is... well, it's kind of over, you know." He quickly glanced up at her and then went back to extracting another chip. "Once the excitement's over."

Heather smiled gently and waited a second to catch Dave's gaze. "If a relationship's good, Dave, it doesn't really have an endpoint: you're always on a journey together, so you're always enjoying it."

For some reason, Dave's heart had started hammering on the inside of his chest like a wrongfully imprisoned inmate. He went to pick up a chip with a large sweeping movement that he hoped would mask the trembling of his hand but instead, it sent the whole bowl scuttling across the table. It skimmed over the menus and beer mats and as it reached the table's edge, Heather reached down and calmly caught the bowl, complete with all its chips.

"Good catch," Dave said with a nervous half-laugh. "So uh, did you want to go see a film?"

Heather tucked a few wayward strands of hair back behind her ear. "Sure, sounds good," she said. "I don't really know what's on at the moment."

Dave took out his phone and bought up the cinema listings. "Uh, there's one called Don't Knock Twice. It says 'a group of six teenagers on summer vacation trek out into a supposedly deserted section of the woods when they come across a mysterious cabin...'"

"With hilarious consequences?" Heather suggested.

Dave scrolled down the through the rest of the synopsis with a raised eyebrow. "Yeah, I think it must be a romantic comedy."

Heather chuckled. "Anything else?"

Dave swiped the screen. "There's one called, Tears of the Father. 'A heart-warming story of one boy's journey to manhood as he seeks to become reunited with his estranged father in 1930's Germany.'"

"Huh, okay."

"Sound any good?"

"Do you think it has a scene where a motorbike jumps through a helicopter?" Heather asked.

Dave scrolled through some more of the review, "Hmmm, it doesn't really say here. It might do." He looked up. "Are you going to be disappointed if it doesn't?"

Heather curled her lip as she considered it. "There's really only two things I look for in a movie," she said.

"Is one of them a motorbike jumping through a helicopter?"

"Yeah."

Dave smiled. "And if it doesn't have that?"

"I'll probably settle for an incisive deconstruction of society. But only if we're taken on that journey by vibrant, believably-flawed characters and an emotionally engaging narrative."

Okay," Dave said, swiping through to another film. "What about The Judginator? 'Max Razorsteel is the toughest cyborg justice-ranger on the bench, but when international terrorists kidnap his girlfriend, executing the law becomes personal.'"

"A cyborg justice-ranger?" Heather repeated sceptically.

"Yeah."

"Who is literally rescuing a damsel in distress?"

"That's what it says."

"That sounds like it could be really nuanced."

"That was certainly my first thought."

"It might even hit both my criteria. We should get drunk and go watch that."

Dave grinned. "That sounds like a terrible idea," he said and took a long drink of his ale. He rested the empty glass back on the coffee table. "After some intensive consultation, I've reconsidered my position: let's do it."

FEBRUARY IN CAMBRIDGE

D ave trod carefully over ice-coated cobbles in the dim, morning twilight, his breath a visible, dissipating sigh of water vapour. The hotel room had been comfortable but his anxiety over the impending TED talk had robbed him of the slumber that he had needed. He had finally succumbed to the inevitability of being awake and so had quietly closed the hotel front door behind him to wander the town.

Cambridge had an obvious overabundance of history. It was tough to walk down a street without bumping into something five hundred years old or to find an informative plaque marking the geographical genesis of some commonplace concept or technology. He walked past listed townhouses with their frost-stained windows illuminated by the half-light of an unblemished blue sky. Which forking paths would have led him to call any one of these places home? Maybe out of university he could have gone into research or engineering, joined one of the many high-tech industries that huddled around the university town for its academic warmth. He could have gone into finance like some of the other physicists from his course. They earned many times what he did, but he often wondered whether their happiness had scaled by the same amount. He imagined himself living in London with a studio apartment of exposed red brick, a bike stored in the hallway next to a vintage elevator with its metal lattice, sliding door. He imagined a coffee house across the street, rough wooden floorboards and a large front window where on rainy Saturday mornings he would sit drinking, listening to the conversations around him, watching rivulets bead down the glass. Wherever he went, Dave imagined alternate versions of himself, versions running alongside him and he often wondered how easy it would be to jump the rails and settle onto one of these other tracks. It wasn't that he was unhappy with his current life or the choices that he had made, he was just curious to know how differently things could have turned out and where he might have ended up. The different people he might have met, the different women he might have dated, they all crowded along the edges of his imagination.

A young woman cycled past on a creaking bike, her perfumed wake lingering in the still, cold air. He could have studied here, joining one of the Cambridge colleges and taken his place in an eight-hundred-year lineage that spanned the waxing and waning of kings and queens. It was tempting to imagine that by walking the same streets as Newton once had, that he could perhaps have become something more, something greater. Dave knew that this was the great myth of location, that greatness was somehow a product of the environment. Wandering down an old cobbled street was no more likely to give him a profound insight into the nature of gravity as walking down a tarmacked twentieth-century one.

Dave stood at the foot of King's College Chapel and ran a hand over the fifteenth-century stonework. He half wished he had already written something for the TED talk, but he had spent three months awaiting a flash of inspiration that had never arrived. He now had a little less than five hours to come up with something coherent and professional sounding. The easy option was for him to embrace everyone's expectation and to talk about Dynamic Enacting Ratios as though they were a valid construct. In some ways it didn't really matter that it was bullshit: the world was full of people who'd made successful careers out of selling bullshit, the question was more, why shouldn't he? Alternatively, he could always offer some version of the truth by explaining his flawed methodology and calling for an improved scientific literacy amongst educationalists, but there was a good chance that many of those in his audience had already bought into the whole ratios thing. In his experience, people were usually resistant to being outed as fools.

He ran his fingers over the ridges in the stone, artefacts of a chisel from six hundred years ago. He began imagining the life of a fifteenth-century stonemason, but then stopped himself. Imagining an historical other carving a stone was no more an insight into their life than it was into his. This was the trivially uncomfortable truth of gazing wistfully at history: that history wipes away all who contribute to it. All that remained of the engineers, stonemasons and artists who built the great chapel, was the physical product that they had once spent a bit of their time working on. Nothing of their laughter, friendships and loves had survived. Even those historical names we remember are little more than a hollow proper noun. A collective historical memory of a great battle has little use to the long-dead victor. The buildings, the carvings, the well-worn slabs, they were the lone survivors of an erstwhile present and for any Ozymandias willing to listen, they spoke softly of their future anonymity.

Dave sighed heavily under the weight of perspective. The longer he remained at Woodford School, the more of Martin's job he would end up doing, a role that, beyond witnessing a slightly different range of absurdity and incompetence, held no joy for him. His hand rested on the stone buttress, its broad rise bearing the load of the chapel roof. He had spent fourteen years teaching physics at Woodford and a lot of the time he had enjoyed it, but the idea of simply slotting back into full-time teaching now felt like a retrograde step, not from any sense of superiority or because he had grown accustomed to a lighter timetable, but because it felt pointless. Society seemed to consider his job a dumping ground for failed professionals; the school's lack of funding had precipitated conflicting priorities between educating the students and remaining solvent; and those entrusted with power seemed more intent on short term personal gain than from the collective good. Whilst many of these elements had been true in the past, the rapid demise of Woodford's Science department had catalysed Dave's awareness of them and his sense of ennui.

The sound of wood vibrating across stone echoed off the chapel wall. A barrister was placing an A-board outside the coffee shop opposite. He should probably try telling Heather how he felt about her again and see where that left him. Dave wandered back across the grass and hopped over the low wall. Existence might well be meaningless, but right now, he really fancied a strong black coffee and a chocolate brownie.

TED TALK

The lights came up on the TED stage and Dave walked out to the sound of applause. Behind him were two giant screens. One screen displayed his name and the title of his talk, which he had cautiously given as 'Improving Teaching'. The second screen displayed a video feed from the cameras positioned around the stage. Dave had watched the other academics and headteachers confidently deliver their talks: schools being set up in a jungle, unmanned drones providing Wi-Fi for remote communities and one bold academic proposing that computer hacking should become a GCSE. Dave knew that the giant screen was there, but he was unprepared for the surreal experience of walking out onto the stage whilst simultaneously watching himself do so. It gave him the unnerving sense of being bifurcated, as though he was acting out one experience whilst observing another. The result was that neither felt completely real. The evening before, the organisers had strongly suggested that Dave get comfortable with the theatre environment by practising his talk on the stage, but Dave had politely declined since he was unable to practise something he had not yet written. As he looked out at an audience obscured by bright stage lighting, he understood why they had suggested this practice.

The applause died away and Dave wondered how many other contributors had reached this extraordinarily late stage without really knowing what they were going to say. He had given the organisers a PowerPoint with three slides on it. The first was a catchy phrase he had come up with that morning whilst sitting on the toilet, the second was a montage of press clippings praising Dynamic Enacting Ratios. The third was there in reserve: a graph showing a spurious correlation that he could use in the event of deciding to deliver a grand debunking. However, despite having decided upon these waypoint slides, he was still unsure what route to take between them. In front of him was a large digital clock with red numbers counting down from ten minutes – the length of his talk. It currently read 9:57.

"So there's a five-year-old kid and it's break time," Dave began, slipping easily into the same mode he used to deliver his physics lessons and to address assemblies. So long as he didn't rush, his mind could easily stay ahead of his words. "His friend comes running out of the toilets, and he's frantic: there's a serious problem - at least serious in the minds of five-year-olds."

All good TED talks seemed to start with some sort of establishing story, so Dave decided to use one of his own childhood experiences for the purposes of an analogy. It was an analogy he had often used when discussing teaching with Heather. However, he had shifted it into the third person because he wanted to avoid it coming across as self-promotion: the important thing in TED talks was not to whom the story had happened, but the idea that it communicated.

"A tap is stuck and nobody can turn it off. So one by one all of the strongest kids in the school, they go over to the toilets and they have a go at stopping this tap. Each of them presses down, putting their weight onto the tap and making lots of noise. But there's no change. The water just keeps on flowing and everyone else just keeps getting more and more anxious. So, this five-year-old steps up. Now you have to understand that this five-year-old is pretty spindly, they probably have just enough muscle to help them move around. So, for all these big kids, this is hilarious. But this little guy ignores them and carries on because he's noticed something. Instead of pushing down on the tap, like everyone else has been doing, he just pulls the metal cap upwards. And the tap turns off."

There was a relaxed chuckle from the audience, a sign that on some level, his story had been engaging. The clock read 9:00.

"So what can we learn from this? Well, maybe that five-year-olds don't really understand plumbing. But like a lot of us, they were succumbing to a really common mistake - something that psychologists call 'framing'. Now in framing, we make assumptions about a situation and then we restrict our thinking to only operate within the boundaries of those assumptions. The five-year-olds had made an assumption. They had assumed that pushing down would turn off the tap. So, all of their subsequent solutions were about providing a bigger downward force. And they were undoubtedly successful in this. They found the strongest and heaviest students and they all piled onto that tap. But none of these solutions helped them because the problem of turning off that tap was never about a lack of downward force."

"Now with a problem as simple as a tap, when we hit upon the correct solution, it's obvious: the water stops flowing. But when the system becomes more complicated, it can be much harder to see whether our solutions have been effective or whether we're just pushing down harder on the tap. And this is a central problem for what is becoming our country's most important industry: teaching."

The clock read 7:52. Dave took the clicker out of his pocket and moved the presentation onto his first slide.

"Teaching is the industrial base of a knowledge economy."

Dave had absolutely no supporting evidence for this assertion but by slowing and emphasising his delivery, he managed to make it sound slightly profound. There was a murmur of interest from the audience. Whilst they might forget the majority of his talk, this was the sort of phrase that was likely to stick in their heads.

"Now if you want to be an industry world leader, you have to find ways to improve. But with teaching, this is far from straightforward. There are a huge number of variables that can alter outcomes: the teacher, the students, their ability, the subject, the location, the time of day and then on top of that, it's not always obvious what we even want those outcomes to be. Sometimes we're just interested in exam results, but other times it's about the students' conflict-resolution or problem-solving skills, their resilience, their creativity, their lateral thinking or their attendance or maybe even how community-minded they are and what sort of citizens they might become. Teaching is nowhere near being a tap problem. Teaching is far more like..."

Dave paused. The clock read 6:58. Unfortunately, he didn't know what teaching was more like. He had only ever considered what teaching wasn't in this context but now his sentence had unhelpfully stranded him at the requirement for a positive analogy. He knew it had to be something complex with lots of competing factors and it had to be something that people would recognise. 6:57. He also felt like it should be vaguely related to his tap analogy, but that felt like an unnecessarily difficult restriction to accommodate in this moment. Maybe if he had a few days to think it through and talk it over in the pub, but... 6:56. Something that was both commonplace and yet complex? He remembered reading somewhere that nobody really understood how paracetamol worked. Maybe something like that...

"...like a pharmaceutical problem," Dave said, hoping that the pause had come across as dramatic rather than incompetent. He began to explore this new analogy at approximately the same rate as the audience.

"With pharmaceuticals, you might have a drug that works brilliantly for some people, but for others, it has negative side-effects, or if used in the wrong dose, even harmful ones. And this is also true in teaching: why would a strategy that works well with a group of high achievers necessarily work well with a remedial group? It might, but you can't assume that. And sometimes a perfectly good drug can end up being far less effective because of extraneous factors like your patient's age, lifestyle, diet, community or even genetics. But when it's important to know whether a drug works we use randomised control trials and employ powerful statistical tools to cut through that complexity."

Several other examples of how else teaching could be parsed through this analogy queued up in his mind, jostling for attention. He glanced down at the clock. 6:11. His point had been made and spending any more time here ran the risk of becoming boring. He should move on.

"And there are studies that do this for teaching. But for some reason, schools still end up foisting poorly tested methods and philosophies upon a nation of students."

Dave paused. Like a mountain ranger who had walked a trail whilst staring at his feet, he wasn't entirely sure where he was and so he took a moment to look around and consider his position. His speech, improvised sentence by sentence, had seemingly delivered him to a point where his only coherent option seemed to be debunking his own study. But rather than the moment being some momentous Rubicon, it felt disappointingly banal. Telling the truth didn't feel controversial.

"Let me highlight this with a specific example. Dynamic Enacting Ratios, or 'duh'. Right now they seem to be a very popular technique in teaching."

He clicked his slide and projected behind him was a montage of article headings, all extolling the virtues of DER.

"A lot of schools are trying out this new system because it promises simple, straightforward improvements and claims to have a scientific basis – that there's some solid research to back it up. The claim is that each class has a perfect ratio of the teacher explaining ideas, to the students working on those ideas. Now, I know something about this system because I'm the author of the original paper. But I have a confession to make. Dynamic Enacting Ratios has no evidential basis. It's completely spurious."

There was another murmur of exchanged words and Dave tried to get a read on his audience, to establish whether the murmur was born of interest or irritation. But in the gloom behind the bright stage lighting, he was unable to make out any facial reactions. His eyes snagged on the glowing red countdown: 5:15. It was probably too late now anyway, he would have had some difficulty walking back DER from his outright denouncement.

"To get published I deliberately used a small sample size and employed an unscientific process called p-hacking. Now in p-hacking, you work backwards, you keep tweaking your initial data until the most statistically significant relationships emerge. You can p-hack your way to correlating all sorts of nonsense."

On the screen, Dave projected his reserve slide: a graph correlating number of deaths from automobile accidents to butter consumption. The p-value was significant at 0.98. A few of the audience chuckled at the absurdity. The heading at the top of the slide said 'Correlation is not causation.'

"Now I wasn't doing this to expose a shallow lack of rigour in some educational publications, nor was I intending to highlight the willingness of schools to jump on an educational bandwagon. Originally, I just needed to submit a research paper to tick an education-outreach box for my school. The content was unimportant, and so I wrote the paper more as a joke, expecting that it would be rejected. But for some reason, it wasn't. And even more strangely, it started to be enthusiastically adopted by schools."

There was another murmur of what Dave now took to be dissent. The glowing red digits read 4:30. He imagined a theatre full of irate headteachers, all shifting in their chairs as their patience evaporated. He had to find some way of softening the tone, of absolving those schools who had spent money on what they would now view as his scam. But he didn't want to just capitulate into an apology, he wanted to make it look like it was a part of his talk. He had to work in his original analogies.

"Now I'm not blaming schools here. I'm saying this is perfectly explained as a framing problem. If a school's management believes that improving teaching is a tap-problem, when someone comes along with a simple way to make their staff more effective, this would sound completely reasonable to them. Why would they not give that a go? You pull up on the tap; the teaching improves."

The murmuring began to subside. "If however, management were to think of teaching as a pharmaceutical-problem and someone turned up and introduced Doctor Winger's Miracle Cure, a technique that collapses down all of the myriad complexities that have previously hampered their efforts to improve... well, then they are much more likely to be sceptical. Extraordinary claims require extraordinary evidence."

"So this might explain why DER was adopted, but it doesn't explain why so many schools reported that it worked. Now there is an outside possibility that in making up these ratios, I accidentally stumbled onto a genuinely useful process. But this isn't really supported by my data. What I imagine to be more likely, is that these schools are experiencing something similar to the Hawthorne effect: a brief improvement in productivity that comes from the additional attention and interest being directed towards the students. The Hawthorne effect is short-lived, but it's long enough to convince a school that's already invested time and money into DER, that they made a wise choice. After all, nobody wants to look like a fool."

He glanced at the clock. 3:10. With only three minutes left he really had to think about how he was going to bring this thing into land. What was his take-home message going to be? If he had been vaguely organised he would have summarised his key points and put them onto a slide, but he wasn't even sure what those key points were.

"Now I'm not saying anything new here. There are plenty of academics out there who undertake exactly the sort of systematic analysis that I'm advocating and to their collective credit, they all identified the evidential basis of DER as being terrible. Which is comforting: it is. And there are groups like the Evidence Based Teacher Network who do great work pulling together all of these systematic studies and doing a cost-benefit analysis of the different techniques. And again, DER scored terribly. Which it should: I made it up. But despite all this, DER still spread amongst schools like a rash."

The clock read 2:30. Two and a half minutes in which to wrap up the whole thing? Dave glanced around the stage. There was a large flipchart of paper behind him. For some reason, one of the previous speakers had used it to scrawl a circle with the word 'learning' in the middle. Dave took a step back and moved the board closer to the middle of the stage.

He glanced at the board's little shelf for a pen, but this one was empty.

"Firstly we need to recognise that by treating teaching as having a single success metric, such as exam results, we are framing it as a tap-problem. And when we do that, we restrict our ability to move forward."

Fortunately, a decade of teaching had conditioned Dave to feel naked if he went anywhere without a board pen. He pulled a black pen from his pocket and as he was talking, scribbled:

1. Teaching is not a tap-problem.

"It would be like a pharmaceutical company obsessing over headache medication and constantly trying to improve paracetamol at the expense of every other product line. We need to think bigger than that."

2:08. Two minutes remaining. Dave tried to recall what else he had said.

"Uh, secondly, schools are eager to improve, but what they don't need is a collection of anecdotes about what worked on a small, specific group in some suburban London school. That's not data, that's a series of anecdotes. What they need is good quality, evidence-based research with datasets large enough to reach significance levels and an academic review system that rejects statistical manipulation and spurious pseudo-science."

He continued talking as he wrote:

2. The plural of anecdote isn't data.

"Ideally, evidence shouldn't be taken from just one study, but rather from the aggregate of multiple studies investigating the same technique."

1:30. He still didn't have a clear idea of how this was going to end but he imagined going back to Woodford and how difficult it would be to explain these ideas to Martin. Maybe his third point could be something about demoting Martin?

"Thirdly, we need to support schools' management in their scientific literacy. It's the management that organises the training of their staff and we need to give them the skills to help identify the academic junk-food of poorly researched flimflam."

He wrote:

3. Evidence-based, not eminence-based.

"The value of a teaching technique is established not through its popularity or how many headteachers have recommended it, but through its evidence."

Whilst this did not specifically call for Martin's dismissal, it did strike at the heart of Martin's belief system. Martin assumed the wisdom of crowds was absolute. Dave looked at the board with its three bullet-points. There was space for a fourth, but with only a minute remaining, he worried that he had been too critical of schools. The fault was not entirely theirs to bear.

"Finally, all these ideas need to be baked into not just how schools and teachers approach education, but how the government does. The education system is laid down by the government and in their guidelines and if the government isn't using evidence to inform their education policies, then progress becomes that much harder."

He wrote:

4. Evidence-led policy.

"With the government's help, we can secure the future of our knowledge economy."

He looked down at the clock. He had somehow managed to arrive at an ending with only three seconds remaining.

"Thank you for listening," Dave concluded and inclined his head at those gathered in the gloom beyond the lights. He had expected disgruntled mumbling and perhaps a polite smattering of jazz-club applause but to his surprise, there was a crescendo of clapping.

THE ASCENT OF DAVE

♦ ♦ ♦

Dave was accustomed to being essentially anonymous at meetings and social events and so found it profoundly weird that every stranger he met for the rest of the afternoon knew who he was. He was unable to hide or sneak off anywhere, because whenever he tried to leave, people would walk over and start thanking him and asking questions. Many of them were sympathetic to his talk and expressed an optimism that teaching was heading in the right direction. Quite a few of them thanked Dave for having the courage to stand up and apportion some of the blame onto the government, which Dave could not recall doing. However, he smiled and nodded regardless. Several headteachers had asked Dave how they could harness the power of the Hawthorne effect, which again, struck Dave as quite a severe misreading of what he had said. It seemed like everyone he met had taken something slightly different away from his talk, but all of them were united in imagining that Dave had agreed with them.

THE BEST LAID PLANS

Two months later, his TED talk went up on the web. Dave knew this because on the same day, Katarina called him into her office and complained for ten straight minutes over his failure to mention the school's vital input in supporting his groundbreaking research.

"But I debunked the study?" Dave said looking confused. "The whole point of the talk was about needing evidence in teaching."

"No, the point of your talk was to raise the school's profile and you didn't mention the school once," she fumed. "You completely failed." She went on to remind Dave how tight the school's budget was and how a smart promoter would have reached out to the wealth of educational industries. "We could have become an academic hub," she said standing up and moving over to the window to walk off some of her tension. "We could have had academics and industry using us as a testbed for their theories."

"They'd be unlikely to do that. Testing theories within a single school leaves you open to correlated errors."

Katarina ignored this and instead criticised Dave for his lack of vision, concluding that Gary would be very disappointed. Katarina's concern was almost comically misplaced. The Science department had all but imploded. John had left to teach in Dubai, Mary had taken up her job in Oxford and Growler had returned to his antiques business. In their place were three newly qualified teachers, none of whom had the requisite science specialism or any A-level experience and all of whom desperately struggled with classroom management. They spent as much time learning their new subject as they did planning, spent more time planning than they did teaching and spent more hours teaching than they did sleeping. To make emergent bad behaviour easier to stop, the sleep-deprived NQTs had stopped doing practical lessons and simply made the students work out of textbooks. When the progress of entire year groups began to plummet, Gary decided it was time to appoint an executive headteacher, a man named Daniel Pike. Gary put him on the same salary as Katarina and told him to improve the school's performance, restore discipline and to solve their financial problems, something the additional salary did little to help. Pike had absolutely no experience of teaching and held a corresponding lack of curiosity when it came to possible causes for the school's decline in performance. However, he did have a justified reputation for being a hard-ass.

Pike's role was ostensibly to operate in partnership with Katarina, but after a few weeks, he had found that it was much easier just to overrule her. In their first senior management meeting, Pike had actively encouraged the team to put pressure onto the expensive, experienced teachers and had made no pretence of hiding his intention to replace them with cheaper NQTs. He instigated an immediate campaign of zero-tolerance discipline with, his most controversial rule being that students should move between lessons in silence. Those students who struggled with this dramatic change, quickly escalated through detentions to expulsion, a strategy that did not so much deal with the discipline problem as it did transfer it to another school. Many of these expulsions were questionable but since they were often targeting the most vulnerable students, parents and carers were either unaware that they could challenge the decision, or did not care. When parents did complain, Pike would prevaricate and stall for weeks, often reinstating the student only when legal action was threatened. He would then repeat the whole process anew by expelling the same student over some different issue a few weeks later, his strategy presumably being one of attrition, forcing parents to ask themselves why they would want to send their child to a school that clearly did not care about their education. It was, as Dave explained to the regulars down at the pub, a perfect of example of how a sociopath would run a school.

Dave leaned over his pad of A4 and scribbled the words 'bike mechanic' and 'deputy head' to a list that stretched halfway down the page. Tomorrow was the last day of the Easter term and as usual, Dave had arranged to meet up with Heather for a celebratory drink. He added the words 'education consultant' and 'pirate ninja' to the list. The difference this time was that Dave had finally decided to leave Woodford School. He finished his cup of strong black coffee and listened to the rain lashing against the pub window. He had listed all of his career options, but Dave could not decide on any of them, not until he knew how Heather felt about him. He crossed out 'deputy head'. If she was interested, he would stay around, but if not, well, then he would just start afresh elsewhere.

He turned over a new page of A4 and asked Mike the barman for another cup of coffee. Tomorrow, he would tell Heather how he really felt, but Dave was unsure what he would say or how he would introduce this topic. It was so easy to talk with Heather, his concern was that they would discuss work, global politics and history and then towards the end of the evening he would have this rapidly closing window in which to communicate all his feelings.

He wondered whether he should start by complementing her clothes, or her perfume, or how her eyes always seemed to sparkle or how she looked when absent-mindedly playing with her hair. He scribbled down some of the instances in which she had set his pulse racing and considered how he could mention them without it seeming tacky and weird. He took a sip of coffee and spent a few minutes reviewing what he had written. He crossed them all out: they were all tacky and weird. The whole list was superficial qualities that could apply to any beautiful woman, but he wanted to write a list specific to Heather. He was not attracted to her because she was beautiful: he was attracted to her because of who she was, because of her kindness, her generosity, how she made him laugh, how she made him think and how she challenged him. Making beauty the basis of attraction was like putting a bowling alley on a boat. He wrote a new list of what made Heather wonderful and then after a few minutes' consideration, crossed them all out. He wanted to tell her how he felt, not freak her out.

He wrote down the different topics he could use to springboard the conversation in the right direction and then began rehearsing both sides of the conversation, imagining Heather's possible responses and composing contingencies for them all. It was a chaotic task, with small verbal variations sometimes sending his imagined conversation down quite different routes. After an hour in this garden of forking paths, he abandoned the approach and decided instead to focus on a monologue laying out how he felt.

He went to bed practising various lines and woke up the next morning doing the same. When he got to his office, Dave printed out his notice, signed it and put it in an envelope. It felt strangely liberating, as though shrugging off a weight that he had unwittingly borne. In the afternoon, Daniel Pike assembled the senior management team so he could spend an hour shouting at them. Dave sat there mentally rehearsing his speech to Heather as Pike threw pieces of paper around and shouted about something or other. It made sense to start out talking casually, to ask how the last few weeks had gone. "Dave!" Pike shouted. He knew that she had had a difficult term and talking it through would be cathartic. "Dave!" Pike shouted again. Dave mentally retuned his focus to find that everyone in the room was looking at him.

"Yeah," he said.

"Are you even listening to me?"

"No, I was just thinking really hard about what you'd just said," Dave lied and then added. "Powerful stuff."

"Well, I'd appreciate it if you paid attention. You're one of the worst offenders for this."

"Absolutely," Dave agreed, having no clue what Pike was talking about. Pike resumed his criticism of Dave for the poor academic progress of the entire school. For some reason, losing a swathe of experienced teachers had not helped the students' progress, but Pike seemed convinced that if they could only apply stronger discipline, learning would spontaneously occur. Dave, however, was weak on discipline, and thus responsible for everything that was going wrong.

It was a curious argument and Dave listened with a slightly puzzled expression. He contemplated slamming his resignation envelope down, overturning the table and then storming out the room, but he lacked the anger. Pike was essentially a more aggressive version of Martin. He wanted to make things work but he had so little understanding of the system, he was unable to see his own hand in steering the school across the event horizon of collapse. Pike was now telling Dave something to the effect of how worthless he was, but Dave was only half-listening, giving the criticism the same weight as he would the verbal slings of a five-year-old. He smiled and nodded his way through the rest of the meeting and at the end handed Katarina his envelope.

"It's been an interesting experience," Dave said. Katarina looked blankly at the brown envelope for several seconds. She had dark rings under her eyes and her complexion seemed more drawn than it had a few months before.

"You can't leave," she said imploringly. "You're the only one that does anything." Dave smiled. When Katarina realised that this had not convinced him she added: "Think about the students. You can't just leave them. What about their lives, their futures?"

Dave shook his head. "If emotional blackmail is the mechanism by which an industry has to hold onto its workforce, that industry probably needs reviewing," he said.

He walked down the hill towards the pub, his stomach fluttering at the prospect of the forthcoming conversation. Heather was standing outside the pub waiting for him. She wore a bright-red raincoat, a dark-grey, knee-length skirt and boots.

"Before we have a drink, can we go for a walk?" she asked.

"Uh sure," Dave said and followed her down the steps to the riverside path.

"These last two terms have been really difficult. And I know they have been for you as well," she said. "It's been really helpful having someone around who understands the situation and appreciates how crazy it all is."

"Yeah, likewise," Dave said carefully, unsure where this was going.

"I've not been doing this for as long as you have, but for me, it seems like these last three or four years have just gotten steadily worse. We've talked about this loads, you know, about focussing on just exam results and more recently, about trying to keep the school solvent." She scuffed a foot on the path as she kicked a stone into the water. "I'm tired of parents who think it's okay to come and shout at me and who have no understanding or respect for what we do." She stopped at a bench that overlooked the river. "And management who seem to have the same problem. It's so depressing to come back each September and see that nothing's changed," she said, sitting down and tucking her feet under the bench whilst leaning slightly forward. Dave lowered himself onto the damp wood, watching Heather closely. Her talk felt like it was heading somewhere bad. His chest felt warm and sweaty, but his hands felt cold and had begun to tremble. He tucked them into his coat pockets to both warm and restrain them.

"I'm an industrial chemist. I could do so many other things. But I happen to like teaching. I think it's really important." Heather sighed and looked down at the muddy path. "I was talking to a friend of my mum's at Christmas. She's taught abroad for the last thirty years and she was saying that it's really a cultural thing. In a lot of countries, teachers are highly respected. She reckoned that the worst places she'd worked were here and in the States. Over here, people pay lip service to respecting your role, but really, they think of you more like a garbage collector: they're grateful that you do the job, but they imagine that if they had to, they could probably do it just as well. But they don't tend to think that about doctors or lawyers or entrepreneurs."

Heather looked up at Dave. His heart jumped a beat as he looked into her brown eyes. "I need to tell you something," she said. Dave felt light-headed and gripped the base of the bench to steady himself. "It's something I've been thinking about for a long time, but it was this last term that really decided it for me. I've been accepted for a job at an international school in Hong Kong."

"Oh," Dave said. Piece by piece the information floated down through his mind. Heather was leaving the country. He would no longer see Heather. The warmth of her company would be gone. The little pieces of his broken future fell like snowflakes, piling up until under the cumulative weight of realisation, the bottom fell out of his world. Dave found himself in emotional freefall. He looked across at Heather's beautiful face, her smooth skin and her gentle, caring smile.

A chill gripped his stomach and he began to shiver uncontrollably under his coat.

"Are you okay?" she asked, her soft voice wrapping around him like a duvet.

"Yeah, I'm really pleased for you," Dave said weakly as he tensed his chest muscles in an attempt to suppress the shiver. "That's really great... it's great news. You'll have a great time."

"It's an amazing opportunity," Heather said.

"Yeah." Dave heard himself say. Everything felt distant and attenuated like he was experiencing it through polythene. "I guess you won't have to pay any tax," he mumbled.

"No and the pay is more than twice what I'm on now," Heather said, watching Dave closely. "It's a really good school. An old friend of mine works there. She says the levels of respect for a good teacher are orders of magnitude higher."

"Orders of magnitude," Dave repeated with a weak smile. The sadness began crushing down, shortening his breath and restricting his peripheral vision. "I can see how that would be better." He said staring at the pebbles compressed into the mud. "It'll be a big change though."

"Yeah, in some ways, but I'll still keep in touch with all my friends. We use a chat group most of the time anyway, so I don't think that'll be all that different. But yeah, I know what you mean: Hong Kong's a big city."

"Chat group," Dave mumbled, staring at the mud. "That's great." There seemed little point in telling Heather how he felt now that she was walking out of his life. He wanted to go home where he could be alone.

"There is one thing I'd really miss, Dave."

"Reality TV shows?" He said thinking about how he could exit gracefully. It had been a long day. He could say he was tired, suggest they do this another time.

"No Dave, they have the internet. I won't miss any crappy TV."

"I dunno."

Heather leaned forward and spoke gently. "I'd miss you."

Dave nodded but he didn't look up from the mud. "Sure. I'll miss you as well."

Heather reached down and gently turned Dave's face towards hers.

"No," she said. "I would really miss you. But I don't want to miss you."

"What do you mean?" Dave said furrowing his brow. He noticed the smooth skin of her fingers still resting against his cheek.

"Why don't you come with me, Dave? The school I'm at, they're desperately looking for a physicist."

"I... I don't know," Dave said dumbly, his brain lurching back into action and frantically trying to assess this completely unexpected situation. Alarms and sirens were going off in his mind: what if she was inviting him just as a friend? He needed to tell her how he felt... he had planned this... what was the first thing he had planned to say... he had rehearsed it to death. I mean, obviously, he wanted to go with her, but what if he had misunderstood why she was asking him..."It might be awkward," he said.

Heather leaned forward and kissed him softly on the lips. "I doubt it," she whispered.

Dave blinked. His brain was completely silent. He could still feel where Heather's lips had pressed against his. She moved back slightly and smiled at him, waiting for his reaction.

"I gave in my notice today," he said, still frozen in the position where she had kissed him.

"I thought you might."

"How? I didn't make the decision until yesterday."

"Dave, you've been ready to quit almost the entire time I've known you. Your school's a mess. It seemed logical."

"You just kissed me," Dave said.

"I did," Heather agreed.

"What did you mean by that?"

Heather leaned in and kissed him again, her hand pressed against his cheek. He reached up and rested his hand on hers.

"What do you think that means?" She asked, lowering her hand but keeping hold of Dave's.

"I don't know? I mean, I know what I hope it means. I've just never been sure if you liked me." Heather pulled a 'are you kidding?' face. "When we first met, you were really quick to tell me you had a boyfriend."

"Well, that's because at the time I had a boyfriend."

"Right, so I just figured you weren't interested."

"Dave, I dumped that guy four years ago."

"Yeah I know, but..."

"I dumped him because I fancied you."

"You did?"

"Yeah."

The information triggered a gestalt switch in Dave's head. Every interaction he had with Heather, he now saw in a completely different light. All the times she had smiled at him, the times she had gently laid a hand on his arm, all the walks they had gone on, all the beer they had drunk. How she had always made an effort with her clothes and how at the end of each evening she had always given him a hug. He realised that they had always been expressions of affection. Of her wanting to be with him.

"Oh," Dave said. "I didn't realise that."

"No, I know," Heather said with a smile. "I was never quite sure if you liked me back, but I just got bored of waiting."

"To be fair, I had planned to tell you how I felt today," Dave said defensively.

"Well I beat you to it," she said.

Dave smiled as he suddenly realised something. "So I can kiss you and you won't mind?"

Heather laughed. "Dave, for someone who's so intelligent, sometimes you say really stupid things." She pulled him towards her and gave him another kiss.

If you have enjoyed The Ascent of Dave then please help others to discover the book by posting a review on Amazon or by recommending/lending it to friends and colleagues.

If you are interested in other writing by Andy R, you can follow him on twitter @AndyRwrites

Printed in Great Britain
by Amazon